THE
RAVEN
SONG

THE RAVEN SONG

A NOVEL

LUANNE G. SMITH

Published by 47North, Seattle

www.apub.com

Amazon, the Amazon logo, and 47North are trademarks of Amazon.com, Inc., or its affiliates.

ISBN-13: 9781662505782 (paperback)

ISBN-13: 9781542035026 (digital)

Cover design by Shasti O'Leary Soudant

Cover image: © Triff / Shutterstock; © Dina Belenko / Arcangel; © Jorge Royan / Alamy Stock Photo / Alamy

Printed in the United States of America

Meddle and mell
Wi' the fiends o' hell,
An' a weirdless wicht ye'll be;
But tak' an' len'
Wi' the fairy men,
Ye'll thrive until ye dee.

—old Scottish rhyme

Chapter One

The mourners had convincingly shed tears between bites of lemon cake, kind words had been read over the grave, and the body of Mary Blackwood had been buried six feet deep in the ground at Saint Albin's Cemetery. The photographer who was to capture the image of Edwina's dearly departed sister had turned on his heels and left at the first sight of the body dripping with seaweed in the coffin, but Edwina needed no photographer's proof to remind her of her sister's state. Three days later the image of Mary lying inside the coffin with sopping wet hair laced with algae had hardly left her mind. The memory circled inside her head like a bat trapped in an attic without windows.

The calling card, too, preyed on Edwina's thoughts. Tucked inside the lining of the coffin, the note implied someone had been watching her. The proof was in the single blue orb placed in Mary's dead hands. Only someone who'd witnessed the sisters' exchange atop the bridge's tower would have known what Mary had dropped in the water. But who? Did they know the value of the orb to Edwina? She'd proclaimed its importance aloud that night. Had someone heard? Did they know the orb contained the memories of a man she'd fallen in love with?

Edwina stood behind the shop counter and took the card out of the envelope for what felt like the hundredth time. The lettering was written with the same iridescent green used by most witches. The ink was charmed so it would shimmer on paper for those with arcane sight, but the enhancement was undetectable to the mortal eye, appearing an ordinary black. A convenient, if rather informal, means of announcing oneself to other witches without being detected. But most calling cards she'd seen were professionally printed by tincture witches who specialized in the grinding of beetle shells in enchanted mortars to make the ink. This one had been written by hand and was missing the all-important name of the person who'd sent it. As she tipped the card toward the light coming through the front window, the telltale sign of ink bleeding into the paper from the nib of a fountain pen confirmed her suspicions, though it didn't tell her much other than the author had access to a not readily available product. And something was off about the iridescence. Had he made his tincture? And why did the note give her a prescient sense of smoke and char in her lungs?

The question of who had sent the card remained. There'd been no clue but the anonymous signature: An Ardent Admirer. A tinge of fear touched a nerve, and she tossed the card down. Why would anybody be interested in her? But of course, she knew. If they'd witnessed the exchange with her sister, then they also saw her shape-shift.

She wasn't so naive in the small world of witches as to not recognize the rare value of her gift. In addition to her ability to shift into the form of a raven, she also had the talent to spot gold, silver, and jewels by their spark—be it on the muddy foreshore, in a city gutter, or dropped and forgotten in the long grass of a sunny green. While it was against the law to use one's magical talent to provide oneself with egregious wealth, Ian had reminded her there were always greedy ne'er-do-wells floating about in the sea of supernaturals willing to take the risk, even if it meant forcing another witch to do their bidding.

Edwina flipped through the pages of her grimoire, looking for a protection spell she might cast over herself and her shop. Something to fend off this man in the shadows. Listening to her intuition, she stopped about midway through the book, landing on a page she'd written when she was nineteen. She remembered the intent behind her writing quite clearly. The emotion and anger had been aimed at Freddie Dankworth, her one-time suitor. She'd made several notes about hexes that would blister the skin, citing stinging nettle, hemlock leaf, and poison ivy as ideal choices to grind in the mortar while uttering an incantation. She'd never gone through with that particular spell. Writing it down had appeased her instinct for retaliation against a young man who she suspected had only ever been after stolen kisses under an elm tree, all of which he'd taken freely from Mary.

Edwina turned the pages, back on the hunt for a protection spell, when her fingers landed on an entry she couldn't account for. While smudged slightly from what looked like a dried water spot, the handwriting was distinctly Mary's. On the bottom right-hand corner of the page, she'd drawn a hollow crescent moon, the sigil for silver, and written the letter *E* next to it. Below that she'd made the mark for Mercury, a circle and cross with a crescent on top. There she'd written "quicksilver" and the letter *M*. Edwina traced her finger over the ink, wondering what her sister had meant by marking up her grimoire. Was the doodle merely another of her inexplicable jests? Or was there some message in the symbols? If so, the meaning had found an ignorant interpreter. Aside from recognizing the symbols for silver and Mercury, she couldn't guess what Mary had meant by it.

After staring at the marks for several minutes, Edwina closed the book and walked to the front of the shop, keenly aware of her sister's absence once again. The tide was out. She'd felt it recede inside her as if her own blood had withdrawn from her veins. A week ago she and Mary would have skipped down to the foreshore to scavenge for whatever precious metals the river had churned up at low tide. Now she couldn't fathom walking among the sand and rocks ever again. She couldn't imagine doing anything without her sister going forward. They'd always been a pair, however mismatched they'd turned out in the end.

For appearances, the shop remained closed out of respect for Mary, yet part of her missed the bustle of opening the front door first thing in the morning, curious to see what business the day might bring. The irksome boy no longer haunted her doorstep, thank goodness, taunting her with his insidious nursery rhymes, though she almost preferred Benjamin's hollow-eyed stares to this new threat hanging over her.

She leaned her shoulder against the window frame to watch the street from the shadows. Looking from one face to another, she couldn't shake the feeling that her "Ardent Admirer" could be spying on her at this very instant.

On the street, a woman in a black straw hat and checkered coat with a shiny brass pin in her lapel—a circle with crescent-moon horns up on top—approached the shop carrying a bundle wrapped in brown paper. The woman tried the handle, but finding the shop was still closed, she rapped on the door, rattling the glass.

The woman pressed her cupped hand against the glass and peered inside. When she caught sight of Edwina through the window, she made it plain she was waiting to come inside, lifting the bundle in her arms as proof they had business together.

Thinking the woman likely wanted to offer an item to sell on consignment, Edwina opened the door, eager to let her know that was not the shop's policy. "I'm sorry, we're closed, and I'm afraid we don't—"

"And a lovely day to you, miss," said the woman. Middle aged and less well put together face-to-face than she'd appeared through the wavy glass, the woman stuck her lace-up boot on the threshold as if to block the door from closing again. "Pardon the intrusion during your mourning period," she said with a nod to the crepe myrtle wreath hung on the door. "Only I have a special delivery for ye, if ye be Miss Blackwood." Edwina sighed and retreated, allowing the woman inside once she saw velvety red rose petals poking out of the top of the bundle.

Ian had been a comfort and a blessing, as the old ladies liked to say, since the odd incident with Mary in the casket. He'd been scheduled to return home on the train but stayed in the city after the anonymous note had lit a torch of protectiveness in him. Since then he'd spoiled her with two bouquets already. One, a posy of blue forget-me-nots tied up with black cord in consideration of her mourning, and a second smaller nosegay bursting with sweet peas, sprigs of lily of the valley, and a single red rose tucked in the center. Ian had used the fashionable mortal language of flowers to heartily express his own version of ardent admiration. According to the botany notes written in her grimoire, the flowers represented pleasure, passion, and a declaration of love. The feeling was mutual, but this third delivery of flowers was verging on lovesick mania.

Edwina shook her head at such lavish attention. The woman laid the flowers in her arms, gentle as a babe, then hovered for an awkward moment. Edwina produced a small coin for her trouble, but the woman waved it off.

"Never ye mind that. Just make sure ye get them in some water right away," the woman said with a wink, taking a long gander at the shop before letting herself out.

Edwina unwrapped the brown paper on the shop counter to reveal a dozen long-stemmed red roses. "Oh, Ian, you shouldn't have," she said to herself as she inhaled the splendid scent from the bouquet. They must have set him back a week's wages or more. She would never have taken him for such a romantic. In the short time they'd known each other, he'd laid open his heart honestly for her to see, but there'd never been any hint he held such depths of sentimentality within. She scarcely experienced such starry-eyed emotions herself, but since meeting Ian she'd let herself indulge in the most romantic fantasies. That is, until Mary's death, and now even her dreams as a woman falling in love wore the heavy veil of bereavement.

Edwina scanned the shop for a container. Not having a proper tall vase to put the roses in, a large pitcher from the kitchen would have to do. She'd just filled it with water from the upstairs living quarters and returned to the shop when Ian walked through the front door. "Hello, thoughtful you," she said with a smile.

"Am I?" Ian shut and locked the door behind him. He'd had a haircut and shave and smelled deliciously of soap.

She beamed as she arranged the roses in the pitcher one by one. "I've never been so spoiled."

He eyed the shop door. "Dinna we agree to keep the door locked until we figured out who's behind that mischief with your sister?"

"Yes, of course, but I couldn't ignore the roses you had delivered."

He took notice of the bouquet and shook his head. "I sent the posies, aye, but I dinna send you any roses," he said and approached the counter. The lines on his forehead drew together in disapproval as he examined the flowers and the paper wrapper they'd arrived in. "There's a card," he said, sweeping aside a few bruised leaves that had fallen.

Edwina picked up the last stem to tuck it in the water but froze midway. Hidden from her eye earlier beneath the flowers had been a scribbled message on a calling card. The handwriting, marked in luminescent green ink, was immediately recognizable. She dropped the last rose as if it might be poisonous to the touch. "What does it say?"

Ian turned the card around and she read it aloud for herself.

Dear Miss Blackwood,

"One fire burns out another's burning. One pain is lessen'd

by another's anguish."

I do so look forward to getting better acquainted soon.

Your Humble Servant and Ardent Admirer

"But what does he mean?" she asked.

"It's from a play about a pair of lovers," Ian said. "But why that quote?"

"Is he doing what you do?" Edwina asked. He raised a curious eyebrow at her. "I mean, using poetry or writing to say something more."

"But how would that—"

Suddenly, the color faded from the roses. The petals withered and turned black, emitting a foul odor as the flowers smoked and drooped in the pitcher. Edwina and Ian gagged and covered their mouths at the foul sulfur-like stench.

"They've been hexed." Ian had grabbed the pitcher of roses to get rid of them when the wilted buds burst into flame. He snapped his hand back, burned by the flash. "It's spellfire," he said, pulling Edwina out of the way as the flowers spit flame onto the counter and floor.

"We need a counterspell!" she urged, covering her face with her shawl.

Ian took a defensive stance and reached out his burned hand. "Earth and water bind and conspire, put out the flames of wind and fire." The elemental request only made the hexed blaze leap higher, as if he'd thrown water on an oil fire. Tongues of flame licked the walls and ceiling, igniting the wood and blistering the plaster. Black smoke coiled above their heads like a snake ready to strike. "Get out! Now!"

Edwina watched in horror as the shop ceiling became engulfed in flame. She had just enough time to grab her grimoire, hat, shawl, and a handful of jewelry from a display table before Ian rushed them to the front door.

"Locked!" Edwina fumbled for the latch as the smoke burned her eyes, creeping inside her nostrils and seeping into her lungs. Ian nearly disappeared in a haze of smoke beside her before she found the bolt and forced it open. The door swung wide, crashing against the wall.

The gush of city air, however befouled by the taint of heavy industry, was a welcome relief. Edwina gulped it all in as she ran outside. Ian scrambled out behind her before bending over the pavement and coughing until his lungs and eyes cleared. Horses and autos slowed in the street, their owners gawping at the black smoke and orange flame engulfing the shop until shouts of alarm grew louder than the commotion of traffic.

In the time it took Edwina and Ian to stop coughing, the blare of the fire brigade horn wailed from the next lane over. Three horse-led wagons piled with ladders, a boiler, and a dozen firemen stopped in front of the corner shop. Edwina's entire life was contained inside—a photograph of her father, her hope chest, her mother's cloisonné clock, all those discoveries made on the foreshore . . . She could remember when and where she'd found each of the items on the display tables: The silver spoon with the grapevine design on the handle uncovered in the sand beneath Graham's Quay. The broach with the missing stone found wedged beside a horse trough on Barkley Street. The hatpin decorated with mother-of-pearl she'd plucked out of the rocks and seaweed at the bottom of the embankment stairs, and all the keys to all the unknown locks scavenged from the cracks in all the roads she and Mary had ever traveled. All of it turning to molten, anonymous metal before her eyes.

And then the upper floors burst into orange and black. The attic room she'd shared with Mary caught fire. Edwina clasped a hand over her mouth to contain the wail rising in her throat. The city hadn't proved to be the sanctuary their father had hoped for, but they'd found a patch of freedom on the rooftop, where stars twinkled above the smudgy air. Two sisters with the uncanny ability to change into ravens sipping their father's sherry at midnight and casting dreams of the future, with secrets shared under snug wool blankets after the lamps had been blown out. Now even those untainted memories of Mary were covered in soot.

Edwina watched through tears as the flames scorched the roof and a blaze danced behind the attic window where she and Mary had once flown to and fro. As the firemen aimed their hoses at the inferno to preserve the adjacent buildings, she felt a gentle tug at her elbow and didn't resist when Ian urged her to fade into the back of the crowd.

"Not sure we want to stick around and answer the sort of questions spellfire is going to raise among the mortals." Ian kept their backs to the wall behind the gawpers on the street.

Shaken by the abrupt loss, Edwina caught Ian by the arm when he suggested they leave, desperate to salvage at least one thing. "Do you have your memory?" she asked.

"Aye, it's in my pocket."

Then there was nothing left to stay for, only what lay directly in front of them on the road ahead. Edwina wrapped her arm around Ian's and the two walked away, not looking back.

Chapter Two

Ian seldom felt the kind of rage inside that threatened to undo him. He'd seen it in other men often enough. Or rather the aftermath of their actions, once they'd lashed out. Crimes of passion, they called it. Fury, violence, and haphazard spellwork coalescing with an act of revenge. He'd seen victims killed or maimed in his work with the Northern Witches' Constabulary. The grievous injury one human could do to another tainted his half-shadow memories with images he would have been happy to forget. But it wasn't always physical damage done. Sometimes the poor sods had their minds affected by a vicious hex and their thoughts cast to an internal hell where they would never function normally again. Was that what he felt boiling inside him? The urge to lash out at whoever was threatening Edwina and damn the consequences? If not, he was very near the line and more than willing to cross over it if provoked.

Ian encouraged Edwina to walk casually down the pavement away from the fire. He didn't dare let go of her, keeping her arm firmly entwined with his, while he searched each face they passed for a look of grim satisfaction. Surely, the man was watching even now. That was his game, wasn't it? Spying on her from somewhere in the shadows, relishing her distress. Undetected, undeterred.

So far.

"Where to now?" she asked when they came to the corner.

"This way." Ian directed them around an open-mouthed merchant who'd stopped his cabbage cart in the lane to gawp at the firemen leaning their ladders against the building.

Ian took a split second to think about where they should go. Instinct under pressure had always been his greatest talent, having kept him alive during dire times. "Just keep walking," he said as his eyes locked on another man's in the street long enough to raise the hairs on his neck. The man glanced away at the smoke, and Ian pulled Edwina close, shielding her with his body as they walked past.

Following a hunch, he led them to the embankment. Zigzagging between crowds of pedestrians and coaches, they walked far and fast before turning away from the river again. There they veered right down a narrow commercial lane leading to a market square until Ian felt confident that no one had followed. To be sure, he stopped and checked his watch, letting the cogs and flywheels inside spin long enough to detect any supernatural entities in the vicinity.

They stood for a moment among the merchants' sacks of flour, bags of grain, and fresh-cut flowers laid out on tarps to be sorted into small posies, watching, waiting. Hawkers called out, advertising their goods as fog crept in at their feet.

"Nothing yet," Ian said.

"Perhaps whoever sent the spellfire is content to let us out of their sight. For the moment."

While Ian continued to surveil the crowd with his watch, Edwina wandered a few feet away, drawn to a shop window. He caught up to her on the pavement, where she stood staring intently at a seamstress's shop. The latest electric sewing machine was on display in the window with a sign that promised it could do twice the work in half the time.

"What is it?" he asked, confused by her sudden interest in the mortal device. The poor lass was understandably all a muddle from the shock of seeing her home go up in flames.

Edwina quickly wiped a tear from the corner of her eye. "My mother," she explained. "She's a seamstress. I've often wondered if maybe she's taken up work somewhere in the city. If, all along, she's only been a few streets away the whole time she's been missing."

"Missing?" Ian's instinct prickled. "I thought you said she left."

Edwina gazed up at the building to where the window of a flat looked out over the shop entrance. "Gone is gone. What's the difference?"

"Could mean the difference between *wanting* to be found or not."

She nodded. "If she or my father ever wanted to get in touch again, they'd go to the shop. But there isn't a shop anymore. One of their daughters is dead and the other is"—she looked at the unfamiliar street around her and shrugged—"adrift."

"Aye, lass, I'm sorry about your shop," Ian said, squinting from the irritation roiling beneath his regret. "I wish I'd thrown the flowers outside on the pavement the minute I knew who'd sent them." He rubbed his thumb along the groove of mortar in the brick wall out of frustration with himself. "And then to only make it worse with my clumsy spell. Can you ever forgive me?"

Edwina lowered her head and turned from the seamstress's window. "He knew we'd use a water spell to quell the fire. Who wouldn't? He set a trap and we fell right in it." She shook her head, still in a distracted daze. "But what does he gain from flushing me from my home? My business? Was it mere cruel sport? Did he mean to kill me?"

It was an unsettling thought. Ian had even begun to wonder whether Edwina was under the influence of some curse, the way her life had turned so topsy-turvy. The circumstances of her parents both disappearing were odd. The depraved life and untimely death of her sister were a tragedy no sibling should have to bear. And now her home, her livelihood, presumably all she owned save for what was on her back, had been destroyed by fire.

The Raven Song

"It feels like my life is spinning out of control," she said. "I don't know which way to turn. I . . . I don't know whose face I can trust."

"You know mine," he said, taking her face in his hands. Despite the flow of people going about their shopping, he held her in his arms as the old ladies in lace balked and the young men winked and tipped their top hats. "Whoever this madman is, he tried to kill you," he whispered. "I'm not keen to give him a second chance. We have to get off the street." He released her from their embrace and gripped her shoulders. "We can go north, ye ken?"

After seeing Mary's coffin defiled by the anonymous card writer, Sir Henry Elvanfoot had offered Edwina sanctuary in the north. Ian hadn't yet told her, but he had a ticket for her in his back pocket as well as one for himself, courtesy of the old wizard. All they had to do was board the afternoon train.

"I hate giving a madman the satisfaction of scaring me away," she said, dabbing her nose with the back of her hand. "I've been run off most of my life."

He handed her a handkerchief. "You've done what you must to be safe."

"Where will I stay tonight?" Edwina looked at the paltry jewelry she'd snatched from a display table on her way out the door. "It won't even buy me three nights in the doss-house." Her face crumpled, and she wiped her eyes with the cloth.

"Come, lass, you've a place to go. A safe place where you'll be well taken care of."

The concern of impropriety showed on her face as plain as if it were written in witches' ink. An unmarried woman traveling alone with a man on a train would raise eyebrows, aye. He thought briefly of asking her to marry him, of traveling north as an engaged couple, but the words got hung up on his uncertainty.

Edwina wandered a few steps away from him, her eyes on the worthless items in her hand. He thought she might see the truth of her

13

situation then, realize she wasn't safe in a city alone with nowhere to stay. But then she turned around with a gleam in her eye. "The witches' safe house," she announced. "I can go there. And then tomorrow I can return to the shop and see if there's anything to be salvaged."

Ian felt a deep desire to grab her by the wrist and drag her toward the right side of reason when a man in a gray homburg bumped his shoulder, jostling him and reminding him of the market crowd around them. "Pardon me," Ian said. The man tipped his hat in apology without looking back as he brushed past. For some reason, the gentleman's hat struck him as extraordinarily lavish for a day trip to the marketplace, with its gray silk banding, crisp brim, and buckle. And he was carrying a silver-capped walking stick? The man was taking dandy to a new level.

"It isn't that I don't want to go with you," Edwina continued, "but if either of my parents do return, I need to be here so I can explain. About the shop. About Mary."

"Aye," he said, though his mind was still preoccupied with the man who'd bumped into him. He looked over the heads in the crowd and spotted the gentleman pausing under an archway to check his watch before tucking it away and walking on. Out of caution born of professional experience and a heaping dose of suspicion, Ian checked his jacket pockets to see if anything had been lifted from him in the encounter, but his watch, pipe, coins, and papers were all there. Everything was accounted for until he checked the back pocket of his trousers where he'd kept the train tickets Elvanfoot had bought.

Gone! And so was the man.

"Damn it."

"What is it?"

"That man. He stole something from me. Wait here." Ian took off, running after the thief as he squeezed between shoppers in the marketplace. When he got to the archway, there was no sign of the man in the homburg. There were only two directions the pickpocket could have gone, but he seemed to have vanished in the crowd. Had he overheard them talking and snatched the tickets? Or was it *him*? The stalker? Ian checked his watch. A faint glow indicated the presence of three magical folk. He could account for himself, but not the others. And then Edwina caught up to him.

"You were supposed to wait for me," he said.

"I'd rather not be left standing alone on the pavement with thieves and attempted murderers lurking about just now, thank you." Edwina adjusted her shawl and straightened her shoulders as she braved a look in either direction. "I'm going with you."

He exhaled, taking her point. The third figure lighting up his watch was traveling north, but there was no way to know if it was the pick-pocket or merely a witch walking up a busy commercial lane. He chose to follow anyway. If it did prove to be Edwina's stalker, he was in the proper mood to see the matter put to an end once and for all.

"Come on," he said, and together they followed the small dot on Ian's watch in the direction it traveled.

Five minutes later, certain they'd been on the trail of the pickpocket in the gray homburg, they determined their mystery subject was instead a man in a black suit and matching derby with a walking cane at his side. He was stepping inside a men's haberdashery when they spotted the faint purple aura spilling out above his collar. Witch-born, and not the man who'd bumped into Ian and stolen the tickets. The gentleman witch gave the pair a disapproving look before he entered the shop, where he was greeted with a cheery "hello" from the owner. Also not the man they were looking for.

"I thought for a minute it was your 'admirer' who'd nicked the tickets," Ian said, shaking his head at himself. "Just another common mortal pickpocket. But how did he know I had train tickets in my pocket?"

"Tickets?"

He caught the dubious tone in her voice. "Aye. Elvanfoot had bought two tickets, expecting I'd be able to convince you to travel north."

"I see. We make quite a pair, don't we." Edwina leaned against the wall outside the haberdashery as traces of fog coiled at her feet. "I've been burned out of my home, and you've lost the only means of returning to yours." She hefted the worthless jewelry in her palm again, the weight proving too slight to be of any value. "Shall we both try our luck at the witches' safe house, then?"

He shared her frustration. The entire city seemed to be conspiring against them. But she'd correctly identified the one place they might yet depend on. All it required was a ride through the dark and a brush by the city's old plague pits.

"Let's head back to the marketplace and see if we can turn that secondhand jewelry of yours into enough coin for a pair of third-class tickets to the East End," Ian said and readied his watch for the journey underground.

Chapter Three

An hour later, Edwina and Ian knocked on the door of the witches' safe house. Abigail Featherstone, the seasoned witch who guarded the property, opened the door. This time, she smiled to see the familiar couple on her doorstep.

"Come in," she said. "I thought I should be expecting you."

The pair entered the slum house at the end of the dingy dead-end lane. Looking around, Edwina swore the same bowl of uneaten mush sat on the rickety table as the last time they had been there a week ago, though she knew the appearance was merely part of the illusion of the place being a common slum house. And while the austere front room did a good job of souring expectations on one's initial entry, it hid a cozy and well-furnished interior that waited beyond the broom closet. All the visitor needed was the spell to let them pass.

Abigail noticeably sniffed at the odors rising off their clothing. "Char and smoke."

"Hexed spellfire destroyed my home and shop," Edwina explained. "It's why we're here. We have nowhere else to go."

"Right," the old woman said, peering at them. "You've also got the scent of trouble on your tailwind." Abigail waved them in past the pile of never-finished washing in the back room. Charlotte, the young witch in training, stopped pretending to scrub a man's shirt against a washboard when they walked in.

"Gran said you'd be back." The girl picked up her white rabbit from an empty washtub and cradled it in her arms, neither excited to see them nor troubled by their sudden appearance. "Should I send them through?"

Abigail nodded. "If you please, Charlotte."

The girl twitched her nose and recited her words, and Ian and Edwina passed through the broom closet into the hidden space beyond. Abigail followed close behind, telling Charlotte to keep an eye on the lane for any stragglers wandering about.

Once inside the brightly furnished sitting room, with its velvet chairs and library of grimoires filling the bookshelves, Edwina spun around to confront the safe-house witch with a curious look on her face. "Abigail, what did you mean you were expecting us?" she asked. "Did someone alert you we were coming?"

"Call me Abby. Most folk do," she replied as if she'd said those words a hundred times to a hundred different strangers already. "As for your question . . ." The old woman held up a finger as she opened the top drawer of a mahogany writing desk in the corner. From it she pulled a black leather book and flipped through the pages until she came to the entry she was searching for. "Here it is." She tipped the book toward Edwina so she could read for herself. Ian leaned in as well to discover it was some kind of ledger.

Edwina took the book in her hands, staring in disbelief at what had been marked down. There beside her father's name, Alfred P. Blackwood, was a "paid" stamp.

"Your father prepurchased safe passage for you and your sister out of the city, should the need arise. The agreement which he signed expires next week, so you're right on time. I meant to show it to you last time you were here, but you ran out so fast I never got the chance."

"I see." Edwina closed the book and handed it back to Abigail. An uncomfortable cramp formed in her stomach, thinking that she and her sister could have safely left the city if only she'd intervened sooner in Mary's life. "Thank you."

"Will you take tea?"

"Aye, that would hit the spot," Ian said, shucking off his jacket. He sat in the wingback chair nearest the fireplace with an audible sigh of exhaustion.

After their hostess left, Edwina reached up to remove her hat, but in her hurry to escape the burning shop, she'd never put it on, apparently losing it somewhere in the hubbub of the street. Instead she secured the pins holding her hair in a loose knot at the nape of her neck. The scent of smoke lingered on her person, just as the old woman had said.

"Are you going to call him?" Edwina asked, sitting in the chair beside Ian. "Hob will be worried sick when he can't find you at the shop."

He reached out for her hand. "Give us one moment alone first before the old woman comes back."

"It's unusual, this." She gave him her hand, and he tilted his head as if he didn't understand her meaning exactly. "You and I," she said. "Thrown together by an unfortunate twist of fate. Two weeks ago, neither knew the other existed. Now I don't know what I'd do without you."

"Aye, true enough. The Fates play the most elaborate games. Only . . ."

He squeezed her hand to reassure her, but the effort failed.

"Only what?" she asked.

"Only it isn't exactly true that I didn't know about you before we met."

"Well, yes, you followed my sister and me to the foreshore that night," Edwina said, sorry she'd brought up the uncomfortable details of how they'd come to meet.

"No, before that. Before I came to the city to look for Elvanfoot's son."

Now it was Edwina's turn to tilt her head in ignorance. "You knew of me before that? How?"

He cleared his throat. "Not by name, of course. Or even by sight. More like a rumor."

At the mention of the word, Edwina dropped his hand and sat up, worried he was going to say he believed something unsavory about her family, her past, or perhaps some vulgar gossip he'd heard. Rumors were like weeds, setting their roots deep and flowering quickly so they could go to seed and release their nonsense and be carried away on the wind. Edwina shuddered inside. Without money, family, or even a place to live anymore, her magic and reputation were all she had left. Her mind scanned over who might have a grudge or the calculating cruelty to start rumors.

Freddie.

If her one-time suitor had been spreading lies about her or her dead sister, she swore she'd hex the man so all his teeth would fall out and he'd never be able to say an intelligible word again. "What had you heard?" she asked, almost afraid to hear the answer.

"Just pub talk."

"What does that mean?" she asked, growing more unsettled at his admission.

Ian looked away sheepishly. "It's been hanging in the air for a while now that there were shape-shifters in the south. Reports of girls turning into birds. Had no idea I'd actually see you for myself one day."

"So, I'm back to being a freak now?" Edwina jumped to her feet, propelled by agitation.

"No, of course not, but people are naturally going to talk when they hear of such a thing. And by 'people,' I mean the fair folk. They've been whispering about the existence of a pair of raven sisters for years."

She sat back in her chair. "What is it about this room that starts the most fantastic tales spinning out of your mouth?"

The last time they'd visited the safe house, they'd ended up arguing until Edwina stormed out, offended by accusations against her sister. They'd fallen out briefly, but the attraction between them was too strong to keep them apart for long. Following that vein of thought, she tamped down her growing ire and tried instead to understand. After all, he'd been right about Mary in the end.

"It's nae a tale. Are you not proof enough of that?" Ian crossed his legs and reached in his side pocket for his pipe. "Do you think I might find some tobacco here? I'm nearly out."

"Don't change the subject. What do you mean the fair folk were talking about me?"

He tapped the pipe against the heel of his hobnail boot to loosen some stubborn residue before dumping it in a stand-alone ashtray beside his chair.

"Have you any clue how rare and ancient your gift is?" he responded. "Magic like that must go back to the beginning, ye ken." He looked up from stuffing the last of his tobacco into the pipe with his thumb. "The fairy courts, the prophecies, the infusion of magic into the bloodline of our ancestors." When she stared back nonplussed, he lit his pipe with a flame he summoned on the tip of his finger. "Have ye no idea of your people's own history?" Ian's mouth filled with smoke as he drew air through his pipe.

"The first witches were what you'd call acolytes," he explained. "They were mortals who served the fair folk in their ceremonies and rituals. Paid homage with their stone carvings and tree blessings. And when this world could no longer hold all the fair folk and their magic, most left for the Otherworld, but they left behind the gift of spellcasting for those who'd served them. So they might continue as guardians to protect and preserve the secrets of the natural world." He puffed again on his pipe and blew out a cloud of smoke in the shape of an oak leaf. "In a way we're all touched by the fair folk, you might say, though some might be more favored than others."

The top of Edwina's head buzzed as her intuition recognized the truth of his words. There'd always been tales about the earliest witches. Stories that said they were born in storm clouds or sprang to life from the cracked limb of a tree hit by lightning. None of those were true, of course. But she was certain there was a grain of truth in the notion of modern witches evolving from that first transference of magic from the fair folk.

"Tea," Abigail announced as she entered from the broom closet carrying a tray with a charming black-and-gold-rimmed teapot and two matching cups. If she sensed she was interrupting, she didn't let on, setting the tray down and pouring Edwina a cup and then Ian. "Sugar?"

Edwina shook her head, still lost in thought, but Ian answered by raising one finger, then blew out another plume of sweet and fruity smoke.

"I always did love the smell of pipe tobacco," Abigail said, stirring the sugar into the tea. She wore an amiable smile on her face, as if a pleasant memory had been conjured back to life by the scent of smoky cherries and plums. She was relaxed, the perfect hostess, until she handed Ian his cup of tea. Her hand suddenly shook, and the tea sloshed over the rim of the cup as the china rattled.

"Steady, missus." Ian brushed hot tea off his trousers. "Are you all right?" He took the teacup from Abigail and helped her onto the opposite velvet settee.

"Blow your smoke out again," she said, perched on the edge of her seat like a cat waiting to pounce.

Humoring her, he set the cup down and took a deep draw off his pipe, then puffed out a white cloud that encircled his head.

"Is the smoke enchanted?" she asked as her eyes followed the wispy trail.

Edwina, sensing something was terribly amiss, leaned forward. The static in the air had changed. A tingly sensation crackled in the ether. Abigail's eyes tracked from the smoke to Edwina.

"Aye, I got it from a tobacconist shop in Coven Park." He took the pipe out of his mouth to inspect it. "Is there something wrong with the smell?"

"Abby?" Edwina's intuition flared.

The old woman's eyes followed some invisible line on the floor that snaked from Edwina to the broom closet and presumably beyond, by the way she stared at the door. "There's a spell attached to you," she said.

"What kind of spell?" Edwina squirmed in her chair, trying to detect what the older witch had. "What do you see?"

"Puff out more smoke." Abigail waited for Ian to exhale yet again; then she pointed. "There, do you see? A trail of where you've walked. The smoke illuminates it."

"Bloody hell, she's right!" Ian blew a stream of smoke across the floor. Shadows of Edwina's steps led out through the front door. "That's how he's done it. He's put a tracking spell on you. And to think I only helped him follow you with that fog-casting spell of mine."

"Is it my boots? Should I take them off?" She undid the buttons running down her ankles, took off the boots, and set them on the hearth in front of the fireplace. She returned to her chair, but the smoke still revealed her movements.

"Yes, both fog and smoke would make your steps light up like fairy lights." Abigail had regained her composure and consulted the pages of the black book where Edwina's father was mentioned.

"Then he can find us here." Ian looked around the room as though searching for a back exit. "We have to leave. He's already tried to kill you once. I'm not giving him a second chance."

Edwina hugged her shawl around her. "We have no money, no friends to call on. There's nowhere else to go."

"Not entirely true," said Abigail. "I don't know who's following you or why, but you're still entitled to safe passage for two." She checked the small watch hanging from her chatelaine. "You'll need to move quickly. I was going to put you on the morning train tomorrow, but perhaps it's prudent to have you hop on now. There ought to still be room. Tell me, is there luggage coming? Only you didn't arrive with any, so I assumed it was being transported by wagon. Charlotte is standing watch on the pavement for it to be delivered. The timing will be tricky, but I think we can manage."

"Train? What train?" Edwina asked.

Abigail clasped her hands together and took a calming breath. "I showed you the ledger, dear. Your father paid for your passage to safety, and that's what I deliver. It's fortunate you didn't use up the service last time you were here. And I assume," she said with a nod toward Ian, "that this man will be going in your sister's stead, as her name has faded from the registry. Dead, is she?"

"Going where?" Ian asked.

Abigail shrugged. "That's up to you."

"North," Edwina said. "We need to go north."

"Then you're in luck. The northbound is on its way. Now, fasten your boot buttons. You've just enough time to make it down the stairs." When Edwina didn't immediately put on her ankle boots, Abigail clapped her hands. "You've got a tracker on you, so unless you want whoever is following to find you, dear, I suggest you move like someone who doesn't wish to get caught like a fish on land."

Ian and Edwina exchanged a glance. While she slipped on her boots and fastened as many of the buttons as she could manage without a hook, Ian explained they had no luggage.

"All the better," Abigail said. "Let's go."

The old woman led them to the back of the room, where a full-length mirror in an ebony frame hung on the wall. The reflective surface had the sheen of mist floating around its edges. Abigail blew against the glass. The fog closed in to swallow the hard reflective surface, creating a portal to a hidden corridor behind. The trio stepped through the mist and descended the brick-lined stairway. Abigail went with them only as far as the first landing before she handed them each a brass token to use as payment. "This is as far as I go. If you are being followed, I need to check on Charlotte. She's a fierce little spellcaster, but she's never had to defend the place against a witch hunting another witch. Not alone, anyway.

"Follow the stairs to the bottom and wait on the platform," Abigail instructed. "The next train is due in three minutes. Your tokens are for a compartment in the middle car. As you're unchaperoned, you might not wish to draw the shades. But for your safety, only open the door for the conductor."

Abigail returned upstairs while Edwina and Ian stared at the gaping dark corridor ahead lit only by gaslights that wavered from a weak supply. The level of trust they had to invest in the safe-house witch tested their resolve. Ian did a quick scan of the dungeon-esque stairway with his pocket watch, then nodded. The space appeared to be clear of the wrong sort of supernatural element.

After corkscrewing downward seven steep levels, Ian and Edwina emerged on an empty rail platform. A red-bricked tunnel, smudged with smoke and soot, emptied into a dark void in both directions. Only the steel tracks and the faint sulfuric breath of something moving in the tunnel beyond assured them this was how they would be leaving the city. Edwina, forced once again to retreat from comfort and familiarity by forces beyond her control, stared into the darkness, pondering what new gamble awaited her in the north.

Chapter Four

Ian's pocket watch lit up like a comet when he made a second scan of the underground platform. Several bodies were moving toward them, one in the immediate vicinity. Yet he hadn't seen anyone else, and there were no annexes or side tunnels off the platform other than the open freight lift rigged on a pulley.

"There's someone down here with us," he said.

"Who?" Edwina retreated from the tracks so her back pressed against the brick wall. "It couldn't be him. It just couldn't."

Ian checked the stairs to see if they'd been followed by Abigail after all but didn't see or hear her or anyone else. He returned to the platform, where a whoosh of warm air was expelled from the tunnel, ruffling the fringe on Edwina's shawl. "Nothing," he said as the screech of faraway wheels speeding over steel rails was accompanied by the piercing whistle of an oncoming train. "Could still be Abigail," he said. "I may be getting interference from the bricks."

"What if it's him? What if he followed my footsteps?" Edwina opened her grimoire and started thumbing through the pages. "We'll need a strong defensive spell."

"I thought we'd have time for tea together before riding north," said a small yet familiar voice that echoed off the platform walls. "I'm a little peckish."

"You!" Ian glanced again at the face of his watch, then put it away with more relief than he let on. "What the devil, Hob? You're supposed to be home."

Edwina closed her spell book. "Hob, thank goodness. We thought . . . Never mind. I'm glad you're here, um, wherever you are."

Ian's hearth elf popped out of the rubbish bin on the other side of the bench and pulled a greasy sheet of newspaper off his head. "Battered cod," he said, taking a whiff of the oily wrapper. Hob gave the paper a lick before stuffing it back down inside the bin. He jumped to the ground and approached Edwina, only to have his stomach grumble loudly. "Pardon my rumbling, milady, only I haven't had breakfast for two days."

"What are you on about?" Ian asked, glancing down the track. "Why haven't you eaten?"

The hearth elf sighed. "Too late now. The train is already here."

The ghostly glow of a headlight came into view through the darkness beyond. A thundering engine chugged toward them, slowing just as it came out of the tunnel. The engine rolled past and five passenger cars, painted burgundy and gold, came to a stop in front of the platform. The nervous face of a woman in a black velvet bonnet holding a cat peered out of the only window without its shade drawn. She watched as two men and a woman disembarked, then pulled her shade down as well. While the passengers' luggage was shunted off the train and onto the freight lift, the conductor approached Edwina and Ian to ask for their tokens.

"How far are you going, then?" asked the conductor. "We're limited-stop on this line. Calling at Black Ash, Hurley Burn, Everly Station, and Oak Stone. If you're going west, you'll need to transfer."

The woman in the compartment with the cat peeked out from behind her shade as if waiting to hear the answer.

Ian asked Edwina, "Will Everly do?"

She took a breath as one does before taking a giant leap over a puddle and nodded. The conductor dropped their tokens into a metal counting box and, after winding the handle around once, punched them out a ticket each. Hob produced his own token, presumably out of thin air. Confused, the conductor looked to Ian for guidance on what to do. "What's this one need to ride for, then?"

"He's with me."

"Why don't he just pop out like normal?" the conductor asked.

Hob growled low in his throat.

"All right, all right. Only asking the question. Your lot don't often travel overland, is all. Got the safety of me passengers to consider. Top priority."

The conductor cranked out another ticket, and the hearth elf jumped on board. Ian and Edwina found seats in a middle car as Abigail had instructed. Hob, being furrier than the average passenger aboard, was meant to ride in the baggage car, but he slipped into the compartment behind them.

The scent of rose water lingered inside, likely from the woman who'd just disembarked. Edwina suggested it was a form of spellwork meant to keep harm at bay. "Perhaps to protect her from a former lover," she said. "Roses give protection to those who still believe in love's virtue."

"Unless they're hexed to burn you alive," Ian said with a look of warning.

"That was a ruse." Edwina took the spot beside the window, still cradling her grimoire. "If he was watching, he would have known you'd sent me flowers twice before, so he assumed correctly I'd be duped into believing you'd done so again."

Ian made sure Hob was inside, then shut the compartment door. He exhaled in relief when he finally sat on the bench seat beside Edwina.

"He's been watching for weeks," Hob said, checking the seat cushions for coins and finding a single copper.

Edwina looked up from her book in alarm and peeked through the side of the shade to check the platform. "How do you know that?"

"That's why I haven't eaten. I've been helping Sir find the origin of the big spell."

"Did Elvanfoot have any luck?" When Hob slumped on his seat, Ian reached in his pocket for a tin of kippers in tomato sauce he'd been holding on to for breakfast. "Here, eat these before you topple over," he said as the train rolled forward after a small jerk in the slack. "And then you can tell us what you learned."

The elf ran his finger over the metal rim until it popped open. He swallowed the can of herring in one sloppy gulp, licked his lips, then wiped his mouth with the back of his hand. He unbuttoned his green tweed jacket and let a small burp escape before begging Edwina for her forgiveness.

"Never mind that," she said. "What have you found out?"

The elf folded his hairy arms over his middle. "Been running up one length of the isle and down the other looking for obscure pages of grimoires and dusty history books to take back to Sir."

"And?"

"He's looking for answers to thorny questions. Oh, and he suspects you're being tracked with a spell that reveals your whereabouts."

"Yes, we've already discovered that for ourselves," Ian said. "Enchanted smoke and perhaps fog appear to reveal Miss Blackwood's footprints."

"Sir's mind is like the insides of your watch. Always turning, always working to make some puzzle make sense." Hob took his pipe out and lit the bowl with the end of his finger. He exhaled, and the smoke lit up Edwina's footprints inside the compartment as if they were made by pixie dust. "He'll sort it out with all the other knots he's working on," the elf said and closed his eyes.

Whether conscious of the act or not, Edwina scuffed the soles of her boots against the floorboards as though she might loosen the spell's hold. As a private detective, Ian had seen a similar spell used once by a jealous husband who'd tracked his wife's movements from one day to the next, one lane to another, hoping to catch her in a lover's arms. That man hadn't relied on footprints, though. Instead, he'd gifted the wife with an atomizer of perfume induced with an enhanced elixir. The scent trail had coalesced with the static in the air, leaving a ribbon of color like the northern lights. If one wore an enchanted pair of spectacles, the lights shimmered for the viewer in her wake as she passed. But the stalker hadn't had that kind of access to Edwina, had he? It seemed unlikely, so how had he cast the spell? Whatever the means, the notion that he believed he had a right to track her made him arrogant and dangerous. Greed was a likely motivation, but it didn't make the man's intentions any less devious. The sooner they got their feet on northern soil, the better.

Thoughts of home settled Ian. He would be on his own patch again soon, and while his memories were supposedly thin in some places, he was ambivalent about the effect on his mood. He could not know what he didn't remember and therefore didn't have enough awareness to miss it. His fingers curled around the orb in his jacket pocket. Such a small thing and yet all his memories were apparently contained within it, plucked from his mind by a witch who had needed no spellwork to carry out such magic. No, Mary's fiendish ability had been innate, part of the odd creature she'd been born.

He glanced at Edwina as she unfurled her shawl to get comfortable on the seat beside him. He thought he'd seen magic done in every form, from incantations and potions to scrying and hexes. Those were the tools of the witch, aye. Yet another kind of magic floated through the ether as thick as heavy fog in the north. Inborn in some. Passed from bloodline to bloodline. The magic resided in the trees, rocks, streams, and wild hearts of the animals that roamed the moors and mountains. As old as the earth itself. The magic was imbued in the first beings to walk the land, the fair folk who'd harnessed the energy of the ethereal force to create the peaks and forests, the lakes and valleys. Creatures like Hob. And, he suspected, perhaps Edwina too. Was that the source of her ancient magic? Was she, like his own distant kin, part of that tribe of enchanters?

Ian released the orb in his pocket. He still had the option of reabsorbing the stolen memories *if* they were his. The bauble had been tossed in the river, seemingly lost for good, until it showed up again in Mary's coffin along with a note from Edwina's stalker. Aye, Sir Henry Elvanfoot had a spell to return the memories held within, but even with the old wizard's assurance, he didn't yet know if the risk was worth recovering the memories it held. There was the taint of the watcher's energy on the orb. The damn thing could be hexed for all he knew. If he should swallow the remembrances and they brought him naught but a ruined mind, there'd be no one to remove the corroded memory now that Mary was dead.

He twisted his neck to the side, cracking his upper vertebrae to release the tension. In some ways he thought Mary had done him a favor. When she'd plucked out his memories, she'd taken everything, good and bad. What Hob restored with his elf magic had the sheen of optimism on it, something Ian wasn't sure he'd always carried inside him. Shadows of thoughts still lingered in the outer reaches of his mind, imprints reminding him of tragedies, misfortunes, and disturbing scenes that had once haunted him. Silhouettes of the cast-off memories remained rooted in the muscle and tissue. He knew the source of at least one, so deeply had the memory embedded itself in his heart: the murder of a child by her parents after they'd believed her to be a changeling. The callous, superstitious abuse he'd witnessed was the reason he'd quit the Northern Witches' Constabulary. But while the echo of the memory hovered in his periphery, he no longer lived with the detailed images of torture and neglect—only the occasional pang of regret that knocked in the center of his chest whenever he saw a child alone on the street.

"Penny for your thoughts," Edwina said with a look that said she'd attuned to his reflective mood.

"Just thinking about how fortunate I am to be the first to show you around my home city once we arrive," he bluffed as the train rumbled through the dark.

Hob's long ears pricked forward. Aye, the elf knew the truth. Their hearts and minds were synchronized and had been since Ian was a babe. The old fellow certainly couldn't read his mind, but some sort of vibration existed between them. A humming connection almost like an invisible umbilical cord, he mused, though the maternal image wasn't ideal. He sometimes lost patience with the imp's place in his life, but who wouldn't be grateful to have one of the fair folk personally watch over them?

He thought again of Edwina and her stalker. She and all the wary fellow passengers on the train were running from a similar threat. Someone or something was chasing them, forcing them to seek safe passage on a metal beast hurtling through the underground. None had anyone to watch over them, no fair folk guardian to work his tutelary magic and restore goodwill in their lives. But he could be that for Edwina now. The circle of energy flowing in the ether from hill to hill around the city could sweep the uninitiated off their feet if they carried even a remnant of the old blood in their veins. He was certain the current would call to her, attracting like to like. And then what would she make of her gift?

Chapter Five

Edwina startled awake. She'd been leaning against the compartment wall, trying not to contemplate the source of the dark-brown stain on the half-drawn window shade, when she'd nodded off in the tunnel. Now watery sunlight seeped through the clouds aboveground. She sat up. "Where are we?"

"Welcome back," Ian said. He sat beside her with his arms folded across his chest and nudged his chin toward the view outside his window. "We're just coming into Everly Station."

Somewhere en route the train had emerged from underground to follow the track north over the open moors. "Have I been asleep the whole time?"

"Aye, but dinna fash. Your snoring dinna keep me from nodding off for a minute or two myself."

She blushed from the implication that they'd both slept on the same bench. "But we can't be there already."

Hob leaned over the rim of the luggage rack above the seat. "After Hurley Burn Station they induce sleep on the train to calm the passengers." He pointed to a vent, where the scent of lavender still stirred in the air. "Too many witches all fretting together can cause a spark, so they use a calming spell," he added.

"But not you, I take it," Ian said, yawning and fishing in his pocket for a packet of shortbread wrapped in brown paper.

"*I* am not a witch." The elf grinned at them.

Ian tore open the grease-stained paper and offered Edwina first choice, though most of the biscuits had gone crumbly. "No, because no witch would be so daft as to ride a train in the luggage rack," he said to Hob.

"I'm hiding."

"From?" Edwina asked.

A tap at the door alerted them to the trainman making his rounds. The conductor opened the compartment door and tipped his cap at Edwina. "Begging your pardon, but we'll be arriving at Everly Station in five minutes," he said before searching the compartment with his eyes. "Mixed mortal platform ahead for those disembarking. Your, er, pet has got to get out of sight now." An angry hissing noise ensued from the rack above as the conductor left and repeated the same arrival message to the compartment across the aisle.

"All right, calm down, Hob," Ian said as the train slowed. "The man's right. Off you go. Let Elvanfoot know Miss Blackwood has arrived."

The rattle of baggage trolleys, the clop of horses, and the general muttering of people congregating in a confined space interrupted the quiet sanctuary of the safe-house train. A flutter rose in Edwina's chest at the thought of disembarking among a crowd of strangers in a new city and with an apparent madman stalking her. She peeked out from behind the shade. Everly Station was a surprisingly bustling place with multiple trains parked side by side. An enormous arched bridge spanned the railyard of what must have been at least a dozen tracks. Their train, she noticed, had lined up on the track farthest from the main building before a separate platform. Ian urged her to gather her things as he opened the compartment door and checked the aisle. How had her entire life come down to collecting a shawl, a book, and a handful of secondhand jewelry rescued from a fire?

"You're not checking your pocket watch," Edwina said after they disembarked. Meanwhile, she scanned the platform up and down, watching every face for clues to a sinister heart as they were swallowed up in the crowd of passengers coming and going through the busiest terminal in the isles.

Ian shook his head. "A tool like that is only good for when you're working down south, ye ken?"

"Er, no, I do *not* ken," she said, hurrying to keep up. She'd observed him rely on his watch's sensitivity to detect the presence of supernatural elements ever since he awoke in her father's bed after his memories had been restored.

He smiled and escorted her down the platform toward the main station, where a magnificent stained-glass oculus winked from above. From there, they walked up a jolly green-and-white stairway that led to a footbridge on a level above the station. "An instrument like this, even one as sensitive as one designed by Sir Henry Elvanfoot himself, does me no good in a city where nearly half its inhabitants claim to be descended from a magical bloodline."

"Half?"

"Aye." Ian escorted her to the busy street outside. Hansom cabs queued aside the pavement, picking up and dropping off passengers. "Who else could have conjured a city like this?" He gestured toward the skyline, where blackened spires pierced the rust-gray crown of smoke encircling the city beyond the bridge. A man in a plaid coat walking past in the opposite direction offered a wink and a nod to Edwina as if to say it was true.

Edwina cast her eye at the magical horizon, from the fat buttress of a stone castle to the spindly Gothic pinnacle atop a narrow monument to the familiar sight of a clockface held aloft in an obelisk-shaped tower. Enchantment radiated between the spires, the stones, and the mossy slate rooflines. She felt a tingle of energy skitter along her skin.

Luanne G. Smith

The threads in her shawl felt it, too, ruffling the fringe as though lifted in a breeze.

"It's mesmerizing," she said before Ian tugged her by the hand toward a quieter side street away from the congested pavement outside the station.

Ian found a place to stand at the base of one of the city's infamous closes. A double set of steps angled up a steep incline, climbing between buildings to a street on yet another level above. They'd walked less than a quarter mile and she'd already witnessed three distinct elevations of the city. Built by witches, indeed. Any mortal would have sought flat ground to suit their flat vision, but here the landscape was well matched to the ambitious, magical eye.

"This will do," Ian said.

"Do for what?"

He raised a teasing eyebrow at her before leaning over a moss-covered stone balustrade. Behind it was a small triangular recess at the rear of a building whose front presumably faced the street level above. He called out, and Hob's head popped up briefly before Ian squashed the elf back down below the height of the rail. Even in a city of witches, one apparently needed to be discreet.

"Sir has sent transportation," Hob said. "He was most pleased to learn milady had made the journey."

The little fellow shook out his furry head, and a cloud of fine golden dust blossomed around him. Some of it settled on Edwina's outstretched palm, a gossamer sensation brushing her skin. It felt like the entire city was coated in the stuff, the way her body tingled.

"That doesn't work on everyone, ye ken." Ian nodded toward her hand. "It's the fair folk in your blood. Draws like to like."

"You think there's a long-lost fairy relative perched in my family tree?"

Ian and Hob grinned as though she were joking before the elf dropped down and disappeared through a drainage pipe that led to some other realm. "Have you never suspected as much?" Ian asked.

He was, of course, referring to her ability to shape-shift into a raven. He wasn't the first to speculate about where the source of the unique magic had sprung. At one point or another, she and Mary were thought to be descended from an ancient goddess or some dusty old magician from an eon ago or even a medieval sorcerer with the power to fool a king with his shape-shifting tongue. Her ancestral history had never pointed to anything of the kind, but there was always the possibility of a lover's tryst between a witch and fairy somewhere in the tangled branches of her family tree.

"I suppose I never had any reason to before," she finally answered as a rattling four-wheeled contraption rolled to a stop at her feet.

Ian gave her a look of disbelief before greeting the driver. "Aye, I see Elvanfoot has sent the dogcatcher after Miss Blackwood, then."

The driver chuckled, then sobered when he met Edwina's eye. "Pardon, miss, it's only because they call this thing a dog cart, so the lads like to have a laugh."

The "cart" was actually a motorized vehicle with two rows of seats. Like a horse-drawn bounder, one seat faced forward for the driver and one faced backward for the passenger. A fringed canopy covered both. Edwina had never seen a contraption like it before, but coming most recently from the busiest city in the world, she was disinclined to think a small horseless cart was something that might catch on in the narrow lanes where horses and omnibuses practically ran over each other.

"Any bags can rest here by my feet," the driver said.

"We're traveling rather light today," Edwina said. After a quick exchange with the driver, Ian folded down the footrest and she climbed up, moving over on the seat to make room for him. When he put the footrest back up without joining her, something inside her unraveled. "Aren't you getting in?"

"No. I've my place to check on after so much time gone. If I can remember which lane I take to get there," he said with a grin.

He'd made a joke about his somewhat faulty recollections, faulty because her sister had stolen his original memories. "I could still remedy that for you," she said with a nod to his pocket where he kept the remembrance.

"I know." The smile on his face faded, stirring her guilt. He looked as though he wished to say something more, but a sideways glance at the driver had him hold his tongue. "Dinna fash. Elvanfoot has promised to take good care of you."

"How will we see each other again?" she asked. Already Edwina could feel comfort and familiarity recede. Had she really traveled four hundred miles north only to be abandoned? Surely he would kiss her until they met again.

He did not. Instead, he held her hand in both of his, self-conscious at the public display of affection.

"I'll call on you at Eidyn House as soon as I can," he said.

"Eidyn House?" One more confusing thing to add to her already dizzying new existence.

"Aye, that's what Elvanfoot calls his wee abode," he said, letting her go. "The main thing is you'll be safe there. Until we're more certain about . . . you know who." Again, he glanced at the driver as if to say she shouldn't trust anyone, not even those around Elvanfoot. Not yet.

Edwina nodded and prepared herself for the bumpy journey ahead by holding tight to the handle on the side of her seat. Ian waved as the car jerked into gear and sputtered forward. She waved in return, watching as he stuck his hands in his pockets and slow-walked down the street until he was out of sight.

Shuttled from one city to the next, bereft of home and family, Edwina was now a woman left alone among the bustle of a strange new place. She suddenly felt as lonely as she ever had in her life.

Chapter Six

As soon as Edwina was out of sight, Ian removed his pocket watch and took a reading. Despite what he'd told her, his watch was finely tuned to the idiosyncrasies of his densely populated home streets. The difference between entities was often subtle, but after long months of practice, he could differentiate between the regular witches who sold tinctures and balms on the high street to old men with arthritic knees and those who skulked in the narrow closes willing to sell bottled curses for tuppence. Aye, if he tilted the device just right and uttered a well-chosen incantation, he could sometimes see spells forming in the aura around the subject visible on his watch. And right now, it was telling him the creeping sensation of disquiet he'd been feeling ever since they arrived in the city was justified.

His intuition had gone on alert as soon as their train pulled into the railyard. A familiar summons from the unknown had tapped him on the shoulder. The city could be complicated at times, with its crosswind of magic. The mix of fair folk and witch with mortal and cunning folk sometimes made it tricky to know who to trust and who to avoid. But something had called to him. Some unresolved business with the Otherworld. And since his instinct felt the summons strongest along the city's trough, he could only assume the sensation was related to his work. Some of his most reliable informants dwelt in the dingy underbelly, where they waited and watched for scraps of information to fall through the cracks of the high road above.

But who had called, and why? His underlying uncertainty gave him pause. He'd only just returned home, and already he feared the worst. Could he have lost the memory of a dagger-sharp threat that lurked in the shadows of the low end of the city? Latent memories of a dead man tickled his throat, where he'd experienced the horror of a blade slice across his skin. An experience that wasn't his own. Aye, a man's memory was a delicate, marvelous thing. No witch should have ever been born with the power to remove another's essence while they still breathed. With his blood rising, he turned the corner onto the fishmonger's close—a narrow bricked-in passageway tucked between buildings where men's breath was forced to mingle in the air as they passed on a cold night.

An unsettling sense of déjà vu overcame Ian as the tall buildings of the lane closed in on him. Once again, he found himself regretting his unfortunate encounter with Mary Bewitched. The fallout may have left a bigger gap in his memory than he'd feared. Halfway through the close his body was remembering things his mind could not, tingling with the anticipation of danger with every step he took toward Oxgate Road at the bottom of the hill. He formed a defensive spell on the tip of his tongue as two men passed him going the other way, but each tipped his hat in greeting and carried on, making him feel like a skittish cat.

When he reached the bottom of the hill, he turned right onto Oxgate and glanced at his watch. An eerie pulse echoed ahead under the King's Bridge. He approached the darkened underpass with a healthy dose of skepticism.

"Whispers on the wind said you was back."

A voice from the shadows.

Ian looked to his left. There, in the arched entrance to a slum house, where immigrants from across the narrow sea were forced to live ten to a room to survive, stood a dark-haired man in a ragged coat hand-rolling a cigarette. He licked the edge of the paper and nudged his chin to ask for a light. Ian approached, recognizing the face but not a name to go with it. Following his intuition, he snapped a flame to life on his fingertips and lit the man's cigarette, though on closer inspection he was no longer inclined to call the smoker a man.

The creature laughed. "Conjuring right out in the open," he said, blowing out a stream of smoke and glancing up to the bridge as if watching for trouble. "I'm flabbergasted."

The creature's tattered black trousers had faded to gray from time and wear, but his pointed shoes were oddly new and the leather still had a shine to it, as did the pair of rings on his fingers. The contrast stirred a sense of familiarity loose.

Without forcing it, the name came to Ian like a swimmer breaking the water's surface after a long dive. "Finlay," he said, noting the furtive sprite's face and hands were covered in soot.

The creature smiled. "That's right. Now follow me," he said with a jerk of his head.

Knowing he had some forgotten business with Finlay, Ian followed. They walked single file down another narrow alley that felt more like a crack in the city than a shortcut between streets. The pavement reeked of human waste that would take a day's steady rain to wash away. Above, a bank of coal smoke sank in a dense cloud, rendering the air barely breathable. "Keeps the overly curious out," Finlay said when he noticed Ian gagging.

"And the sane." Ian held his elbow over his face while they sidestepped an old man sleeping rough with his face toward the wall.

"It gets better on the other side," Finlay said. He sprinted up a set of stone steps on short, springy legs. Despite being a foot taller, Ian had to work to keep pace with Finlay. He didn't know why, but he trusted the quirky little fellow enough not to keep checking over his shoulder to see if he'd soon be set upon by a pair of accomplices out to relieve him of his earthly possessions.

41

The close led to an abandoned street and an unfamiliar section of tunnel beneath King's bridge, only this opening was much narrower and darker than the first. Ian hesitated and Finlay stopped.

"You dinna wanna be left behind now," Finlay said, grinning.

His smile was hideous, with pointed teeth that looked sharp enough to tear human flesh. And yet Ian took a deep breath and joined him under the bridge. Midway inside the tunnel, Finlay crouched by the wall. He tapped the stones three times. The illusion of a wall fell away and a passageway opened. A gauze-thin memory of the place surfaced.

"You can stop blaming the wee witch who made mincemeat of your mind. She isn't the reason you canna remember the place." Finlay raised his hand to shut Ian up when he began to speak. "Aye, I know you're confused. Step inside. You'll find it all comes back to you." The sprite made a gesture with his outstretched arm, inviting Ian to go in first while he watched for onlookers down the road.

"I must be daft," Ian said, crawling inside the hole in the wall despite the fear of having his heart torn out by the sharp blade hiding in his companion's smile.

Inside, the veil was lifted. Ian found himself in the familiar setting of a snug room hidden under the bridge. Gnarled roots from an abandoned tree formed the ribs of a dome overhead while luminescent mushrooms hung in vivarium globes from the ceiling, providing a soft candlelight glow. A small desk and chair made of driftwood sat in the corner with a stack of old books on top whose covers had frayed and peeled from the humidity. And just beyond the reach of light was the vague sense of a tunnel lurking in shadow. Its breath was sweet and earthy, like a truffle newly dug up from the ground. Ian took in a cleansing breath, recognition permeating his senses.

"Fin, you bastard," he said. "I told you, you dinna have to use spells to guarantee my confidentiality. I agreed to do the work like you asked."

"It's a precaution. To keep your heart true. And *safe*."

"Aye, and every time I pass through the door, I forget you and this place again." Ian walked over to the pile of books and opened the top one. He scanned his last entry, reading his notes about the surveillance he'd maintained on Oxgate Road and several surrounding passageways. "How did you know a witch had taken my memory?" Ian asked, casually turning the page. He looked up from the book when Finlay didn't answer. The sprite's puckered lips and guilty eyes said it all. Ian was incredulous. "Are you saying the Blackwoods are part of this investigation?"

Finlay sat on a stool and crossed his arms over his chest. *Bracing himself to resist saying more than he should?*

"There are some who think so," the sprite said, relenting. "The sisters have been attracting unusual attention lately."

"For obvious reasons," Ian said. "I got a firsthand demonstration of what they're capable of."

Finlay nodded. "We've known about the shape-shifting since they were born."

"*We* being your mysterious employer?" Ian had sorted out that Finlay wasn't the rogue sprite he'd initially taken him for when they first met. No, his manner was more refined than his outer appearance would suggest. And those shoes. The sprite's vanity wouldn't let him trod the earth in human-made shoes, and yet he didn't think the spry fellow had the polished disposition to be closely associated with the Seelie Court.

"More like an elder who asked for a favor," Finlay replied, parrying the speculation. "No one has officially taken credit for the sisters' gift." He hesitated. "It's one of the reasons we brought you in. The prophetess foresaw you meeting them. I need you to write up a report about what you witnessed about the sisters. The other reason is I'm not allowed to go near the gateways, given the trouble."

Ian had been hired to investigate a ruffle in the fabric between the realm of the fey and the earthly world of mortals and witches. There was already a natural thinning taking place in the veil between the two, like a deer shedding its winter coat as the end of another cycle wound down. Every thirteen turns on the fairy calendar, which roughly translated to a year in human time, the ancient inhabitants of the land—sprites and goblins, pixies and elves, water nymphs, tree spirits, and fairies— returned to reaffirm their queen as leader of the fair folk, as much for themselves as for the sake of those who occupied the land now. Still, fewer and fewer of his fellow city dwellers seemed to pay attention to the old stories anymore, not with the shiny new attractions of science and industry overshadowing ancient magic. Mortals were unlocking a magic all their own from pure ingenuity: Cars that ran without help of a horse or mule. Wires that could relay messages over hundreds of miles in mere minutes. Even a machine that could clean a man's shirt through agitation, though not nearly as fast as Hob's trusty whisk broom.

But there was something different happening this Midsummer cycle. Someone, or *something*, had been going back and forth between another part of the veil for nearly a year. Yet, according to Finlay, no one on either side could account for the disturbance except to say the gateway was somewhere in or around the seven hills that made up the city landscape.

Finlay had called on Ian, being the only supernatural private detective in the isles, to help identify the trespasser. The admission that the prophetess had seen Ian in one of her visions and that she knew about the sisters had just altered the scope of the case. Even though the fair folk had initially hired him to uncover the anomaly, he'd now become a part of the investigation through his association with the Blackwood sisters.

"By the way, it's only the one sister now," Ian said, correcting Finlay. "They fished Mary out of the river earlier this week."

The sprite cocked his head to the right as if he'd missed something fly by on the night air. "And the other?"

Now it was Ian's turn to be coy. "Safe for now," he said and left it at that. He didn't think Finlay had been stalking Edwina, but he wasn't ready to rule out the possibility just yet, not after learning the sprite knew who she was. The fair folk operated by different rules than the mortal and witch isle residents. They were flighty, capricious, fickle. Yet they had honorable hearts and occasionally showed kindness if you remained in their good graces. But cross them and your life wasn't worth spit.

Finlay's impish smile fanned out across his face, revealing his pointed teeth. "She's here with you, then. You wouldn't consider anywhere else safe." The sprite nodded, thinking to himself. "And yet it makes sense that circumstances would bring her here."

"How's that?"

"The Gathering has already begun," Finlay said. "Midsummer forces are drawing in the revelers." He tapped impatiently on a glass orb to make the mushroom lamp glow a little brighter before pulling the chair out from the desk and pointing to it. "You must find the hole in the fabric between worlds. Consider using the raven woman. With her instincts and unique talents, she might be sensitive to such things in ways you are not."

Ian raised an eyebrow. "And she can go near the portals when you can't?"

Finlay arranged the book and pen atop the desk. "Aye, that's right. Now write quickly. I must fly and let my people know about the dead sister. Someone's trying to cover their tracks, and it doesn't sit well so close to the Gathering to have things out of order."

Ian sat at the driftwood desk. The fair folk had misjudged his size when they built the damn thing, but he squeezed into the tiny chair, dipped the pen in ink, and began to scratch out his report on the parchment paper bound in leather about Edwina and Mary Blackwood and their ability to transform into creatures of claws and feathers. He spared no details while describing Mary's unnatural attraction to corpse lights and her ability to steal memories before her death. He wanted his account duly noted in the record, being that he was one of her victims.

Chapter Seven

Sir Henry Elvanfoot's "wee abode" turned out to be a turreted manor house located a few miles south of the city. Edwina twisted around in her seat to better see the grounds as the chauffeur pointed to the ivy-covered house, as promised, when they'd arrived. A kitchen garden bursting with basil, lemongrass, garlic, comfrey, and just about every herb needed for tinctures, potions, and spells wrapped around a solarium on the east side of the property. Beyond that, a five-foot-tall hedgerow ran along the back and sides of the house, terminating at the wrought-iron gate at the end of the carriage drive. There, flanking the entry, stood two lampposts adorned with rearing unicorns that held up a brass nameplate declaring the place as Eidyn House.

The gate opened of its own accord to allow the dog cart and driver to enter. Edwina felt a nervous flutter upon arriving at such a grand house with her back turned as she sat in the rear-facing seat. Surely that was a bad omen? Adding to that, she'd arrived with nothing more than her mourning dress of black crepe, the shawl her mother had made her, and her personal grimoire, which she clutched in her hands. Everything else she owned could fit inside her pocketbook, if she had one.

Although happy to be out of harm's way, Edwina found seeking refuge at the home of the famed wizard of the north was fraught with an altogether new source of peril for one not acclimated to socializing with the upper class. The situation had been different while he'd visited her store. That was her domain, one she felt comfortable in. Here, she didn't know any of the rules and feared Elvanfoot would see her as little more than a penniless charity case.

Edwina nearly made the driver turn around and take her back to the city center to inquire about the nearest witches' safe house, but then a wave of the same skittering energy she'd experienced outside the train station wrapped around her, sending a tingle up the base of her neck to her temple. Oddly pleasant, the sensation nudged against her intuition, convincing her to set aside her doubts and disembark from the vehicle.

Elvanfoot's butler, a red-haired man in black livery that included a green-and-gold plaid waistcoat, greeted Edwina at the door. "Miss Blackwood," he said with a bow before inviting her inside. The faint glimmer of a golden aura peeked out above his collar. "Sir Henry is expecting you."

Embracing her newfound courage, Edwina entered the grand house. A large entryway with wood-paneled walls, marble floors, and an enormous grandfather clock greeted her. In the center stood a round table with a towering vase filled with purple foxglove. A small collection of calling cards had been tossed down on the table alongside the afternoon post. To the right, a majestic double-wide staircase with a hand-carved railing and red carpet led to the landing above, where a portrait of a bearded man with crystal-blue eyes and a crisp ruff stared down from its place on the wall. She was still gaping at the painting when the butler closed the front door and instructed her to follow.

"He's in the library just now," he said, stopping before a door halfway down the hall. He knocked on the doorframe to announce her arrival.

"Ah, Miss Blackwood," Elvanfoot said, looking up from his chair by the fire, where he'd been relaxing with a book three times the size of her meager grimoire. "What a relief to have you arrive at last. Do come in." He stood and greeted her by gripping her hand in his. "And may I offer my condolences once again for your loss."

Edwina felt the tingle of energy transpire between their fingers. Disguised as a gesture of heartfelt welcome, it was more as if he'd taken her mystical temperature the moment he'd clasped her hand. He presumably found her off balance and quickly offered her the chair opposite his.

"Tea, Yates. A *Camellia sinensis* variety will do." The butler retreated through a side door, leaving Edwina alone with the wily old witch. "Now," he said, "Hob has filled me in on the fiery circumstances leading to your decision to come north. You will be perfectly safe here. The house and grounds are both protected with enchantments and charms to ward off the odd hex or ill-aimed curse."

Edwina described how the roses had burst into flame after she'd read the peculiar note accompanying them. She dug the card out of her grimoire, where she'd tucked it away before gathering her meager belongings during the fire. She presented the soot-smudged card as evidence of her ordeal. "Hob mentioned you were looking into the tracking spell to see if it can be traced."

"Did he?" the witch asked, looking up from the card. "Ah, yes, he's brought me a wide assortment of books on many subjects." Elvanfoot gestured to a stack of dusty tomes on the side table before setting the card down on his desk and retrieving a leather-bound book stuffed with loose papers. "I've confirmed it is possible, at least theoretically, to attach a tracking spell to an individual without actually making contact," he said, scanning his notes. "A sort of telekinetic airborne toxin could do it. Obviously, taking advantage of physical proximity to attach such a spell is the easiest and most likely scenario, but since we don't know who this so-called admirer is, it's impossible to say whether or not it's someone you've met or had recent contact with. Thus I thought it wise to explore other options."

It was a frightening thought. She'd assumed the watcher had to be a stranger, but what if it was someone she knew? Somebody she had daily contact with? A customer she'd shared a laugh with, or the lamplighter who showed up outside the shop each evening to climb his ladder, or even Mrs. Dower? No, not Mrs. Dower. Despite her intimate work of preparing Mary's body for the funeral, which made her suspect in the appearance of the orb inside the coffin, the poor woman was as mortal as they came.

"Do you yet know if there's a counterspell?" Edwina asked.

"But of course," he said, shaking himself free of his thoughts. "We mustn't waste time on simple pleasantries when there's mischief to be undone."

Yates came in with the tea along with some heavenly-looking sandwiches. The butler poured two cups, while Elvanfoot reached for a stick of incense from atop the mantel above the fireplace. He lit the incense with his fingertip, then let the smoke trail around the floor near Edwina's shoes, assuring her there was a spell for everything. They both watched as the shape of her footprints materialized on the rug.

"As I suspected," he said. "The magic employed is as ordinary as treacle and molasses. Only the modus operandi employed by our suspect could be described as an above-average application. I believe we can have your predicament sorted before Yates clears the tea tray."

Elvanfoot sat back in his chair and picked up his teacup as the smoke from the incense continued to swirl from a burner on the table. The aroma had a vague familiarity about it, one of those scents from childhood so distinctly entwined with memory. Yet for Edwina, the smell kept reminding her of a garden she was certain she'd never been in, one full of roses, lavender, and jasmine flowers. All the same, the memory, or at least the *feeling* of a pleasant memory, relaxed her so that she no longer dug her nails into her grimoire.

"As I imagine you are eager to be rid of this hex, we've already begun with a cleansing spell," he informed her.

Of course, she thought, the smoke from the incense would carry away any toxins in her aura. She hoped its effects began to work soon. He might have muttered a few words of an incantation to boost the power, but then she recalled he'd claimed he'd done magic so long he no longer needed to say his spells aloud. He invited her to pick up a sandwich, so she ate as daintily as she could while waiting for the smoke to wash through her like a fresh breeze wafting through the mind and body. She even closed her eyes at one point, as much from the hope of a cure as the overwhelming tiredness and relief she felt at being in his home and having something to eat besides crumbled shortbread.

Elvanfoot nibbled on a biscuit, commenting on the fresh buttery flavor while encouraging her to take another of the small finger sandwiches. Though wary of accepting too much hospitality, she was absolutely famished and took a hearty bite of a second cucumber, soft cheese, and watercress sandwich. Better than any smoke spell, the tea and food filled the empty corners of her stomach until she'd nearly forgotten the trouble that brought her to his house in the north.

"We grow the vegetables ourselves," Elvanfoot said and pointed to a set of double glass doors that led to the backyard garden. "The watercress does marvelously in a shady corner by the heron statue. I sprinkle in a bit of powdered gingerroot to give the plants vigor. You'll find there's very little here not touched by magic. I'll show you around later, if you like. Perhaps in the morning, when you're feeling better."

"Better?" she asked, before swallowing a bite of sandwich.

"The compounds in the enchanted watercress will flush the traces of spell out of you in no time. I apologize, but it was the quickest and safest solution."

Edwina tossed the rest of the sandwich onto the plate and peeled the bread apart. "Watercress? That was your counterspell? But I thought the smoke . . ."

"Watercress is an excellent detoxifier. Doubly so, when mixed with a little garlic." Elvanfoot called out for Yates. "Yes, I think it's time to have Mrs. Fletcher show Miss Blackwood to her room," he said after the butler returned. "The burgundy room, as we discussed." He turned to Edwina the moment she felt the first cramp. "I had a strong suspicion the original tracking hex was ingested. Surreptitiously added to your tea or milk perhaps? This allowed the invisible spell magic to seep through your aura to create a sort of shadow energy, culminating in the impression of your footsteps on the pavement. My deepest apologies, but you'll be somewhat miserable in the short term while the detoxification continues. Do trust that the discomfort will pass shortly thereafter and you'll be good as new. In the meantime, I've put you in the recently remodeled wing of the house. We've begun adding indoor plumbing, if you can imagine! Not quite the first flush toilet in the region—Lady Everly is always the first to have every newfangled gadget—but there you have it."

Edwina's stomach did a somersault. "You might have warned me first," she said. Bugger the upper class and their rules of etiquette.

Elvanfoot deliberated her objection with a nod of his head to either side. "Perhaps, though surreptitious magic is often best dealt with using the same secretive application. The body has a strong inclination to protect itself from known harm. And this way you're already on your way to a clean slate."

Edwina fumed. She resented being treated with the same level of concern one reserves for a farm animal afflicted with parasites, yet there was little argument to be made with his logic. Yates, perhaps intuiting the need to intervene before sparks flew, urged Edwina to follow him out of the sitting room. "This way, miss," he said as he escorted her to the bottom of the stairs, where he pulled a cord on the wall that apparently called the housekeeper. Mrs. Fletcher, dressed in a plain gray dress, white apron, and crisp white cap, met her at the top of the grand staircase. From there they traversed a corridor with a balustrade overlooking the main hall, climbed a second set of stairs, and followed another long hallway until it turned sharply left for another twenty feet. Mrs. Fletcher marched with quick little steps, like a woman afraid of falling behind in her work or one grown accustomed to traveling the hallways of a big house several times a day. But after a long train ride, a bumpy journey on the back of an open dog cart, and a potent cleansing spell churning in her stomach, Edwina wasn't sure she'd make it to the room before collapsing.

To her great relief, the housekeeper finally stopped midway down the hall, excused herself after a small coughing fit, then opened a solid oak door. Edwina momentarily forgot her ills as she took in the grand interior, which was adorned with a four-poster bed, silks and brocades that framed the windows, and a view facing the back garden. Heaven. Mrs. Fletcher made fast work of pointing out the extra blankets in the wardrobe and the toilet items lined up on the vanity table, and then she showed off the en suite bathroom. Indoor plumbing indeed. A flush toilet and a bathtub with hot running water! Edwina didn't think she'd ever leave the room again.

"A right grand idea, is it not?"

"Fabulous," Edwina said and then begged to be left alone before she truly passed out, though maybe she already had and this was all just a dream. Surely no one who lived on this grand a scale would offer a common shopkeeper sanctuary in their beautiful home. Her stomach did a backflip, signaling her intuition might be onto something. And, of course, she knew. There was always a cost to such hospitality. She was an anomaly under the roof of a master wizard, one whose mind craved answers to magical conundrums, and she and her preternatural shape-shifting ability were an enigma.

At least this time around, she thought, surveying the luxurious modern facilities, she was a well-compensated freak.

Chapter Eight

The piece of black thread Ian had carefully positioned in the doorjamb of his flat was still there at the bottom, near the floor. A good sign no one had broken in through the front. It didn't, however, preclude the idea of someone getting in another way. And for some, a mere crack was all they needed to enter. The thread was for the detection of mortals; the protection spells were for everyone else.

Ian turned the key, pushed the door open, and was hit by the stagnant odor of a flat left closed up for nearly two weeks. He'd been gone longer than he'd planned, but there was no foreseeing the entanglement with the Blackwood sisters. Well, apparently some prophetess had seen it, according to Finlay, but that was a problem for another day.

He crossed the room and opened the heavy green drapes, sending a million dust motes aloft in the air. Aye, it was a fair view of the river, the spires, and the murky foul air. He was glad to be home.

"You smell like mushrooms." Hob poked his head out of the pitcher nestled in the washbasin beside the nightstand. "Why didn't you go with milady?" he asked.

"We have a wee bit of work to do first."

"Not on an empty stomach, I hope."

Ian opened his coat and tossed two mince pies and a slice of honey cake onto the desk next to the bed. "Angus down at the pub says thanks for clearing his cellar of the urisk fella what wouldna stop nipping at the cider. The cake is for you."

"All I did was remind him politely he ought to wait until he's invited before sampling the barrels."

"Manners still count for some."

Hob nodded and took a bite of his cake. "Last I saw, he was headed for the Black Cat pub instead. Maybe the owner there will ask for my help as well."

"It's a fair thought."

The two ate their meal in the relaxed atmosphere of being home again with few immediate demands. Afterward they both lit their pipes, letting the smoke swirl up to the ceiling in the shapes of ships, mermaids, and kelpies.

Hob put his feet up on the bed and let out a satisfied burp. "Sir will have the spell removed by now," he said. "Do you want me to pop over and see?"

Ian shook his head. "No, we'll check in the morning."

"You still love her?"

"Who said anything about love?"

"Your moon eyes did."

Ian balked. "I dinna have moon eyes. I simply enjoy her company."

"She's a bonnie lass."

"Aye, there's that too." Ian blew the shape of a unicorn into the air. He didn't know why he was being contrary to his nature. He had fallen for Edwina, and hard, but he suspected this new reticence had something to do with learning she was somehow connected to the business he'd been conscripted into doing for the fair folk. He couldn't say who he was working for exactly, only that he must finish the job if he wished to be paid in gold. But knowing the Blackwoods were somehow tethered to the coming Gathering had cooled his emotions toward her slightly. Their attraction and budding relationship suddenly smelled of contrivance, and yet he couldn't deny the authenticity of his feelings.

Strange that one could be hit over the head, robbed of his memories, and left for dead yet still develop emotions of trust and admiration for one of the perpetrators. Aye, she did have lovely eyes and a curious nature that sparked a challenge in him.

Ian tamped down the cinders in his pipe. "Come, Hob. It's nearly twilight. We've work to do around the city's portals."

"Does that mean we are going home?"

"Aye, eventually. I've been asked to investigate all seven gateways, including the one on Hare Hill."

Hob beamed and put out his pipe. "Unusual request."

"The veil is thinning but not yet lifted," Ian said. "Someone's been slipping through one of the portals ahead of the Midsummer Gathering. Certain entities want to know who and why."

Ian grabbed his night cloak and a flat cap from a hook by the door, and he and Hob left the flat and crossed the river. The setting sun's last rays grazed the back of Ian's cloak as he took the road that wound behind the castle on the hill. Across the city skyline, soft golden light rested on the shoulders of the towers and spires as well, while in the recesses below, the night shadows had already crept in.

Traffic on the terrace road was quiet, with only the occasional horse and carriage passing by to take some merchant or banker home for his tea. All the better, Ian thought. Maybe he'd get lucky and find the hole in the veil between worlds on his first try. Being a born cynic, he flipped the collar of his cloak up and prepared for disappointment as Hob trailed behind him, employing his usual fashion of transportation by hopping from one downspout to another.

Soon Ian came to a strip of abandoned land that ran beside the terrace road. Derelict and forgotten with broken pottery and wooden crates dumped over the side, the sloped terrain appeared as if it still served as a midden for the castle. And yet green grass poked up around cinquefoil bushes, and small colorful birds sang their last calls of the evening from the branches of a shrubby rowan tree. At the far end of the road, a stairway connected the upper terrace to the market street below.

The strip of land wasn't a naturally beautiful spot, but appearances weren't important. The hill upon which the ground sat was endowed with an ancient legacy, part of a network of fairy mounds where gateways allowed for magic to breathe between one world and the next. A place where the ancient ancestors could reenter the world they'd left behind. On ceremony days, the courtiers came to pay homage to the flora and fauna they'd nurtured into being when the world was made of magic and springy hope. They would step through the portal in their physical form and walk the earth once more, but afterward they would have to return to the Otherworld until the veil thinned again.

This coming Gathering was a different affair, however. The Seelie Court would be returning to this world not only to celebrate the glory of Midsummer but to reinstate their current queen as sovereign over all that was green and good. For one full day beginning at midnight, they would dance, drink, and feast as they relished the bounty born under the gaze of their summer queen. A sight to see, Ian recalled, but also an ideal opportunity for mischief.

He jumped over the low stone wall and tromped through a patch of weeds and grass until he stood on a rounded hump of ground that covered the top of the tunnel on the road below. There, in among the curly dock and thistle, sat an abandoned spring. The sunken ground, lined by exposed rock and lichen, was no bigger than the baptismal font in yonder Saint Maggie's chapel, but while that one obliged the mortals with an eye on heaven, this one served the fair folk. The weedy gateway situated above a bustling market street might seem an unlikely entry point to the human eye, but the hill and castle made the site a tempting location for the fey-born. The more Ian thought about it, the more he believed the site to be an ideal entry point for one of the fair folk wishing to slip through to walk among the city dwellers at night. A creature who'd mastered his human appearance and attire to blend in on the street—someone like Finlay—could easily come and go from a spot like this one and not raise an eyebrow.

Nothing appeared disturbed near the portal opening, but there was only one way to know if the doorway had been used recently. Ian dug through his cloak pocket and found his scrying stone, a lucky find he'd stumbled on at the beach when he was a wee lad still running around in short trousers. His mother had told him to cherish the rock with the hole in the center, for such a stone could only have come into his hands as a gift from the fair folk. And so it was. Over the years he'd discovered there were worlds upon worlds to be discovered by looking through the eye of the stone. Some small and far away, others within the world he walked but invisible without the stone. He'd discovered most of the gateways in and about the city by using the stone.

Ian held the hole up to his eye and peered at the basin of rocks. A shimmer of gold dust clouded over his vision.

"The dust has nae been disturbed," Hob said, poking his head up from behind a row of curly dock.

"Which means this one's still intact and no one's passed through recently." Ian pocketed the stone. Still, he wasn't convinced. In his line of work, he often had to think like a criminal, or in this case a trespasser, to make certain he didn't overlook any clues. He leaned back on his haunches, contemplating how one might get past the opening without disturbing the surroundings, when a man strode past on the road above. He was a merchant with a new foothold on a rung of the middle-class ladder by the look of him. He glanced at Ian with disapproval to see him mucking about in the hedgerow.

"You there, Cameron, what are you up to?" the man shouted, pointing his walking stick at Ian.

Ian had no memory of the gentleman, but whoever he was, he was a mortal who'd called him out by name. "Lost my cat in the verge," Ian called up while Hob rustled around in the weeds.

"But you havna got a cat."

Ian blinked back, wondering which shop he knew the man from. Obviously, there were holes in Hob's reconstruction of his memory. "He's naught but a stray I've taken a liking to," he bluffed.

The man adjusted his glasses and humphed before walking on. "And mind your own business next time, you nosy git," Ian said under his breath.

Once he was out of the man's line of sight, Ian took out his pocket watch and adjusted the knob, narrowing the view to those within a ten-foot radius. They were well within the twilight hour, so if one of the fair folk was near enough on the other side, their presence ought to show up on the watch. He let the gears spin a few seconds and thought he noted a brief flash but then gave up as a large hare poked its nose out of the bushes. The gateway was clean as far as he could tell.

"How long's it been since you traveled back and forth through the gateway at Hare Hill?" Ian asked Hob.

The hearth elf scratched the hairs on his chin. "It was the Gathering before your grandfather was born. Aye, that was the time when Annag was raised up as Queen of Elfhame."

"And do you never miss it there?" Ian thought of the golden light his scrying stone had allowed him to see just beyond the gateway of the Otherworld during a previous Gathering when he was a young man with new whiskers. He'd gotten a smack on the back of the head from a sprite who'd called him an idiot and asked him if he wanted to be taken as tithe to the Otherworld. And yet the beauty he saw and felt through the stone had inspired a level of awe he carried to this day.

"It's not so long ago since I was there." Hob paused while the hare nibbled on a thistle. "Besides, my purpose now is here. With you."

"Aye, as my self-appointed guardian." Ian had replied with the same knee-jerk response he always did, but only because he often resented having a shadow. Yet he knew it was only because of the hearth elf watching over him that his mind and memories had been partially returned. He immediately regretted his words. "I dinna mean to . . . It's only . . ."

"It's my place to be here now. And when it no longer is, I'll go back." The hare gave one of its ears a good scratch before scurrying off for a quieter patch of grass a few feet below. "Shall we spy on another gateway this evening?" Hob asked, rubbing his hands together in anticipation.

Ian checked the time. "One more and we'll retire for the night."

"We have to go check on milady tomorrow morning," Hob said.

"Aye, that we do."

"Sir believes he can rid her of the hex, but it won't remove her from danger."

Ian stood and brushed off his trousers. "Is there something you're not telling me?"

"No." Hob took on a sheepish look, as though searching for the nearest hole to escape. "Only trouble can travel on a train north, too, so why would Sir think she'd be any safer here than in her own city?"

"Because she's here with us, where we can protect her."

"But you were with her before and someone almost killed her."

Ian glared. "'Almost' is the key word there."

"But if she's being watched by . . ." Hob scratched his chin. "No, that can't be right."

"Watched by whom? Hob, if there's something you know, tell me now."

Hob gazed into the font. "There is no coincidence. Only the revelation of time and circumstance."

Ian arched a brow. "Have you been nipping the whisky down at Angus's pub since we got back?"

The hearth elf shrank and looked away. "It were just the one." He waved the confession away with his hairy hand, then grew pensive. "If you must know, she is one of your kind. And she is not."

The way the elf spoke, with his eyes gazing into the Otherworld through memory, Ian was reminded that Hob was part of an ancient clan he had no claim on, even if his family boasted of being distant relatives of the first inhabitants. "I saw her change into the raven," Ian said. "Gave me a shiver. Like a bolt of lightning under the skin. Like I was seeing the old magic done before my eyes." Then the truth hit. "That's why you call her 'milady.' Because she holds some place in the hierarchy."

Hob grinned. "Aye, milady holds a place." He watched the hare nibble a dandelion with one ear bent in their direction. "Which one remains to be seen."

This was only more evidence that meeting the Blackwoods was no coincidence. Perhaps as Hob suggested, the truth would be revealed after time and circumstance made their peace. In the meantime, he had his own position in the hierarchy, working for a ruffian sprite who liked to lurk in shadowy back lanes under bridges.

"Come, Hob. Let's see what the next gateway tells us." And together they traversed the length of the Queen's Mile to the foot of another great hill that marked a portal between worlds.

Chapter Nine

The skeleton key rattled appropriately in the lock of the old cottage. It had been enchanted to work solely for its new owner *or* his servant, should he wish it. His plans had unfolded delightfully since he'd mastered the art of summoning. Even though his energy was taxed from the long train ride north, he would call forth his demon this very evening. There was much to talk about.

The house exhaled its stale breath as he removed his cherished gray silk homburg and tossed it on the wicker settee. The dead did sometimes leave an unearthly smell behind if the body was allowed to linger too long on the kitchen flagstones. It was not unlike rubbish bins left to swelter in the sun, he mused, as he swept his hair back in place. A week spent in the southern capital hadn't been long enough to air the place out as he'd hoped after having the troublemaker dispatched, but one couldn't leave the windows open while away. Not even a crack. Not with *her* in the cellar. He was confident his entrapment spells were lock-tight, but then he'd always been cautious and proficient when it came to his craft.

The floorboards creaked underfoot as he set his valise down. For the sake of appearances, he ought to keep a manservant on at the cottage to assist with his belongings, but trust was such a tricky emotional state to maneuver anymore now that his plans were in motion. So, even though it was degrading for a gentleman of his standing to carry his bags from the train station and turn down his own bedcovers each night, he found that looking after himself while hidden away in the rugged north country had become an invigorating adventure. The same went for keeping watch over the woman, though he'd grown dead weary of listening to her pleas for mercy. She'd proved nothing but a drain on his energy. Regrettably, his demon had made a good argument for keeping her alive. For now.

Yes, he must speak with Maligar. There were new developments to discuss after his encounters with the sisters. One dead and the other afraid for her life and unsure of which way to turn. She was nearly ready to be plucked off the street. The vigor of summoning magic exhilarated him, as it should, but when he was able to shape that power to manipulate others' emotions, the particular sensation of control filled him with an exhilarating buoyancy. And yet the craving for more was never truly sated.

A knock sounded from below the floorboards. She'd survived the week he'd been gone to the city, then. Still, he'd been too generous in only binding the one leg while he was away. He would need to harden off yet another corner of his heart if he wished to attain the destiny he deserved.

After changing out of his suit and washing his body of impurities with a damp rag, he put on his blue robe, emblazoned with quarter moons and five-pointed stars. He settled the golden headdress bearing the circle and half-moon symbol of the ancients on his head. After securing his scarab amulet ring, his cherished symbol of transformation and protection from the ancient world, on his finger, he got to work. It was the twilight hour, and the evening was filled with the sort of electrified air the Otherworld found attractive. Bees and tiny moths flitted from tree to flower while shadows swelled in the hedgerows to cover up all manner of lustful sin.

He closed the curtains, pushed up his sleeves, and slid the sitting room furniture against the walls to create an open space to work in.

His blood simmered with anticipation as he rolled up the rug with the tribal medallion design to reveal the grand pentagram that had been carefully painted on the floorboards. The cardinal directions were also represented with a crossroads drawn in black through the center, which he paid deference to by tracing their directions with his hand across his chest.

The robed man lit a fat white candle with a matchstick from the mantel and placed it inside the circle. Softened wax oozed from the top and trickled down the sides from all the times he'd lit the wick previously. The woman banged on the cellar wall again, interrupting his concentration, so he stomped his foot on the floorboards.

Help is not *on the way, madam!*

He raised his arms in a V, reflecting the carriage of a man prepared to accept the All Powerful's gift. With his mind recalibrated, he stepped inside the pentagram and drew his knife, tracing a magic circle around him. Deep in the pocket of his robe he kept three amulets: citrine, garnet, and lodestone. He placed the gems on three of the five points, spacing out their fiery energy. On one of the remaining two points, he set the fat candle. On the other he placed an offering of licorice allsorts kept in his other pocket, which Maligar insisted upon. The treat was tied up in a paper bag for easy nibbling.

With his offerings spread out, he centered himself and raised his arms once again for the invocation. The silk slid across his skin, reminding him he was naked beneath the robe. He harnessed the excitement that followed, using it to propel his magic. "Doorway deep I knock on thee, call thy spirit willingly. Summoned here to do my will, be it good or be it ill. From your hellish depths afar, rise before me, Maligar."

An unseen force, like a change in the weather, sent a wave of static electricity skittering through the room. Could *she* feel it too? Had his magic grown powerful enough to affect the entire household? The beams of the cottage gave a little shake, and he smiled as the shape of a manlike creature swooped into the room, riding a wave of atmospheric energy. The being materialized in the shadows, where the drapes rippled in folds of dark velvet. With deep purple eyes that seemed to drown the candlelight's reflection, the being blinked from the dimness before grinning conspiratorially.

"I have summoned thee," the man said to the creature, feeling for the security of his protective ring. "You are bound and thus must do my bidding." He tossed the licorice allsorts outside the pentagram for the demon to devour. Such an infantile appetite for a creature of the netherworld, he thought, then quickly marked where his feet stood within the protective circle to make certain he was safe.

"Back so soon?" Maligar stepped out of the shadows and popped a candy in his mouth. "How fared your travels south, good sir?" The demon's cheeks caved in and his eyes closed briefly as he sucked on the licorice, savoring the first hit of sweetness against the tongue. "Have we struck the bargain yet?"

"Of course not. She only just suffered the fury of my magic. These matters take time and delicate handling."

Maligar nibbled on another sweet, then tucked the sack in his breast pocket for later. He'd materialized, as usual, in a black frock coat, paisley waistcoat, and pin-striped trousers. The jumped-up demon dressed above his station in his earthly form. When finished with his particular surreptitious talents, the man vowed to give his demon a metaphysical lashing to teach him his place. Perhaps he would lock him away in some cramped vessel or cupboard for a thousand years, where he could reflect on his overreaching faux pas. But first they had to deal with the Blackwoods.

The demon licked a sticky finger. "You don't know, then, that she's already arrived on the train ahead of you?"

"Preposterous. I was on the only northern-bound train. I stole their tickets."

"Not preposterous if one takes a witches' train from a city safe house." Maligar added the inflection of a single raised brow.

The man took a step back, pondering. He'd heard rumors of such a thing. Hadn't a member of the Order of the Night Hunter suspected that an underground track for witches might exist?

There was yet another muffled, angry scream from the woman in the cellar. The man stomped his bare foot three times against the oak planks to shut her up.

The man was constantly astonished by his own power. He'd cast the fire spell on the flowers to intimidate and put the idea in Edwina Blackwood's head that she was in danger, but he'd not counted on a witch-born frightening so easily that she would flee at the first notion of trouble. He'd been prepared to hex her shawl next so her clothes caught fire as well, but he did need her in one piece—frightened but able. Again, Maligar had talked him out of that particular approach.

"I had hoped to perform my ritual before my fellow Order members in the south, but if she's turned up here, then it's a gift we must take advantage of," he said before noticing his heels grazed the outline of the pentagram. He inched forward, keeping his eye on the demon, then pointed a finger toward the ground. "Providence hath provided us with opportunity."

Maligar tapped his polished shoe against the floor. "And how fares our captive? Remember, the bargain depends on her welfare, at least until the deal is secured."

The man rolled his eyes. "Alive, as we agreed. But mark me, that mess you made with the other one still requires airing out. Have a care next time with the details." He swooped his robe up about him as though it were a shield. "Now be gone until I call again."

The demon bowed. "Until we meet again, good sir."

Chapter Ten

Edwina found the wizard in the garden behind the house, snipping the head off a yellow flower. She spied his back, thinking of a painful pinching charm she could flick at the old coot to give him a taste of his own medicine. After being up half the night with stomach cramps, it was the least she could do to repay his peculiar brand of hospitality. Her conscience stopped her just as the butler approached and invited her to sit outside at the table he'd arranged for their breakfast on a brisk, sunny morning.

"Ah, Miss Blackwood," Elvanfoot said, turning around. "I trust you are recovered this morning?"

"I believe so."

"I do hope in the light of day you forgive me for my deceitfulness," he said, tucking the flower into his breast pocket. "It honestly was the least painful remedy. The other option involved leeches, which most people find distressing."

She tried to grace him with a forgiving smile. "Of course."

He bowed his head in gratitude, then gestured toward a patch of green-and-white flowers growing in a clump at the base of a rowan tree. "Please, allow me to show you the garden while Yates arranges our breakfast table."

Edwina had seen the long view of the impressive floral beds from her window on the third floor, but standing at ground level, she had a better appreciation for the care and detail that had gone into his witch's garden. There were rows of garlic, rosemary, Saint-John's-wort, chamomile, and lavender. Fragrant lemon balm grew in a clump, promising relief from heartache and depression for those inclined toward the morbs. Tiny purple blooms of belladonna looked up innocently from the far corner of the garden, but every witch knew and respected their deadly potency once the flowers had gone to seed. It was a garden worthy of the greenest envy, with all the staple plants needed for any spell, potion, or tincture one could dream up. And there were other plants, too, some too foreign for her to recognize. She imagined the elder wizard must have traveled and studied widely to have acquired such an impressive collection of medicinal plants.

"Ah, I wouldn't touch that one if I were you," Elvanfoot cautioned as she extended a finger to admire the three-pronged leaves of a shiny green plant. "Your skin will blister for a week. I use the ivy to protect the purple valerian it surrounds. Brewed correctly, the flower makes a delightful truth-telling tea. I was asked to apply it once to a minister of the exchequer who eventually admitted to pilfering funds. The queen went red in the face for a week. Naturally, the government has been trying to extract my cultivated strain of valerian ever since, but you didn't hear it from me."

"Goodness." Edwina stepped back and rubbed the tip of her finger against her thumb, feeling a slightly prickly feeling even though she hadn't made contact with the plant. "And this?" she asked, clasping her hands behind her back in front of a pinkish white flower to keep from being tempted again. Unlike the other flora, this plant grew from a pile of deliberately arranged stones arranged to the side of the rest of the garden.

"That, my dear, is a rare flower of the mallow family, *Iliamna corei*." He checked the soil around their roots with his finger and seemed pleased with the results. "The only example of its kind in these isles. I'd been corresponding with a fellow witch with a commendable garden across the pond who sent me the seeds. They require scarification by fire to germinate, which makes them remarkably rare but also potent ingredients for resurrection spells. Something I've been experimenting with lately," he said before looking up from the flower heads. "Ah, here is Yates with our breakfast."

A wrought-iron bistro set, coated in white enamel, had been situated on a flagstone patio to take advantage of the morning sun. Edwina sat so she faced the poison ivy, as she didn't wish to turn her back on it. Yates set down a tray he'd been balancing on one hand. In the other he carried a small packet of letters. Steam trailed up from a pot of tea, while two plates covered with silver-plated domes made Edwina's mouth water for a hearty northern breakfast of eggs, mushrooms, tomatoes, and blood pudding. Alas, when the dome in front of her was removed, she was greeted with a bowl of plain porridge paired with a silver spoon atop a clean white doily. Yates presented Elvanfoot with the same along with a stack of mail before he went to stand by the rear entrance to the house.

The sight of the oats didn't disappoint Edwina so much as it wilted her inspiration. With an abundance of beauty, opulence, and potion ingredients at arm's length, she'd never expected to be served something most often described as "good for the constitution," which proved to be the very next words out of the wizard's mouth before he winked and picked up a honey pot to drizzle a little sweetness over his drab meal. Almost immediately a pair of bees buzzed over Elvanfoot's head. He paid them no mind, not even swatting at them to leave him be to eat. Edwina shook out her napkin and dipped her spoon into her oatmeal.

"If you've seen the imp, you'll know I've had him running errands for me," Elvanfoot said.

Edwina dabbed her napkin against the corners of her mouth. "Yes, he did mention something about it," she said, now curious why the wily witch would need to do such deep research on a spell that appeared to have been quite simple to counteract.

"Apologies, my dear, I was speaking to the bees." The witch removed from his breast pocket the flower he'd collected and dabbed a clear liquid from its center on his forefinger. He held his hand out and the bees landed, making jaunty moves that resembled a polka dance. Elvanfoot watched, nodding as they wiggled their bodies. "Yes, yes, he's already collected pages of grimoires from the Hume monastery and Ludo abbey for me in the south, and he even found a relevant page in a sea cave on the outer islands up north." He paused and glanced up at Edwina as if this might mean something to her, but it didn't. The bees continued wagging their bodies atop his finger. "Of course. I'll be in touch when I've sorted out more."

The bees dipped their long proboscises in the nectar on his finger, then zoomed off over the heads of the flowers, flying toward a looming forest behind the house.

"You speak bee?" she asked, astonished.

"Naturally." He shrugged and picked up his cup. "No more difficult than learning Morse code for the telegraph." The old witch smiled and sipped his tea. "I don't wish you to think me impudent, but might I inquire how you came by the enchanted cloak? It appears to be woven from common black wool, yet at times I've noticed it reflects the iridescent hues of green and blue. Like raven feathers."

Edwina sat back and gripped her shawl tight around her. She thought to put him off by suggesting she didn't know what he meant, but he was too clever, and she'd long tired of covering her secrets up from everyone she met, witch and mortal alike. "My mother gave it to me."

"It's almost like a swaddling motion, is it not? The way you keep your shawl held snug around you whenever you're a bit flustered?"

"I'm not flustered. Not exactly." She loosened her grip on the shawl and settled herself. "But when Mary and I were younger, it often helped with the transformation, as you suggest. My mother is a textile witch. She can sew, weave, knit. She made the shawls when we were younger, enchanting them with malleable threads that conformed to our bodies.

You see, it does take a measure of self-control to keep the mind and body housed together when things get stressful. Of course, it's easier now that I'm older."

"Emotions trigger a change?" Elvanfoot sat back and looked up to the second floor, where Mrs. Fletcher had opened a window to air out a room, coughing as though overtaken with dust.

"Strong emotions have always affected our shape-shifting. The day my sister flew off in a rage when you attempted to return Ian's memory was such an occasion. Flight is always our first impulse when threatened. Was," she added clumsily, remembering yet again her sister was gone.

"How did your mother come up with such a fanciful spell? I've never encountered a shawl or any other piece of clothing that could enable a witch to shape-shift."

"Oh, no, you misunderstand me," Edwina said. "The shawl is enchanted with a calming spell that's been bonded to the fibers with a mother's love during the weaving process. That's what she always said, anyway."

"But the transformation? How is it done? What spell do you use?"

"There is no spell," she said. "It's more like how you described yourself once when you said you'd done magic so long you no longer needed to say the spells out loud." Edwina gave a slight shrug. "I merely have to think it and I transform."

He peered at her then as he was prone to do over the tops of his spectacles. Always studying, evaluating, trying to figure out how she ticked. He did it with such a sense of compassionate curiosity that she didn't necessarily feel like she was the subject of a dissection. Instead, the intense observations made the nerves of her neck and temple and even the soft tissue behind her eyes shiver in a soft, pleasant frisson. Still, the constant scrutiny did put her off all the same, knowing what he was dying to ask of her without having the nerve to speak outright.

In truth, she'd never fully understood how the change was propagated, only that she was able to cast off one body for another by focusing her mind's eye on the outcome she wanted. Feeling devilish after the surreptitious magic she'd been subjected to, Edwina pushed her bowl of porridge away, scooted her chair back, and threw off her shawl. It was a rare, glorious northern summer morning, and she needed a stretch anyway. As Elvanfoot had earlier mentioned that the house and grounds were protected by charms, she didn't see any harm in a quick jaunt around the garden.

Edwina's blood surged. Bone and flesh flexed and sponged. Hair and tooth gave way to beak and feather. Lightness filled her being, throwing off the heavy corporal human weight. The eye fixed; the lens flattened. The scent of a dead squirrel on the air alerted her nostrils as she pushed off her seat and opened her wings. She flapped and rose up on a swell of warm air until she reached the height of the roof on the manor house. Weblike filaments from the protection spells grazed the tips of her wings as she circled two of the turrets before glancing at the ground.

The wizard had taken off his spectacles to stare up at her transformation in astonishment. She was relishing the shock on the old man's face, readying to soar over the roof of the house again, when she spotted a bicycle passing by on the road in front of the house. Thinking she ought to get down, she swooped over the garden wall where Yates had been watching her open-mouthed from the rear door to the conservatory.

Edwina's eye fixed on the butler's meek aura in the same way her sight might be drawn by a reflection of the moon on the water. Her eyes were always attracted to whatever shone or sparkled. But then the glow around him wavered, flickering oddly. Suddenly the light burst like a camera flash. The brightness played in her sight, crystallizing in kaleidoscope shapes. Her feet hit the ground and her vision froze, yet her thoughts whisked her away to another scene altogether. In her mind's eye she watched as the red-haired butler fell facedown in the cluster of hemlock growing behind the house. His body trembled and went still. Soon after, a small, wan creature wearing a black mourning veil and tufts of feathery hair dropped from the sky. The fairylike being fluttered its translucent wings and peeked at the back of Yates's neck before extending a finger to touch his skin. The butler convulsed and then went pale. She knew he must be dead.

Edwina wondered if she'd been mentally transported to some other plane of . . . what? Premonition? Warning? Hallucination? The odd vision lasted only a few seconds, but to be yanked out of her conscious thought so violently while in her transformed state left her shaken.

She shape-shifted back into her womanly form and leaned momentarily against the rowan tree to catch her breath before returning to the table.

"Absolutely delightful," Elvanfoot said, holding her chair out for her, oblivious to the inner turmoil still coiling through her phrenological system—a word she learned well enough from the half dozen times her parents had taken her and Mary to an actual witch doctor. He was a friend of a friend who practiced his craft of magic while functioning as a mortal physician. However, his only grimoire seemed to consist of a book entitled *The Constitution of Man*, which asserted the contour of one's head determined the shape of one's behavior. Dr. Samuel Fontanella, as he was called, had examined their skulls, inside and out, using every tool available to him, including calipers for measuring and scrying stones to monitor their auras. He'd also relied upon tick-tock-follow-the-watch hypnosis to bypass the female temperament so one might better get to the heart of the matter inside the head. None of his conclusions accounted for her and Mary's unique ability to transform from one species into another without aid of spell or potion. But after what just happened, she wondered if she were in need of a fresh examination.

Edwina dropped in her chair in front of her cold and lumpy bowl of porridge.

"My dear, I have seen any number of curses, hexes, jinxes, and spells that transform the physical self, but none so brilliantly executed as what I just witnessed." Elvanfoot sat down and removed a small notebook and pencil from his breast pocket as Mrs. Fletcher shut the upstairs window with a small slam. He licked the end of the graphite, then began jotting down a storm of words and diagrams in that fanciful handwritten script of his. Then he looked up.

"Does the change cause you any pain or discomfort?" he asked. "Are you conscious the whole time? Do you maintain your intellect?"

"No. I mean, yes, I remain myself. Mostly. No, there's no pain."

"Can you stay in your altered body indefinitely?" He scribbled down a line of notes. "Do you recite a mantra in flight to maintain the form?"

Edwina answered with a shrug and vague shake of her head, unable to concentrate on anything more he wrote, let alone said. She pondered the strange experience. She'd meant to be brazen and shock the old wizard with the truth of her gift. Instead, the flight had left her feeling as though she'd touched a live wire that zapped her with the electricity of a strange psychotic dream. Edwina reached for her teacup while Elvanfoot wrote down more notes. She hoped the tea would settle her, but her shaking hand fumbled the china so that it rattled in its saucer.

Yates, ever the attentive servant but now with a similar look of awe in his face, reached out to steady her. "Are you all right, lass?" he asked.

He offered his hand, but she recoiled at his touch. *Had* she seen his future? His *death*? Or was she ill? Cursed? Or maybe she'd touched some poisonous leaf in the garden she shouldn't have. Or perhaps Elvanfoot was still feeding her surreptitious food spells and she'd eaten something with a spot of hexed mold and hallucination was the toxic outcome.

When none of those options were made abundantly clear, she answered, "I'm just a little wobbly after so much exertion."

Elvanfoot glanced up from his notebook. "My dear, you've gone pale. You look positively shaken. Is it always so after you change back?" He mumbled something about the ill effects of transformation. "Yates, a bottle of spirits is in order, I think."

With the butler thankfully gone, Edwina ventured to at least partially explain what she'd experienced. "No, I . . . I saw something," she said. "While I was up there." She looked up to the turrets of the house, wondering if one of his spells had somehow interfered with her own magic. "A sort of vision. As if I'd seen someone's future."

The old witch narrowed his eyes. "Have you had such an episode before?"

Episode?

She'd always had the odd premonition—a forewarning about the weather, a feeling she ought not trust the fish from the monger near Blackmoor Lane, or that a somewhat legitimate-looking customer had really come in to nick the shiny silver bell on display in the shop window. And the fire too. Hadn't the scent of smoke and char sparked in her mind flash-powder quick just before the shop was engulfed in flames? Yet this time was different. Her mind had soared into a vision of shadows yet to be, an animated premonition that had left her overcome by a wave of sights until she felt like an hourglass filling up with sand.

Edwina blinked and steadied her breath. It wasn't normal at all, but she wasn't ready to play the part of the wizard's guinea pig. "Perhaps I was mistaken about what I saw," she said, covering up her momentary confusion. "It was a long journey followed by an uncomfortable evening."

"My dear, I'm afraid I'm proving a most unworthy host. Might it be optimal if you had a lie down and got some more rest? I'll have Mrs. Fletcher look in on you in a bit. She'll know what to do. We'll talk about it later." He jotted down another note in his book, punctuating the sentence with a sharp period before closing the leather cover.

Grateful to be out from under the witch's curious stare, Edwina made her way back upstairs, where she closed the door to her room and collapsed on the bed. She closed her eyes, but the vision of the red-haired butler wouldn't leave her. The urge to reveal what she'd seen welled up inside her, as if she needed to sing the vision into the world. But was it real or merely an illusion while in transit? Edwina was unaccustomed to such churning uncertainty. She'd always been the steady one, but now she found herself adrift in indecision.

Where was Ian? And Hob? She could confide in them. Measure the depth and width of her sanity against the banks of their common sense so she might regain her reason. Finding herself without anyone to talk to, the final weight of Mary's absence weighed heavily on her. Yes, her sister had lost her way and done despicable things, but they were blood and bone related, together since the womb. And while she'd often reminded Mary at troubling moments there was no other person in the world who better understood their unique condition, that relationship worked both ways. After her sister's death, she'd lost *her* one true confidante.

Embrace it, Mary would say. *We were born this way for a reason.* But wasn't that what had led her sister to her demise? Had Mary resisted her urges, would she still be alive?

Her curiosity rekindled, Edwina sat with her grimoire and turned to the page where Mary had drawn the odd symbols. Why had she done it? And when? Her sister had marked in her grimoire only once before. It had happened years ago, when Mary had first discovered she could transform corpse lights rising from a body by turning them into small keepsake orbs. Beyond excited, she'd run into the house while Edwina was learning an incantation to make silver polishing easier, stolen her fountain pen, and boldly made her mark in the book, grinning at her mischief. That time she'd left what looked like a roman numeral II, the symbol for Gemini, and written the word "fixed." Edwina had remarked she'd chosen that symbol because they were twins, but Mary only laughed and said Edwina should have read her transmutation studies more closely. Now, she sorely wished she had so she might decipher this latest combination of symbols in what was likely the last communication from her sister.

Too restless to sit any longer, Edwina rubbed her arms and walked to the window to watch for Ian. Instead, she spotted the same man she'd seen on the bicycle earlier, only this time he was riding away from the neighborhood. By the cut of his uniform, he appeared to be the postman going about his deliveries. Such a quiet bucolic lane outside the hubbub of the city's center, and yet she couldn't shake off the feeling that something more lurked in the surrounding fens and forests. She'd thought when she first arrived that the skittering energy dancing across her skin had something to do with the spells surrounding Eidyn House, but now she questioned the very air itself. By the way the young lad sped away while looking over his shoulder, she suspected he harbored the same misgivings too.

Chapter Eleven

Ian swept back the fern leaves covering the opening to the fourth gateway. The crevice, which he knew well from poking around when he was a lad, served as a passage for the fair folk. Set deep between two granite rocks, the doorway was situated just beside the stream that ran through his parents' modest allotment. Their cottage, with its stone walls and thatched roof, sat at the base of Hare Hill on the borderland of the Queen of Elfhame's domain. It was by her leave they were allowed to remain so close to the fairy queen's rumored point of reentry to the world above. His parents, and his ancestors before them, had long and faithfully obeyed the rites and rituals of the fair folk and thus been blessed with bountiful gardens, healthy children, and a roof that never leaked as a result. To do otherwise would bring only ruin.

Curiously, yet somewhat disappointingly, Ian found an intact spiderweb covering the crevice portal. Morning dew still clung in droplets from the delicate strands, sparkling like tiny strung opals. The evidence meant no creature, ethereal or otherwise, had recently passed through. In fact, none of the portals had shown any sign of activity, despite Finlay's suspicions. To be certain, he brought out his scrying stone to see beyond the physical world. Though traces of magic had spilled onto the rocks, a small scattering of golden dust was typical for the area and always had been. He shook his head, flummoxed.

Ian stood and brushed the grass from his trousers. He'd worn his best suit with the slim-fitting waistcoat and black derby hat. Though he wouldn't admit his motivation to Hob, he did wish to make a fresh new impression on Edwina, as she'd only seen him in his tackety boots and the casual clothes he wore to blend in with the city folk in the south.

"Aye, did I nae say so," his father said over Ian's shoulder. "A few fair folk came prancing by on their wee white horses in May, but no more since that I've seen, as is proper."

Ian stood and faced his father, whose salt-and-pepper hair stood on end in the breeze, making him resemble a startled Dumpy chicken with its feathers ruffled. The gray-and-white plaid shirt his father wore beneath his gray wool waistcoat did little to dissuade Ian of the image.

"Aye, I believe you," he said. "There's nae a mark around the opening to suggest otherwise."

"Your mother's had a notion there was something afoot a time or two, but not enough to swear to it by spit or moonlight." His father, always one to observe the old ways, turned his coins over in his pocket at the mention of moonlight. "Are you sure you canna tell me what all this is about?"

Ian shook his head. "A case I'm working on. That's all I can say for now."

"An investigation involving the fair folk on our doorstep and you dinna think we might be interested in the details?"

"It isn't just this one, ye ken? I'm checking on all seven." Ian scanned the ground again for any missed sign of disturbance. Seeing nothing of interest there, he looked toward the strip of forest at a mile distance. A thin stream of smoke swirled upward into the sky above the treetops. "Someone staying at the old Osborne place?"

"Och aye," his father said and spit on the ground. "Osborne's relatives finally sold it off six months ago to some city fellow. A sassenach. Mainly keeps to himself when he's here. Spotted him a time or two foraging in the woods, wearing a suit and carrying a walking cane to pick mushrooms and moss off the forest floor." His father rolled his eyes.

The news surprised Ian. The place hadn't been lived in properly for nearly twenty-five years after Old Man Osborne died. He and the other lads used to dare each other to look in the windows at dusk when the bats circled in the sky above and the swifts called out for the last time before going silent for the night. And while there had been desperate holiday goers over the years who were willing to pay just about any price to spend the summer out of the foul city air, rumors of curses and ghosts kept the mortals away from the Osborne place. The occasional witch did rent the house, hoping to commune with the energy of the surrounding woods for spellwork and gathering ingredients. Still, the thought of someone buying and living on the property was a welcome thought, especially with his parents getting older with few neighbors nearby, aside from the fair folk.

"Come in and have a cup of tea before you go, lad," his father said.

He didn't know why, but the casual invitation from his father strummed an odd emotion in him. Ian wasn't the sort to suffer from melancholy, but as he touched the blue orb he kept in his pocket, it struck him how much of the ordinary life, the affection-filled parts that made up the connective tissue between the big memorable moments, he could have lost if not for Hob. He'd nearly lost that sense of home and belonging and place in the world, all that George Elvanfoot had lost during those three weeks he went missing and was forced to live on the streets in anonymity.

"I'd like that," Ian said and clapped his hand on his dad's back as the pair walked inside the cottage.

Turning from the stove, his mother, a middle-aged woman in a striped skirt, apron, and cotton blouse that ballooned at the shoulders, set a second plate of oatcakes on the table. Evidence of the demise of the first plate was still smeared across Hob's face in the form of blackberry jam and butter.

"Always did have an appetite, that one." His mother wiped her hands on her apron and grabbed a cup for Ian. "Have a seat," she said to her son. "You can stay for a minute before you're off again. Have an oatcake."

"Aye," he said. "If they haven't all disappeared inside his great gob yet."

Hob grinned, making his hairy ears rise atop his head, and took a fresh oatcake. Ian snatched the treat out of the imp's hands and broke it in two.

"I hear you've had a notion of some visitors crossing over a time or two recently," Ian said to his mother after taking a bite.

The woman paused in front of the iron girdle before spreading a third ladle of batter. "A tickle, more like," she answered, hand on her chest. "The way you get a sneeze in your nose when there's a bit of pollen swirling about, but then it never quite goes off."

His mother claimed to be a full-blood witch, but she had the manner of the fair folk too. The family teased there must have been a covert midnight dalliance with a fairy by one of the ancestors a few generations back to account for her uncanny notions. She could read the seasons better than any almanac, predict the rainfall to a quarter of an inch, and detect the presence of the fair folk with a squint of the eye and the skiff of static against her skin.

"'Tweren't the light and airy feeling I normally get," she said. "'Twere heavier. Like a coat of dust that clings to the hairs on the arm and makes you feel"—she paused to find the right word—"grubby."

"When was the last time you had that feeling?" Ian asked.

"Yesterday evening. I was just putting the tatties on to boil. Before that, 'twere maybe a week or two gone by when I last felt it."

"Aye, Maggie, tell him what you told me. About the carrots."

Ian's mother nodded. "'Twere right there in the garden," she said as she pointed through the wall at a specific spot outside. "On the farthest row, all the tops of the carrots had shriveled, so I dug one up and then another. Black as coal, they were. Shriveled, ugly things. Like a hard frost had passed over 'em."

"'Twere the entire row nearest the stream by the rock," his father added. "I meant to show you where she dug them up, but then we got to talking about the Osborne place."

Hob swallowed and sank lower in his seat.

"We've always got along fine with the fair folk, setting aside a pitcher of milk or a plate of bannocks on celebration days," his mother said. "And in the high summer I always leave a bowl of rose hips and lavender for the fair ladies on their white horses. They've no cause to be angry with us. Isn't that right, Hob?"

The woman looked at the elf as if expecting him to nod in agreement, but he'd slunk down even farther in his seat, nibbling away at his last piece of oatcake.

"What's got into him?"

"I'm sure it's nothing," Ian said, then drained his tea. "The portal's nae been used anytime recently." He shook his head, dismissing her suspicions. He knew how important maintaining the family's relationship with the fair folk was to his parents after so many generations living in peace on the land. "The blackened carrots are likely nothing more than a wee hex or blight from the Dunwoodys down the lane. They're probably still holding a grudge for the way you bested them at the market pie-baking contest."

Casting the incident as a mere childish hex seemed to soothe his mother, so he kissed her on the cheek and said he must be going. "Think I'll cut across the south slope to the Eidyn House. On my way to Elvanfoot's to check on the old man next."

"And our Miss Blackwood," Hob said, perking up.

"Oh, there's a young woman visiting, is there?" His mother raised a brow and smiled as she tucked an oatcake wrapped in brown paper in Ian's pocket for the journey. "I thought the cards had been telling fibs this morning when I laid them out for a reading and had all wands and cups turning up."

The skin around Ian's collar got suddenly very warm, knowing his mother's habit of reading the tarot in an effort to understand why he hadn't yet taken a wife. His work as first a constable and later a private detective precluded his pursuing whatever a normal courting relationship was meant to look like. Most young women couldn't abide his odd hours and endless excuses for why he was late or, more likely, a complete no-show after getting caught up in the demands of a case. Not wishing to rehash it all again, he seized the opportunity to depart. He shook his father's hand goodbye, patted his pockets to be sure he had all his effects, and walked out to the yard with Hob. The cool air gave him the reprieve he needed from his parents' inquisitive eyes, and together they tromped through the grassy sward toward Eidyn House with the sound of his mother shouting "good luck" at their backs.

Once they put a little distance between them and Hare Hill, Ian asked, "What was all that shrinking in your chair nonsense at the house?" Hob remained uncharacteristically quiet, so Ian stopped and waited for the elf to say something.

"Mister is wrong about the carrots," Hob said while keeping his eyes focused on their surroundings. "Cold spite can cause such damage, if the wrong being passes by."

"Wait, now you think someone passed through the portal by the creek?" Ian glanced back at his folks' cottage. "But we checked. Nothing was disturbed."

Hob pursed his lips, thinking. "I've been through the doorway many times in my youth." He shook his head. "To pass through without disturbing the strands of a spider's web would seem impossible," he whispered. "But there are some creatures sly and slippery enough to do it."

"You mean one of the unseelie?"

"Shhhhh!" Hob crouched in the grass like a rabbit hiding from a soaring hawk. "You may not mind having your insides shriveled like blackened carrots, but I do."

Ian gnawed on his lower lip, wondering if it could be true. The seelie were about to embark on their high celebration to reaffirm their Queen of Elfhame. And while all of elfdom had a right to participate in the festivities, as he understood their traditions, there'd been a strong and long-standing show of indifference among those who dwelled in the shadows of the above and below worlds. Though all creatures fell under the reign of the Queen of Elfhame, the unseelie made claim to their own vein of power in the realm through their apathy. The unseemly in life was their territory. The awkward moment. The unkind remark. The sense of impending disaster. The particular energy housed in the human heart concerning fear, shame, anxiety, and unhealthy appetites—that was the unseelie's dominion.

Ian's thoughts turned to Mary Blackwood then and her odd compulsion of stealing the memories of the dead and sometimes the almost dead. If not witch-born, he'd have sworn she had the blood of the unseelie in her. Aye, one such as she could shrivel the heart of a man to cold stone with a single look from those smoky eyes.

A worrying thought fluttered through Ian's mind. The unseelie had never bothered his parents before, not in a way that caused any lasting damage, but something was off with this business of the doorways being used by someone who ought not to be passing through. He wondered if he should turn around and go back to help his father with a protection spell or two when Hob tugged at his trouser leg.

"They have protection," Hob said. As proof, his palm lit with shimmering gold light that set Ian's heart at ease. "The house has my claim on it. And all those inside."

There were times when the hearth elf's attention felt like a burden that Ian couldn't shake off, but in the moments when his mind calmed down long enough to recognize the great gift he'd been given through

Hob's friendship, he was enormously grateful. Doubly so, now that there was mischief afoot. "There's a good lad." He handed over the oatcake his mother had given him, which Hob munched in happy satisfaction.

Carrying on, the pair intercepted the road leading to Elvanfoot's house a half mile later. A young man on a bicycle approached from the opposite direction, so Hob hopped out of sight to sift through the red fescue and crested dog's tail. The rider was a postman in uniform riding fast with a face as white as chalk. Spooked by something? Ian turned to watch the lad ride away, and not a minute later the postman glanced over his shoulder.

Mortals carried no magic inside, yet they had an uncanny ability to sense it all around them—or rather the threat they believed the supernatural posed to them. As he understood it, the tiny hairs on their bodies could sense the presence of spell energy, even if they didn't know what it was they were experiencing. In some mortals the experience was heightened into a sixth sense. In others it manifested as pure superstition. A woman once compared the phenomenon to him as having the same sort of effect on her skin as walking into the threads of a spiderweb. So while the postman might not know what threat he was riding away from exactly, from a witch's perspective, his mortal instincts were as good as watching birds scatter from tall grass at the sound of gunshot. Ian had little doubt now there was *something* strange stirring in the air, even if the evidence of it was scant on the wind.

Something amiss this far from the gateway on Hare Hill got Ian's hackles up. A swath that wide had bigger implications than a mere trespasser from the Otherworld. Was that what Finlay had wanted him to discover, knowing his list of portals would lead him to the countryside because of his family ties? Ian was beginning to think the threat went beyond a mere rogue visitor getting an early glimpse of the earthen realm. The possibilities had his intuition flaring like a bonfire as he veered off the lane and tramped through the bracken instead of walking the final distance to the Eidyn House gate.

"Where is Mister going?" Hob asked while running to keep up with Ian's long strides. "I thought we were going to Sir's house?"

"We're taking a slight detour through the park first to Black Briar Pond." He'd meant to put off checking the sixth portal until after his visit with Edwina, but he no longer thought it could wait.

Hob stopped abruptly and made a wee squelchy noise in his throat. Ian slowed and turned around to find the elf surveying the densely forested park ahead. "What's the matter?"

"What if there's something nasty in there?"

"Something or *someone*?" Ian asked.

The hearth elf peered into the shadows between trees. "Both."

Ian consulted his pocket watch. There was only the usual flutter of activity one would expect from the sprites and tree sprits who remained in the above world year-round. Like Hob, some individual beings haunted natural spaces as sentries and guardians while others led a more hermit-like life removed from the duty of such caretaking. They didn't mean to cause mischief; they just hadn't adapted to socializing within the ever-expanding world of humans.

Ian snapped his watch shut and tucked it away. "Do you want me to say a wee spell?"

Hob nodded vigorously, so Ian took a moment to prepare. He didn't have to worry about contriving an incantation incognito to disguise his charmwork. The Northern Witches' Constabulary had little interest in policing spells and the use of magic in the hinterlands. The interference from wooded parks, like those behind Eidyn House, made it near impossible anyway. If they ever tried using spiders like those in the south to detect unlawful magic, they'd never stop jumping on account of the countryside and all its hidden magic.

Ian planted his boots on firm ground and cast his eye on the trees as their shadows bent toward him. "If mischief-makers' pranks decrease, we honor thee and come in peace." He dusted his hands together. "Will that do?"

"That was a very short spell."

"Concise," Ian corrected.

Hob remained wary, but he ventured forward through the ferns. Ian kept the pace slow. Hob could keep up using his special portals if he chose, yet Ian understood the little fellow's apprehension and didn't blame him for sticking so close in the above world. As they walked beneath the outstretched limbs of oak and ash, the air grew thick with the scent of wild things—the slightly sulfuric aroma of a red fox curled up in its den, the soft musk of a roe deer nibbling on tender tree buds, and a rotting carcass no doubt overrun with ants and beetles after the corbies had done their work. A quarter of a mile inside the park, the sun's rays were halved, then halved again beneath the canopy of leaves until the forest's climate cooled enough that their breath hung like mist in the shadowed air.

"It's just this way to Black Briar Pond," Ian said as he led Hob toward a pool of standing water encircled by nine hazel trees.

Hob crouched on a mossy rock and peered into the water. "This doorway is where the water spirits like to come and go," he said. "Nixies and shellycoats."

There was a tone of awe in the elf's observation that Ian couldn't argue with. They were in an ancient space, one where neither witch nor mortal nor fair folk held sway. It was a place where spirits and ether gathered.

"Careful, the Bean-nighe may well do her bloody washing on that very rock," Ian warned.

Hob startled and hopped off. He stood back a few feet from the water's edge with his eyes fixated on the surface. Ian had meant it as a playful tease, but he hadn't done his own nerves any good by mentioning the washerwoman either. He got along with most of the fair folk he'd encountered, but he steered clear of those who called out the dead if it could be avoided.

Hob reached a hand out and rubbed his finger and thumb together as though testing the air for the protection magic Ian had conjured with his spell. "How will you know if any have come and gone through this portal? The door is under the water."

Honestly, he'd not thought that far ahead. With the other gateways, his scrying stone had worked like a charm for detecting traces of fairy magic around the openings, but a small pond was a trickier element to test. There was no seeing into the depths without putting oneself in or on the surface of the water, and that was asking for trouble. The deadly kind, if the wrong sort were lurking below. But perhaps there was another way.

Ian looked around and found a chunk of bark about the size of an otter that had fallen away from its tree. He picked it up and dusted off the bits of fallen leaf and soil that clung to its rough side. "That'll do," he said, then scoured the ground for a forked twig from one of the hazels. When he found the ideal candidate, he stripped off the leaves and placed the Y-shaped stick through a knothole in the bark. With only a little hesitancy, he approached the water's edge and set the bark on the surface, giving it a small push. The makeshift boat sailed onto the pond. When it reached the near middle, Ian said a quick spell: "If all is well, then stand up straight. If trouble lurks, reveal the gate."

Hob stared at the water from the bank and slipped his pipe between his teeth. "Might work. Might not."

The water wand never flinched, not even to stir a ripple on the water's surface. There was the chance Ian's spell hadn't worked, of course, but he was more inclined to believe nothing had been disturbed. Whatever high jinks were happening in the world of the fair folk between his parents' cottage and Elvanfoot's Eidyn House—and there was plenty to inflame his intuition—he could find no evidence of entry into this world through any of the portals.

"Six gateways so far and six seals still intact." Ian watched the boat float to the far side and stall out. "And yet something stirs in the liminal space." Whatever Finlay was hoping to discover was proving to be a myth. Either that or someone had done a fair job of covering their tracks. "Come on, let's get out of here," he said.

Ian and Hob had backtracked a short ways through the trees when a gust of wind hit, stirring leaves and dirt into the air. The gust passed, and in its wake a shadow swept by on their left. Slipping through the trees, the dark shape headed deeper into the thicket. Ian looked up to see if a cloud had passed or a flock of birds had flown over, but in his heart he knew the shadow had moved on its own and that it bore the form of a horse-drawn coach.

Chapter Twelve

The man opened the trapdoor and waited for the stench to clear before descending into the dank cellar. At the bottom of the rickety steps, he struck a match and lit an oil lamp mounted on the wall. The woman rose from the straw mattress on the floor and approached the bars with hateful eyes that peered out from a face smeared with grime.

"Thank you for being quiet this morning," he said. "Now step aside."

Once she backed away and sat on the floor as she'd been taught, he approached the bars carrying a tin plate of beans and bread. He hadn't seen her in a week, yet she appeared somehow ganglier than before. Hadn't he left her a loaf of bread, a brick of cheese, and a bucket of fresh water while he'd been gone? She had nothing to complain about if she didn't eat it, he thought, blinking away the tiniest twinge of guilt.

He lowered the plate into the slot in the bars, but by then he'd already paused too long in thought. The contemptible woman struck out, stabbing her heeled boot against his shin. The pain shocked him into violence. *Ungrateful bitch!* He shoved the tin plate through the slot and dumped the beans on her lap. He wished they'd been boiling hot, but at least she'd think twice about defying him again when she had to recover her meal one bean at a time if she wanted to eat. Plus she wouldn't like it very much once the mice got a whiff of the spilled food on her dress. Yes, the little beasts loved to nibble.

"Enjoy your meal, *madam*," he hissed, seething.

He limped over to the hard chair in the corner to watch the woman from ten feet away. It really was past time he got rid of her, but Maligar had an uncanny sense about these things. While the demon was ruled by the fiery depths of depravation and despair, he had a good head for business. And *his* business was getting what he wanted.

"You haven't worked on anything new," he said after observing the unraveled pile of wool in the corner. He picked up a half-woven shawl that looked like a child had tied the loose ends into knots.

"You're a filthy pig," she said, then spat at him.

The man looked at the dirt under his fingernails. The grime embedded there was more interesting than anything the woman had to say. He often thought of silencing her permanently with a spell by sewing up her throat with a piece of thread dipped in a nettle tea, but he held out hope she would one day give him what he desired. Part of him still believed she had the knowledge locked away in that inferior head of hers. She must, or else none of this had been worth the effort. After so much detailed planning and effort, he couldn't bring himself to give up on his dream, especially not with Maligar now whispering in his ear there might be a better use for the woman.

She took a rag from a bucket and wiped off the front of her dress. She'd called him a pig, but she should see herself. Ragged as a poppet made of twigs and mud. At the thought of her condition, he felt a pinch against the lining of his heart, or wherever it was they said emotions flowered inside the body. But he rode out the discomfort until he again felt nothing but ambition.

"You'll pay for what you've done. I swear it," she said. "Thrice times three and thrice again."

She attempted another of her incantations, but the current that flowed under the words to enact the magic was locked away behind the powerful spell he'd built around her and the cellar. Though witch-born, she'd proved to be like most others he encountered, taking her skill for granted all her life without appreciating her own vulnerabilities. Few had studied the craft as in depth as he had, learning the whys and ways of magic, tracing it back to the original font of power. Alas, the loathsome sorceress did hold one secret he had not mastered: the source of the spell that allowed a witch to transform into a bird.

Chapter Thirteen

Edwina had been sitting on the window seat with her head propped against the glass for the past twenty minutes watching for Ian, but he still hadn't arrived. Closed off in her room and unsure why the man who'd convinced her to flee north with his charming humor and rough around the edges good looks had seemingly forgotten to visit, her mood grew defiant. She wasn't ready to play the martyred prisoner incarcerated in some foreign tower by circumstances beyond her own making. How could another witch, a complete stranger, so easily have derailed her life? How had he tainted her body with a tracking spell without her knowing about it? How long had he watched her? Followed her?

Her "admirer" knew, of course, about her secret. He had to have been watching on the tower bridge that terrible night when she'd confronted her sister. He would have also seen the memory orb fall into the river. How else could it have been retrieved and returned in such a ghastly and disrespectful manner? She closed her eyes and tried to remember the details of that night. The clock had struck midnight. The water was calm but for an approaching ship that made the reflection of moonlight ripple on the surface. And for a brief moment, there had been a man nearby, hadn't there? He'd driven a wagon over the road just before the bridge was raised to let the ship pass. The encounter had felt random—the man had called her a "bloody damn bird"—but she couldn't be sure.

This stranger watching her hadn't demanded anything, yet there was something he wanted from her. He must. What else would compel a person to take such a destructive course of action with someone he'd never met unless he stood to gain something of value? He claimed to be an admirer, yet he'd defiled the dead to make his acquaintance, then further introduced himself by burning down her shop.

Edwina's mind went again to her grimoire, thankful she'd had the presence of mind to grab the spell book before the fire destroyed everything she owned. She couldn't shake the feeling her sister had drawn the symbols inside as some sort of plea to be understood. Edwina hugged her arms, recalling how her parents had tried to detangle the knotted-up mess of their daughters' unusual traits. They'd consulted fellow witches, palmists, and psychics to learn how shape-shifting, something deemed common in ancient grimoires, had waned as a gift until no modern witch possessed the talent besides their daughters. They'd reached out to scholars and philosophers to ask if such a taint in the blood could go dormant only to be resurrected hundreds of years later, but the experts had been flabbergasted by the question. There seemed to be no one left to ask except . . .

Edwina's head snapped up. But of course! Her father had long bragged about shaking the hand of the celebrated witch of the north. She'd never pieced together until this moment that the reason he may have gone to see the man speak at one of his symposiums wasn't because of his famous inventions but because he'd sought answers about his mutant daughters. She doubted the old witch remembered meeting her father, but perhaps the description of a man's dilemma with his unusual daughters had stuck in Elvanfoot's thoughts long after the brief encounter. Yes, it might even be the reason he so graciously opened his house to one so obviously below his station. The shrewd witch had made her his latest subject of study after all.

Nonetheless, Edwina was determined to remain objective. There was a great deal she could learn while in the company of a witch who'd been practicing magic for nearly as long as the queen had been on the throne. Her sequestration in the chilly north didn't have to feel like a punishment. Not while there were vast resources within the house that could help her find some of the answers she sought.

She tossed the book aside and made straight for the stairs. The butler was there at the bottom landing with his back turned to her, winding the great clock in the entryway with a key attached by chain to his waistcoat. Of course she ought to say something to him, warn him about his possible demise, but what if she were wrong? Needing answers first, she slipped past him as quietly as she could while he set the clock's hands to the precise time and closed the glass cover.

Finding the fire lit in the grate, Edwina feared her host might be sitting in the library with a book propped on his knee, but the place proved deserted. She closed the doors behind her and inhaled the scent of leather, dust, ink, and woodsmoke. A dizzying elixir for the witch's senses, but where to begin? When she'd seen the library the first time, she'd been so focused on Elvanfoot, her hunger, and the sandwiches set before her that she'd failed to appreciate the sheer volume of books in his library. There must have been a thousand of them arranged on the floor-to-ceiling shelves.

Not knowing where to start, she went straight to the middle section behind Elvanfoot's desk, where the spines on the books were cracked from frequent use. From there she walked to her right, trailing a finger along the spines until she detected a pattern. They were arranged by subject—alchemy, botany, potions, curses, spells—yet she didn't seem to find any subjects pertaining to a shape-shifting witch experiencing prophetic visions. She settled on two leather-bound books about alchemy, then made herself comfortable on the love seat.

With the heat of the fire warming her feet, Edwina cracked the first book open. It proved to be a treatise on sublimation, the transition of a substance from solid to gas. Not so different from shape-shifting, she thought. She eagerly flipped through the pages, hoping to find something relevant. Alas, it was written by a mortal and had little to do with magical undercurrents that might explain how a body could change from human to bird.

Opening the second book, she found an index of symbols similar to those her sister had jotted down in her grimoire. Her back straightened as she ran her finger down the page, anxious to learn more. She tapped on the first familiar one she came to, the Gemini symbol Mary had written as a girl, which represented a process called fixation. While the subject of alchemy had never excited her the way it had Mary—it was little more than an Old World magician's trick in her estimation—when she landed on the explanation for fixation, the relevance to her sister's predilection didn't escape her. Fixation was about the transformation of a volatile substance into a solid. "Like converting corpse lights into solid orbs," she whispered to herself. "Oh, Mary, you clever girl."

With one hand held to her lips, Edwina scanned the rest of the page to see if she could work out what a silver moon paired with Mercury might mean. Skimming over the descriptions for each, she quickly became overwhelmed by the long-winded explanations of trans-mutation and could find no obvious reason for why Mary had assigned them each a silvery glyph other than relating them with temperament and gender perhaps, both being feminine signs.

Frustrated, Edwina was about to return the tomes to the shelf and leave when she spied the stack of books on the side table, the ones Hob had worn himself out collecting for Elvanfoot by traveling all over the isle. She scooted over on the love seat and explored the titles: *The Jurisdiction of Witches* by Barnaby Simpleton that looked as if it might crumble to dust should she open the cover, *A Compendium of Hexes and Curses in the Middle Ages* by Rufus Hornsby that was missing a perplexing bite-size corner, and a curious little book on fairy lore bound in tree bark and entitled *Enchanters of the Otherworld* by Anonymous.

Drawn to the unusual cover, she flipped the last book open. The pages had an almost childlike quality with drawings and poems of and about fairy creatures, making her wonder why Elvanfoot would be interested in it. Most of the depictions were creatures she was familiar with—goblins, pixies, selkies, and the like—but aside from Hob she'd never had any personal interaction with the fair folk.

Or had she? Edwina recalled the frightening winged fairy from her vision, the one who had placed a finger on the butler's neck. She thought now she hadn't seen the man's death so much as felt it because of this creature's energy in her vision. Would that count as an encounter?

Edwina searched for an example of the fairy among the illustrations when she came upon a section about omens of death. Immediately intrigued, she turned the page. The images were of a shaggy green dog with blazing eyes that carried the dead to the Otherworld and an old woman called the Bean-nighe who washed the clothes of those about to die. A moment later, her veins pulsed with recognition when she saw an illustration of a pair of birds pecking at a bloody spot on the ground. Two black ravens. She and Mary had been aware of the mythology all their lives. Ravens were omens of death for many because of their taste for carrion, but to see their form illustrated in a book alongside the dreaded fey creatures flustered her.

The doorknob rattled and she slammed the book shut.

"Ah, Miss Blackwood, I take it you're feeling better," Yates said, entering the library.

"I'm quite well, thank you," she replied, hiding her disquiet.

"In that case," he said, "I believe Sir Henry has something in his observatory he wishes to show you." Yates pushed both doors wide open. "This way."

Eager for the distraction, Edwina placed the book back on the table and followed the butler to the back of the house, where a spiral staircase led to a small aerie three flights up inside the turret catty-corner from hers. The room was bathed in golden light on three sides from floor-to-ceiling windows that conformed with the shape of the curved walls. The old man sat on a stool before an elevated drafting table that was tilted at a forty-five-degree angle. Around him were odd brass mechanical devices—some ticking like clocks with swinging pendulums, one gyrating on a wobbly axis like a ring around Saturn, and yet another resembling a miniature train engine that puffed out small clouds of black smoke as it chugged along a track mounted to the wall overhead. The floor was littered with discarded mechanical devices, some equipped with cogs and gears and glass eyes that stared indefinitely, the purpose of which Edwina couldn't hazard to guess. And in the corner, an assortment of oddly out-of-place green plants sought the light of the south-facing window.

Yates cleared his throat and tapped on the doorframe with his knuckle. Elvanfoot peered over the top of his spectacles at the intruders.

"Miss Blackwood here to see you."

"Ah." Elvanfoot set his pen aside in the inkwell on his right and covered his work with a blank sheet of paper. "I was hoping we hadn't lost you to melancholia for the entire day."

"Oh, no, I wasn't—" Edwina stopped to stare at a mechanical rat in the window. An automaton of some kind, it moved its head from side to side while twitching its nose. "What a remarkable toy."

Elvanfoot made a low grunt. "Believe me when I say that is no child's plaything, my dear." He held his arm out, and the rat sprang off the windowsill to land on his sleeve. Tiny metal claws pierced the material of his jacket as it gripped its new perch. "This is my watchdog. Er, well, my watch *rat*." Elvanfoot gestured to Yates to open the window. He whispered a spell over the rat's head, and the beast waved its articulated tail and crawled out the window. "It's attuned to the energy of certain spells. They're laid out around the house and surrounding property like ratlines on a ship. The rat will follow the lines of the spells on the ground, sniffing the tension of the magic to make sure all my protections are still in place."

"What if a spell isn't working anymore?"

"Then it'll squawk like a banshee until I rectify the situation."

Edwina moved uneasily from the window, wondering if her own flight that morning had disturbed anything, but as she hadn't heard any squawking, she assumed all was well.

"But that isn't why I asked Yates to bring you here." He dug around on the side table, where several books and loose papers were piled up to his elbow. "Something arrived in the morning's post that might prove interesting. Ah, here it is."

Elvanfoot produced a postmarked envelope with his name and address written on the outside in a fanciful script. The ink had the familiar green iridescence used by witches in correspondence, though this one had a particularly dazzling shimmer to it, like the wings of a rare tropical bird. Before she could ask about the sender, he dug in his pocket for the calling card she'd received in her shop before it burned down, the one she'd shown him when she first arrived. "I took the liberty of holding on to it for safekeeping," he said, setting the two items on his work table side by side. "Note how similar they are in tone, and yet . . ."

The wily wizard took his pen from the inkpot, tapping the end so a drop of ink fell off, then scribbled Edwina's name on a piece of paper, which he then set alongside the other examples. "Now, Miss Blackwood, tell me what you observe."

The variation in tone was obvious when all three examples were placed together. A clear spectrum of luminosity was evident. Curiously, the card from her stalker displayed the brightest ink. She'd expected the opposite.

"They appear the same until set in proximity of one another," she said. "But does the intensity of the ink tell us anything about the sender? My brief first impression had been that he possibly made his own ink."

"Exactly!" Elvanfoot smiled as if pleased she'd picked up on the point of his demonstration right away. "Note that this ink, the one I have made for me in a shop on Cocklebur Road, appears the dullest of the three." He picked up his writing sample and slid it under the lens of a microscope. "It is also the purest of the beetle-derived inks. The witch who oversees the spell work is a very old friend. He reserves the most saturated batches for those of us who do scholarly work on magic. Less showy to use a subtle ink," he said with a shrug after viewing the sample through the microscope. "Take a look."

While no stranger to the extraordinary and supernatural, Edwina had never seen one of these sort of mortal inventions up close. She approached the instrument with caution while Elvanfoot explained he'd tampered with the mechanics of magnification only slightly to make it sensitive to the reflective energy inherent in magic.

Edwina leaned into the eyepiece. Magnified streams of iridescent green-and-black liquid swam before her vision, as if the vivid color were trapped within invisible banks on the paper. The brilliant hue of the crushed beetle shells was only heightened by the amplified view. "And the others?" she asked.

Elvanfoot exchanged papers so that she now looked at the post-marked envelope through the lens. The same brilliance shone through, but the energy of the ink seemed to move at a quicker, more frenzied pace. Compared to the first example, it was like looking at air instead of water.

"Now have a look at this one."

Edwina had to keep her revulsion in check as he slid the "admirer's" calling card into view. The aversion quickly dissipated when the vast difference in the ink's quality was seen under magnification. There was no movement, only a stagnant, reflective shimmer effect that relied on a source of light to give it life. "It isn't the same at all."

"Correct. Which tells us something important about the person who used it."

Edwina backed away from the microscope and waited for him to explain.

"Just as you said, I, too, believe this ink is homemade," he said. "Closer inspection suggests it's been enhanced by spellcasting to make it appear a legitimate witch's ink, but it is not."

Luanne G. Smith

"Which means?"

"It means someone is overcompensating for the talent they lack," said a voice at their backs.

Edwina and Elvanfoot looked up from the writing samples to see Ian standing in the doorway.

"At last." Edwina was so overcome with relief at seeing him she nearly forgot he'd dumped her in the back of a horseless carriage and sent her on her way to a near stranger's house all by herself.

"Aye, well, I got a bit sidetracked on my way here," he said, sweeping his hand over his sleeve to free it of debris.

His dapper appearance made Edwina straighten her back to look at his attractive figure full on. He wore a proper black suit with white shirt and a waistcoat. In his hands he carried a matching black derby. A speck of mud and several small burrs clung to the cuff of his trouser, making her raise her brow in curiosity. She spotted Hob yawning behind him, similarly covered in evidence of tramping through tall grass.

"Ah, red fescue." Elvanfoot extended his hand. "You've walked from Hare Hill, then."

"It's been a while since Hob and I strolled through the sward." After shaking Elvanfoot's hand, Ian gripped both of Edwina's hands in his and gave her a kiss on the cheek, and all was forgiven.

"Where's the little fellow run off to already?" Edwina asked, looking around.

"He ate so many oatcakes earlier he's probably curled up in the kitchen taking a kip in the sunshine by now." Ian emptied his pocket of the brown paper his mother had wrapped the oatcake in and threw it away. "So what kind of experiments are you two wizards up to?"

He was teasing, but in truth they had been conducting an experiment of sorts. "We're comparing inks under the microscope."

"And you are correct, Mr. Cameron," said Elvanfoot, holding up the calling card left by the stalker. "In this case the brightest ink belongs to the dullest witch."

"I don't understand." Edwina set all three examples of the ink side by side again. "How do you conclude the user of this ink lacks skill at their craft merely by the iridescence?" Her mind, unfortunately, went straight to George, Elvanfoot's only son, whose magic was rumored to pale in the shadow of his famous father. But it wasn't just George. Talent was as fickle in witches as it was in athletes or musicians or painters. Yes, hard work could overcome a shortfall in inherent magic, but for some it would never be enough. Still, she failed to see how that equated to the ink one used.

"The evidence is in the carapaces themselves." Elvanfoot sat on his stool and dug around in a tobacco box atop his side table, from which he produced a handful of shiny green-and-copper-colored beetle shells. He scattered them on the table where Edwina had laid out the samples. "Do you know why some beetles shine as they do?"

Edwina had never thought about it before, but logic suggested there was a component of warning to the bright color. "To announce to predators they're poisonous?" And yet as soon as she said it, she knew that couldn't be true. She'd done any number of tonic spells that could have tilted toward poison with a mere flick of the wrist to add too much of one thing or another. None of the spells had called for the addition of metallic-shelled beetles.

"In fact, quite the opposite," Elvanfoot said, as she expected, before holding up a finger to finish his point. "The entire purpose of their brilliant green coloring is to take advantage of the art of camouflage."

"They wish to blend in with their surroundings," she said.

"Yes, though in truth their purpose is much more urgent. The tiny creatures have evolved to blend in with their surroundings to save themselves from being eaten." The old witch paused, tilting his head slightly from side to side as he scooped up the shells and placed one on the shiny green leaf of the hoya plant, where it was much more difficult to see. "Survival of the invisible," he said. "And, if my hypothesis holds, we may be able to say the same for the man who sent your card. Yes, I think that's exactly what's at work here, only he hasn't the skill to do it properly."

"So the man stalking Miss Blackwood is, what, a drab?" Ian asked.

A drab?

"As you said, he's overcompensating," Elvanfoot said. "The tracking spell he used on Miss Blackwood employed mediocre magic at best. We were able to flush it out in a matter of hours."

Edwina's cheeks grew hot pink at the mention of her malady the evening before, but she endeavored to continue the conversation matter-of-factly. "I still don't understand how the ink tells you this."

"Simple inductive reasoning, my dear," said Elvanfoot. "The ink is composed of green pigments, likely from crushed malachite, then given a shimmering glamour spell to make it shine. But it's not a respectable witch's ink. The man attempting to intimidate you is trying to camouflage himself as a witch of substance, but he is anything but in my opinion. Unable to procure the proper ink from a reputable stationer for witches, he conjured his own."

"But he found Ian's memory orb at the bottom of the river," she said. "He cursed those roses to explode into spellfire the moment I read the card. That's no small feat of magic."

Elvanfoot held up the note card for her to read again. "The mysterious words written inside? They basically functioned as a spell. It was *you* who set the roses on fire when you read the incantation out loud."

Ian read the card again. "An incantation incognito committed to paper."

"Er, yes, which is further evidence the person in question wasn't confident of his own skill at hexing. He instead relied on Miss Blackwood to do the spell for him."

"But what about the orb?" she asked.

"As unimpressed as I am with the magic shown thus far by this individual, I wouldn't doubt if he dove in the water after the bauble himself and felt for it in the mud with his toes, which could explain the mess in Mary's coffin."

Edwina was left speechless. She'd feared hexes, curses, and bloody murder had awaited her in the city at the hands of this deranged stalker. She still feared there was something he wanted from her not yet articulated, but if his magic was as toothless as Elvanfoot suggested, maybe he wasn't the menace she'd imagined him to be. Perhaps he merely required the solid walls of an asylum around him.

"But whoever this maniac is, he's still out there and he's still a threat if he's willing to manipulate others into causing destruction," Ian said, turning the calling card over in his hands.

"That I do not know, but I think we can safely determine Miss Blackwood has been sufficiently removed far enough from the man's influence. We'll leave the little common beetle to stumble about in his own ignorance in the south, as it were, until he gets swallowed up."

Ian exchanged a look with Edwina. "I'd be well pleased to think it so," he said.

"As would I." Elvanfoot's eyes sparked with that brilliant starshine as he picked up the postmarked envelope again. This time he displayed a new curiosity about its contents as he flicked the letter open and read the folded card inside. The scent of lemon verbena wafted from the envelope, and a trail of golden dust sifted to the floor as he held up the gilded card in triumph. "Because, monsieur and mademoiselle, now that we have determined you are no longer in danger, we have a Midsummer party to attend. And Lady Everly has asked specifically for the two of you to join me as my guests."

"Us?" Edwina gawped at the envelope.

"It's very last minute, of course, but she's quite eager to meet you," Elvanfoot said. "Shall I reply?"

Ian and Edwina both nodded in shocked acknowledgment that Lady Everly should have any idea whatsoever who either of them were. With the madman's threat declawed and left behind in the south, she agreed a celebration might be just the cure they all needed.

Chapter Fourteen

It wasn't just any party. They'd been invited to *the* Lady Everly's estate to honor the fair folk in a grand fete as they celebrated the affirmation of their summer queen. For a witch, it was a great honor to be asked to attend. Ian had heard rumors about the affair since he was a bairn but had never laid eyes on an invitation of his own, even after he saved the life of the great wizard of the north. It was a shocking development for him and Edwina both.

"The Queen of Elfhame is reaffirmed every seven earth years." Ian held Edwina's hand in the crook of his elbow while they strolled around the grounds at Eidyn House. "Lady Everly throws these parties every Midsummer in honor of the fair folk, but the queen's affirmation is said to be a grand event."

Edwina shook her head at their turn of luck. It did his heart good to see her anticipating something wonderful instead of fretting about the past. Perhaps a bright future waited for them both, should they choose it. He'd been suspicious of Finlay and his ilk already knowing who she was, but he reasoned it was only natural they should have an interest in Edwina. She bridged a gap between fey and witch in a way he couldn't quite explain, similar to the way she appealed to both his head and heart when few others had. Aye, he was done with denials. If she'd have him, he'd be as moon-eyed as an owl.

"The first of the pixies will cross the sward just before midnight with their lanterns held high," he explained. "Others flit through the sky to find a tree branch or vine to perch on, as eager to watch the trooping of the court fairies as the rest of us."

"Aren't they bothered by an audience?" she asked.

"That's half of why they do it." He plucked a twig from a hawthorn tree and broke open a leaf, inhaling the suggestive scent. "It's a parade to show off their glamour, ye ken, but it also reminds everyone they are not gone, just . . . away."

"It will be the grandest event I've ever been to." Edwina glanced down and delicately touched the creped high collar at her neck as though suddenly self-conscious of the mourning clothes she was wearing. Ian was dressed in his finest suit, which wouldn't even get him an interview as a footman in Lady Everly's Albion House.

"We dinna have to go if it makes you uncomfortable," he said. "We could stay here and gaze at the bonny wee stars. There'll be plenty of pixie light to see in the meadow here on Midsummer." Edwina leaned her head against his shoulder, and he had to swallow to compensate for the flush of emotion that overtook him.

She lifted her head again and looked him in the eye. "Would you really say no to a once-in-a-lifetime opportunity to go to the home of Lady Everly herself?"

He swallowed again. "To be alone with you on a summer evening? Aye, I would."

She laughed then, the first hint of joy he'd heard from her in days, before she went quiet again. It was almost as though she were embarrassed she'd slipped out of her mandated mourning behavior.

Ian swept her under the drooping branches of a weeping willow at the back garden. They weren't quite hidden from view from the house, but he kissed her anyway. It was all he could think about since he'd stepped into the wizard's workshop and found her standing over a microscope eager to determine the contents of a flourish of green ink.

Aye, a pretty face could gain a man's attention easy enough, but with some women, the first flash of desire proved as temporary as a ripple on water. Without something deeper beneath the surface, the attraction evaporated in the stagnant shallows.

Edwina tugged at his bottom lip with her teeth as if hungry for so much more when something nibbled at Ian's trouser cuff. He looked down to see a mechanical rat crawling over his boot.

"One of Elvanfoot's inventions," Edwina said. "It's checking the grounds to make sure all his protection spells are still intact."

"Ah." Ian nudged the rat away with his toe. "He used to have a cat that did the work for him until an owl stole it one Samhain." He watched the automaton animal scurry into the bushes as the wires on its nose twitched and sniffed at the magic in the air. While part of him wanted nothing more than to hold Edwina in his arms, Ian's intuition tugged at him until he felt compelled to watch the rat at work. "He checks for fractured spells, does he?" He broke their embrace and squatted beside the bush, lifting the branch under which the metal rat had disappeared.

"What is it?" Edwina crouched, too, gathering her skirt behind her knees. "Has he found something?"

"It keeps running back and forth over the same ground as if it's looking for something." Ian took his pocket watch out and took a reading. There was a faint echo of something nearby, but it was too faint to register properly.

"Is someone here?" Edwina stood, hugging her arms. Despite Elvanfoot's reassurance that the threat to her was nothing to worry about, she scoured the garden's edge with her eyes. After all, *he* hadn't found a dead loved one covered in river slime inside her casket or had his shop burned down by a maniac.

Ian gave the watch a shake, then put it away. He wasn't ready to disclose the work he was doing for Finlay, but there was a great deal else he could explain. "There's mischief in the woods," he said, gesturing toward the thicket of trees far beyond where the black pond was surrounded by the hazel trees.

"Mischief?"

"As I said we're nearing the Midsummer. The fair folk are gathering, which makes them twitchy. They're readying below, stirring on the threshold between this world and theirs, though some already move about in the earth above."

"You mean creatures like Hob?"

"Aye, he's part of the above world now, as many who choose to remain are. But most only return on festival days to keep the connection to their ancestral lands alive, both spiritually and physically. The fair folk continue to be the beating heart of the natural world, no matter where they are."

The rat stopped circling and headed for the blackberry hedgerow at the rear of the property. Its nose wriggled and its articulated legs ambled forward cautiously. There, a palpable spell energy radiated off the brambles. A buzzy sort of static crackled in the air, electrifying the hair on their arms enough to make them rub at the discomfort. Edwina tugged her long sleeves farther down over her wrists, then spread her fingers and stretched her hand out, feeling for the source of the energy.

"Elvanfoot must reserve his most powerful magic for the outer perimeter," Ian said, watching closely in case Edwina detected something more than she bargained for.

"Why, is there something out there we should be worried about?" She walked a short way until she hovered her hand over a break in the hedge. It was large enough for a wee bairn to crawl through on their hands and knees. "I don't feel any buzzing here. Nothing. It's just a gaping hole."

The rat poked its nose through the hole in the hedge. It circled the spot three times before squealing in alarm. Ian knelt and found the leaves around the opening were black and curled, as though they'd been burned by frost. The ripening fruit had shriveled and turned to black mush at the end of the stems, while the air carried the whiff of decay.

"There's something snagged just there," he said and reached out to one of the canes, where a fluff of black fur had caught on a prickle.

"An animal of some kind?" Edwina asked.

Ian removed a clump of the fur and held it in the sunlight. The black sheen was deceptive in shadow. Turned in the full light, the hair had a green cast to it, similar to the way the wing of a blackbird sometimes showed hints of blue and green depending on the angle. He blinked and glanced up at Edwina before sheepishly looking away.

"What is it?" she asked, taking the fur to see for herself.

"It's from a *cù-sìth*, a sort of fairy dog that roams the isles."

"An omen of death."

"You know of it?" he asked, surprised she knew the word.

"Yes." Edwina dropped the tuft of fur she'd collected and wiped her fingers together. She glanced at the house, her gaze full of dread as if she'd seen the dog itself.

"It's nae a concern if you haven't actually spotted the beast." He gripped her shoulder to get her attention, suddenly worried. "You didn't see the hairy dog, did you?"

Edwina kept her eye on the back of the house and shook her head. "No, but I know who might have."

"How?"

"Because I saw the omen of his death too."

"Elvanfoot?" Ian nearly broke for the back door to shake the old man and get him out of the burgh.

"No, his butler, Yates," she said and bowed her head as though confused by her own confession.

"Yates? What's happened to him?"

Edwina explained the strange vision she'd had of seeing the butler facedown in the garden while she'd soared over the house. Ian was accustomed to the strange and inexplicable in his line of work as a private detective, but even he had to keep reminding himself of her unique ability to transform and take to the air. But it was only rare in the world of witches. Aye, for the fair folk shape-shifting was naught but a way of life. The selkies, kelpies, and púca all changed form at will. But they were made of mist and water, smoke and fire. Edwina was a flesh-and-blood woman. Even among the witches of old, who'd mingled with the unseelie at the dawn of magic, their ability to change into hares and cats had generally not been passed on to their offspring.

"Have you had these visions before?" he asked. She shook her head, and all he could do was think of her sister, Mary Bewitched. That one had had an unnatural affinity with the dead and those on the other side of the veil. He wondered briefly if the sister clung on somehow, still working her wickedness in the liminal space between worlds, influencing her twin with visions of those about to die. But even he wasn't daft enough to truly believe it. No, something else was going on.

"At first I couldn't be certain what I'd seen was even real. But now, with a *cù-sìth* showing up at his back door, how do I ignore what I saw? Do I tell Yates? Is forewarned forearmed, as you like to say? Or is it best not to put the notion of death in a man's head and let him continue on as normal until the master of that dog comes to fetch him?"

There was no right answer. A man's fate was not a plaything one kicked about for sport like a football. Tell the man about the details of his death and he might fulfill the prophecy through sheer belief in his destiny. Deny him the knowledge and he was likely to fall prey to some threat that might have been avoided. No, there was a reason such visions of death were not gifted to the earthborn to oversee. Then again, he was talking with a Blackwood sister. The usual rules didn't seem to apply to either Edwina or her departed sister. "We dinna yet know if what you saw was even a premonition."

"But the dog—"

"Finding a tuft of fur in the bushes is a long cry from determining a man's impending doom. We don't even know if he saw the beast. Or if anyone saw it, for that matter. Maybe the dog was just having a sniff around. The old wizard is getting up there in years, ye ken."

Edwina's brows tightened in thought. "No, the image was real. Visceral enough I could have swept a wingtip over his cold skin. But no, there was someone else in the vision who did exactly that," she said, shaking her head. "A shriveled sort of creature with wings, a veil, and tufts of black hair."

"Like a death fairy of some kind?" Ian remembered the shadow he'd seen fly through the trees earlier.

Edwina nodded and knelt down near the break in the protective perimeter again to study the ground the way he would if he were tracking someone. Such a curious creature for a woman, he thought. While he pondered the mysteries of her gender, she pushed back the spindly canes of the blackberry bush. She'd found something and pointed. Ian leaned forward for a closer look. Not only was there the expected paw print of a large dog, but beside it was the track of a small, narrow foot with a pointed toe.

"Mischief afoot, indeed. What do you make of that?" she asked.

"It looks like our four-footed omen of death had a friend with him," Ian said. The footprints weren't much bigger than the dog's. "A shriveled fairy with wings, you say?"

He glanced in the direction the prints were headed. They led toward the hill above the black lake, the site of the last gateway he'd checked and the strange shadow he'd felt go by. Had he missed something on the water? Something neither he nor Hob could see? He'd wanted to keep Edwina out of this business with the gateways, but his client had suggested her instincts might be of help. He could do with a good portion of luck, as he was in over his head with the fair folk and their tricks. Besides, he wanted very much to show her his city with the hope she might find it inviting enough to want to stay.

"Fancy doing a little more investigative work?" he asked. "Get out of that enormous house for a while?"

Edwina stood and glanced at the road and beyond. "I think I'd like that very much," she said as the mechanical rat continued to scream bloody murder on the other side of the garden.

Chapter Fifteen

The demon flipped the woman's ring in the air with his thumb as one might flick a coin. And why not be cavalier with the thing? There were fortunes to be played out depending on the outcome, were there not? The gold band, with its two colored gemstones, glinted brightly as the ring somersaulted in a ray of sunlight. Reluctantly impressed, the man had assumed the ring couldn't possibly contain genuine rubies, not when it belonged to that guttersnipe in the cellar. Despite Maligar's assurances, he'd have bet the ring's stones were made of paste, but sunlight never lied about the multifaceted cut of a ruby.

"Very well," he said, snatching the ring out of the air for a closer inspection. "We'll bond the spell to the gemstones."

Maligar, dressed in his usual garish suit, flopped down on the wing-back chair nearest the fireplace and draped his right leg over the arm. *The insufferable beau-nasty!* And then for the damnable creature to hold that gleam of superiority in his eye, wielding it like the sharp edge of an obsidian blade, as he dug through his sack of licorice allsorts and popped a pink candy in his pointy-toothed gob. Thank the All Powerful for the security of the circle and the grace of the pentagram, he thought, checking his toes hadn't crossed the painted line.

"And then what?" Maligar wiped a finger over his back teeth to loosen a sticky glob of licorice. "We use the woman below as bait? Lure the other one here? On a false promise of reunited bliss? Or would another location prove more suitable? You've already got enough flies buzzing around this place from the stench. How big of a mess will there be this time?"

"None, if she cooperates," the man replied. "But I take your point about finding a more suitable location for the encounter should anything go amiss."

"What about this extravagant affair taking place at the witch woman's estate?" The demon had picked up the invitation sitting in plain sight on the side table and waved the card in the air. "It carries the whiff of lemon verbena, does it not?" He inhaled deeply, savoring the scent as he sucked on his licorice like an impudent yob. "It's meant to entice the receiver into a false sense of gaiety and pleasure. Security. Sounds like the perfect place for you to come out of the shadows."

Damn his nosiness! Lady Frances Everly was a delightful creature of intelligence, grace, and dignity. There could be no greater honor than to receive an invitation to her Midsummer soiree. From the earliest days when he'd created the Order of the Night Hunter, a society for those on the chase to unlock the secrets of the occult, he'd sought her acceptance and recognition. And now that he'd won her approval, he wasn't going to sully it by letting this upstart demon dictate the final piece of his crowning achievement.

"The party is of little consequence," he said of the invitation, waving his hand in dismissal.

Maligar flipped the card over in his fingers in that distractingly quick trick of his where the paper turned so fast the words appeared to stream like a sparkling green ribbon winding itself around the invitation. "Are you sure? I happened to do a little eavesdropping this afternoon. I know for a fact our girl will be attending the party as well. The wizard's web of spells won't protect her outside his home. And the witch's castle is such a large house with extensive grounds."

Yes, he'd summoned the demon for help. He'd required his ancient expertise in this ugly yet delicate matter. And yet he didn't like the way

Maligar tried to steer the natural course of events to his own liking. This was *his* kidnapping, not the demon's. And yet, and yet, and yet . . . Maligar was right. There was a certain poetic charm in making his formal acquaintance with Edwina Blackwood at the home of the authoress of the most infamous grimoire of the century. It would be the birthplace of his greatest achievement. An epiphany in the world of witches, where he would be feted as king of the ambitious and bold.

He cleared his throat and settled back into reality. "Yes, perhaps you're right. I'm already planning on attending the festival in honor of the Midsummer. I'll introduce myself and gain her confidence. I can be quite charming when there's the need."

"I've no doubt you're up to the challenge of winning over Miss Blackwood's good opinion," Maligar said. He was on his feet in a fraction of a second, not a crease in his suit, not a hair out of place. Lightning speed, these demons. "Until then, we ought to make her aware of the stakes." He gestured to the ring with his glittering eyes.

"Ah, yes. The spell." The man contemplated the vast incantations at his disposal. He'd mastered so many. But which spell would bind most naturally to the ruby gemstones? It had to be one deceptive enough to get past the wizard's instincts should he discover the trinket. His feint of acting the bumbling naïf at magic had proved an admirable approach so far. The words of poetry written in malachite ink made him appear mystically challenged, incapable of higher magic. He chuckled to himself to think he might have gotten one over on the famous old witch. Dismissed was disarmed.

"I'll have the flow of energy circulate between the gemstones in an infinity circuit," he said, thinking of the demon's trick with the invitation. "The looping frequency of the spell's power will help disguise the true purpose. Yes, yes, I'll get started on it right away."

He nearly stepped out of the circle, forgetting to first dismiss the demon. The shiny obsidian eyes caught the moment of distraction.

Maligar smiled so that his lips thinned, revealing a line of piranha-sharp teeth.

"I'll just see myself out, then," Maligar said.

"Yes, of course, you're dismissed." The man held his palm out and recited the spell. "Back to the flame and source of fire. Do not return until I desire."

"As you wish."

The demon departed. The man waited a long minute within the protective confines of his circle, punctuated by the hard beat of his pumping heart. The licorice scent lingered, but once he was convinced Maligar had truly cleared the room, he stepped out and closed his magic circle. He lit a fat candle on the desk and meditated on the flame's orange light. The spell needed to be powerful yet subtle. The gems would affect the flow of energy, but that was something he could use to his advantage. Then, when she happened to slip the ring on her own finger, as he knew she would, the energy of the gold against her skin would change the dynamic of the enchantment yet again. Yes, he thought, this could be the perfect spell. Let the chemistry of flesh and gemstone do the work. All he required was a little blood from the ring's owner to seal the deal. He opened the desk drawer and removed the penknife before heading to the cellar.

Pity he needed only a drop.

Chapter Sixteen

As they followed the direction of the fairy's footsteps, Ian assured Edwina that sightings of the *cù-sìth* were a common-enough occurrence. "Dozens of people swear the beast roams the hillsides and city lanes year-round," he said. "I've been called out in the middle of the night half a dozen times to a cottage or a town home where someone claims to have seen the fairy dog on their way home from the pub. Terrified they were marked for death, ye ken? They always beg me to track the animal down and have it exorcised."

"Do you?" Edwina asked. "Hunt the animal down, I mean?" She was curious, yes, but she honestly wanted to hear his reassuring voice at her side more. She would have encouraged him to recite the weather report if it meant listening to his soft northern burr.

"I'd tell them I'd go search high and low so they could go back to sleep. More often than not the thing they'd seen was the tanner's dog off his leash and rummaging through the rubbish in an alley. Or they'd seen the long shadow of a feral cat against a moonlit wall."

"Is that what you think happened today? We're seeing furry shadows?"

The lane they walked on led to a scraggly natural area designated as a city park. A placid black pond sat back from the road, half hidden by the trees. "I'm less convinced it was anything so benign this time," Ian said. "Not with fairy footprints accompanying the dog's."

"And especially not when they were found at the home of a renowned wizard," Edwina said. The protections around Eidyn House were supposed to be fortified with the highest form of magic, forged from Elvanfoot's experience and acuity. And yet a shaggy, smelly omen of death had slipped through the perimeter as easily as if it had broken into a chicken coop.

Ian kept fidgeting with his watch, biting his lower lip as he stared at the gorse-covered hill above the black pond. They'd walked about a half mile from Elvanfoot's house through a quiet neighborhood of large homes with even larger plots around them. Ian seemed to know where he wanted to go, keeping an eye on the trees near the pond. They passed through a wrought-iron gate, and Ian leaped over a low stone wall to get off the trail. There, he scoured the ground and picked up the trail of footsteps again.

"How did you know they would be there?" Edwina asked, staring at the tracks. The fairy imprint had the uncanny resemblance to a woman's button-up boot but in a child's size and with an exaggerated pointed toe.

"I came through this way earlier with Hob," he explained. "I canna say what it was, but I saw, or felt, *something*. A shadow." Ian followed the tracks deeper into the copse of trees, sidestepping the double set of footprints until he stopped suddenly. "They've disappeared," he said, pointing at the ground. "See how they end here, as if the creatures lifted into the air."

Edwina rubbed the gooseflesh on her arms. She wasn't so much bothered by the presence of the fey creatures—she'd easily grown accustomed to Hob and his peculiar ways—but her intuition recognized this pair of creatures, these death omens, had some bearing on the vision she'd had while in flight. Some tethering between her and the fair folk was being hitched together since she'd arrived in the north.

"I'm getting too much interference," Ian said, sighing at his watch. To the north sat the great castle built on the hill overlooking the city.

East of that was another larger hill, where a second castle stood to bookmark the Queen's Mile. Ian looked from one landmark to the other and back to his watch as though trying to get his bearings with a map and compass.

"Maybe you should have Elvanfoot take a look at the gears," Edwina said, nudging her chin toward the watch. "If it's not working properly."

Ian stirred free of his confounded haze. "The thing gives too many mixed signals this near to the city," he said and put the device away. "Half the residents in this part of town are witches. I was hoping I might get a reading on whoever made those footprints, but with some of the fair folk, they can come and go so quickly you never get a proper read on them." He gave the area a final glance before giving up and putting the watch away.

"There's something strange about this place," Edwina said, gazing from the pond toward the treetops and back to the tracks on the ground.

"You mean the park?"

Edwina shook her head. "This northern clime has its own energy," she said, reaching her hand out to feel the charge in the air. "It's in the weather, the angle of the sun, the smell of the earth. All of it. I've felt the change tingling inside me ever since we arrived. Some energy rippling through my blood. And even the vision I had. It was almost like one of those moving pictures, but in my head, backlit by some incandescent lamp radiating from this place. I know it sounds daft, but I can feel it even now."

"No, it's not daft," Ian said. He looked again from one distant hilltop to another. "If you have the time, there's something I can show you that might help explain what you're sensing. We just need to head north toward the old town."

"I have the time, if you do," she said, eager to confirm the nagging feeling wasn't merely her overwrought imagination. And if she got a proper tour of the city Ian called home, a place she may call home too one day, all the better.

Taking advantage of Elvanfoot's hospitality yet again, they waved down his chauffeur when he happened to rumble by in his dog cart while out running errands for his employer. They hopped on the back of the vehicle when he said it was no trouble to drive them into the city. Minutes later, the chauffeur stopped in front of a candlemaker's shop on what Ian called "witch's row," on account of the number of places that sold balms, tonics, and crystals. The couple thanked the driver and jumped out, glad to have saved their feet the two-mile walk.

"We can cut across here," Ian said.

Edwina took his arm as he guided her along a pavement that skirted a narrow backstreet. There, scrawny thistles poked their heads up between cracks in the cobblestones where the sun angled between buildings. He walked with purpose. A man on a mission. For what, Edwina couldn't say, but the tremor in her heart and stomach advised her to be prepared for anything while walking beside Ian. A thing she took full pleasure in.

"Isn't the city center back that way?" she asked, already feeling her button-up boots pinch her toes as they wobbled on the uneven cobblestones. They were traveling in the direction of the large hill on the east end of the Queen's Mile.

"Aye, but what I want to show you is this way. It's a bit of a climb, but worth the effort. The view will help put things in perspective."

Edwina looked ahead at the imposing sight before her. "Things must be very complex if we need to climb a hill that size to get the big picture," she said and followed his lead up a narrow pathway cobbled together with rough brickwork.

The walk up the slope was made more pleasant by a fickle sun that favored them between passing clouds as they passed chapel ruins and a small pond populated with seagulls. When they finally reached the top, Ian set his foot upon a rock and gazed out over the horizon. Pride and purpose showed in his face as he pointed to all the familiar landmarks in the 360-degree view: The castle on the hill. The philosopher's monument atop a crag on the opposite side of the city. The gorse-covered hill above the pond near Elvanfoot's house, along with two more gentle mounds that rose in the distant west and a final one to the south.

"And where did you grow up?" she asked, bracing her hand over her eyes to shield them for long gazing.

"Just there." Ian pointed to the low hill to the south as he placed his hand on the small of her back. "Hare Hill," he said. "The house is just at the base on the right. An old crofter's cottage that's been in the family for seven generations."

Squinting, Edwina spotted the house where he'd pointed. Smoke rose from the chimney of a whitewashed cottage with a thatched roof. She simply smiled at the notion of him growing up in such a quaint home. "And you walked all that way to Eidyn House?" she asked, judging the distance between his parents' cottage and Elvanfoot's manor to be near five miles.

"Unlike some, I dinna have wings to carry me. Nor a horse, for that matter. A friend owed me a favor for finding out who was taking more than the angel's share from his cider barrels, so he offered me a ride to their place this morning in his cab."

"Ah." The reminder once again that he'd visited his parents that morning plucked at her emotions in an uncomfortable way, knowing she'd likely never have such a moment with her own parents again. It had confused her so, to have each kiss her on the cheek, say goodbye, and then walk out the door on the pretense of returning shortly, only to disappear into the city, never to be heard from again. It was like each had turned to vapor, leaving the sisters bereft. No more quiet Sunday roast dinners. No listening to their father read the newspaper out loud at breakfast or washing the dishes afterward in the sink while their mother dried and stacked the plates, complaining about the rain. And now even Mary was gone.

"Were you able to remember everything when you saw your parents?" she asked. "They didn't notice anything amiss?"

In answer, Ian gestured to the forest that ran between his house and a cluster of other cottages on the other side. "The lads and I used to climb those trees when I was barely able to get a foothold on a knothole. We used sticks for swords while we sacked a seaside village or played the part of the highwayman to terrorize Rowena MacTavish and her sister when they walked home from school."

"You didn't play Robin Hood?"

"Perhaps if I'd had a proper Maid Marian I would have," he replied and grinned. "And just there, do you see where the hill looks like a rabbit's head the way it juts out? That's where I ran to when my father nearly skinned me alive after I'd set his workroom on fire with one of my spells." He shook his head at the memories still buried deep in his psyche. "Aye, I seem to remember everything about home. Hob saw to that."

She was glad for him, even if it did churn up the taste of envy.

"Now, as to your earlier observation about our unique energy in the north." Ian turned Edwina around by her waist to look once more upon the surrounding hills in all directions. "Do you see it? The pattern in the land?" he asked, pointing east as he held his cheek near to hers.

With the heat from his body shielding her from the cool wind at their backs, Edwina took in the view with a keener eye. The hills he'd drawn her attention to came into sharper focus, rising from the land in a clear pattern. "Including where we're standing, there are seven of them," she said.

"Seven hills surround us all, seven hills shall never fall," he said. "It's an old saying, but it's more than that. The hills are the original fairy mounds. Each with a gateway that opens between worlds. When the veil thins enough for those on the other side to pass through."

"Samhain."

"Aye, that would be the fall festival. That's when the mischief-makers run amok from the ground below. The complaints of missing pets keep me in business until the end of the year." He pressed his derby snug on his head against the wind. "Beltane in the spring is just as unruly, but the merrymakers mostly take their wildings and fertility rituals out to the green spaces away from the city." He cleared his throat, as if he'd said too much in front of a lady.

"Naturally," she said, feeling the tips of her ears blush.

"Things are much more organized at both Midsummer and Yule," he assured her.

She looked out over the city and the green hills surrounding it. "All of them are fairy mounds? Are you sure? But the city is right in the center of it all. Hasn't that scared them off?"

"Displaced, more like. The same energy and beauty that originally attracted our fey neighbors to this land attract us as well. Mortals, too, even if they dinna know why. There's an enchanted tension created between the hills, ye ken? Almost like we're sitting in a cauldron of magic. The energy travels from under the earth where the ancestor guardians dwell. It goes from the rocks to the trees and to the roots of the plants. And apparently to you. Even the buildings here are changed because of it. From yon high castle sprung from the rocky hill to the city spires that strive to touch the sun, and even in the low spots of the city where naught but cold and shadow thrive, there's a low hum of energy running through everything. I often think the people here are changed by it, their minds so quick and curious and innovative."

"And you think that's due to the energy between the hills?" Edwina wrapped her shawl around herself a little more snugly. "That's the vibration I'm feeling?"

"The seven hills specifically," he said.

"Where the fair folk emerge?"

"Aye, but there's something not right lately. A case I've been working on. I'll show you, if you dinna think the quick path down the backside of the hill is too steep for you."

Ian gestured to the lip of the escarpment. Edwina walked up to the very edge to see over the side. There, a narrow stone-brick trail hairpinned to the bottom on the opposite side they'd come up.

"Easy. You do not want to lose your footing there," he warned, resting his hand on her arm.

Quite the opposite, she thought. The sight of the steep drop had her nearly overcome with the urge to jump and stretch her wings, buoyed by the humming in her veins. Now that she'd seen the view, she longed to glide over the city and hills and map the land with her eye. She and Mary, had they come on their own, would have flown from hill to hill, riding the warm currents through the smoke, then dipping their wings to circle over the city from castle to spire. Conscious of the other walkers atop the hillside, she couldn't risk the transformation, but her shifter's blood was eager to leap and soar.

"Surely you realize by now I have no fear of falling." Edwina hugged her shawl, fighting the instinct to transform even as the toes of her boots inched over the edge of the drop.

Ian seemed amused by her honest reply, yet when a gust of wind hit their backs, he reflexively moved his feet away from the edge, urging her to retreat with him. Of course, it was for his protection, not hers. Or perhaps he did it for the benefit of the hillwalkers gathered on other high points of the ridge who gawped at her daring. Oh, but she wanted to jump! The invisible energy in the air tugged at her, begging her to fly. Her body buzzed with the stuff now that she'd caught the wind at her back.

Ian glanced over his shoulder but took no reading of the people's auras with his watch, determining instead by mere guess that they must be mortal. "The path is this way," he said, leading Edwina to the cut in the escarpment where the lee-side trail began. They ventured down far enough along the side of the hill that they fell from view of the other hikers gazing at the panorama of the city below. Whether it was the wind stirring her shawl, the fey energy crackling in the air, or the warm sunlight conspiring to make mischief, Edwina could no longer deny the temptation to fly. With their backs against the hillside and no other climbers in view, she made a quick apology to Ian for abandoning him on the trail and leaped.

Wing and beak, claw and hollow bone replaced her human form. The thermal updraft caught her underwing, and she lifted high in the air. A sigh of relief reverberated through her body as she soared over the dropping hillside. Ian cursed and scrambled down the trail beneath her. Reaching out to brace himself against the cliffside, he looked up at her in the sky, his eyes wide with astonishment as he watched for signs of alarm from the others at the top of the trail. Had she just acted completely irrationally, practically in sight of a group of mortals? It was the second time she'd given in to such an impulse since she'd arrived. So unlike the practical and careful Edwina everyone thought her to be. But it was a glorious feeling to soar on the currents again, swooping over the city. All she was missing was the company of her sister.

She constantly wondered if there was more she could have done to protect her. But then Mary had always flirted with ruin. They both knew there would be a reckoning for someone who craved the corpse lights while walking among the living. It's why they'd kept on the move, trying to stay one step ahead of the mob they always imagined would come. But in the end it was Mary who did herself in.

With the joy bled out of her airy excursion by memories of her sister's death, Edwina searched for Ian on the ground to see where she might land and transform out of sight. While scanning the ground near the bottom of the trail, she passed over a smallish loch rimmed with wildflowers. A medieval stone kirk stood on a rise above. Below, her sharp raven's eye tracked a movement too quick and agile to be a human, but it was no animal. Yes, there beneath the trees was someone dressed in a black frock coat flitting over the rocks quick as a cat yet as vague as a cloud crossing the sun. And then he disappeared.

She dipped lower, her eye alert for any shift. Two white swans paddled gently away from the edge of the water. A sedge warbler dove after an insect. A squirrel scurried up an ash tree. There, beside the tree! She spotted the creature looking up at her from below the old kirk wall.

Curiosity made her venture closer for a better look, circling with her wings outstretched as she gently descended to just a few feet above. He was a spritely fellow, one of the fair folk by the look of him. Given what Ian had said about increased activity, she counted herself lucky to spot him.

"One should not give in to every whim simply because it is a rare sunny day," the fellow called up as she soared over his head.

Shocked to have been addressed directly while in her bird form, Edwina settled on top of the stone wall and shook out her feathers. A quick glance toward the hillside suggested Ian was halfway down, moving as quickly as he could on the steep terrain to catch up. Before her, the creature's eyes dazzled like a starry night sky. He took a step sideways on springy legs and she nearly flew off, but something about his attention steadied her. She dipped her head in greeting.

"Milady," he said and made a slight bow.

Sheltered by trees and the wall surrounding the old kirk, Edwina felt confident enough to leap from the stones and transform into her womanly body as she hit the ground. "What did you mean just then?" she asked, standing her ground before the otherworldly being. "Why did you call me that? Are you friends with Hob?"

The spritely creature retreated deeper into the shadows where the wall met the trunk of the wrinkled ash tree. "Your gift isn't something to be squandered for your own merriment."

Who was this creature? What did he know of her gift?

"What is it for, then?" she asked.

Even in the deep shadows, his eyes reflected the sparkling quality, drawing her in, yet his smile unnerved her with his too-wide mouth.

"The Telling," he said, as though sharing a secret he wasn't meant to tell.

His eyes flicked up at the road below the hillside. Ian was running toward the loch. Toward Edwina.

"Telling of what?"

"Everything," he said.

Before she could question him further, he scooped up a handful of leaves and seeds and blew them in her face. She flinched, turning away. When she opened her eyes again, the creature had disappeared just as Ian crashed through the gorse.

Chapter Seventeen

"She flew right up to him," Ian said. "Not a care for her own safety."

"Should we open it now?" Hob asked.

Ian looked over at the kitchen table, where Hob sat toying with the string on the large paperboard box Elvanfoot had sent over to his flat.

"Did you hear anything I said? I need to leave," he said. "There's a sprite who owes me an explanation as to why he's suddenly standing outside one of the gateways he's so eager for me to secure, talking to Miss Blackwood while she's flying around over his head."

Hob squatted on his haunches and turned his head away as if he'd been personally rejected.

"Fine, go on, then," Ian said, resisting the urge to roll his eyes. "But be quick about it."

Hob undid the string and stuffed it in his pocket to keep for later. Ian suspected that was all the elf had truly been interested in, so he opened the lid to the box himself. Inside he found a dinner jacket, starched shirt, bow tie, and trousers. A card made note of the fact the items were borrowed from a gentleman of similar build and would need to be returned in good shape two days hence. Ian humphed. How was a man expected to enjoy a party knowing he had to return his suit in good shape before his head had even cleared of the strong drink?

Hob felt the silk lapels with his hairy fingers and gave a grunt of approval. "Milady will be impressed."

Milady. Hob had used the term since the day he'd met Edwina. He'd recognized her as a kindred spirit from the start. Ian had known the elf all his life—he couldn't remember a time when the hairy fellow wasn't beside him—yet there was very little he understood of the life Hob had lived before attaching himself to the house on Hare Hill. For all he'd learned of the fair folk in his official duties as a constable and private detective, there was still a gaping void in Ian's knowledge of the Otherworld.

"Try it on," Hob said.

"I told you, I haven't got time."

"But what if your business keeps you and you're late for the party?" Hob asked. "If you dress now, it would save you having to rush later. It's only practical."

"And go walking around the back lanes of the city dressed like some posh eejit?"

Hob sighed and took the string out of his pocket again. "The suit is merely wool and silk. I can't help what you look like in it," he said, concentrating on the steps of tying a complicated knot.

With no time to keep arguing with the imp, Ian thought it easier to simply comply. And it would save him a trip back across town, if he could leave straight away from the south end of the city to rendezvous with Edwina and Elvanfoot at Eidyn House.

Thirty minutes later, dressed in the borrowed suit, Ian ignored the gawpers and hecklers on Oxgate Road as he pounded on the door to the slum flat. "I know you're here, you lump-headed gibface. Open up."

"Quit yer banging," a woman called out from the window above. "There's no one there. Hasn't been anyone in or out for weeks."

Ian backed up to get a look at the woman's face through the glass. "I'm looking for a wee fellow in a ragged black frock coat and shiny shoes."

The woman waved a disgusted hand at him, uttered something about nutters roaming the streets, and shut her window.

Ian sucked in the insult he wished to hurl at the old besom and instead flipped up the collar on his overcoat and turned toward the brick-lined close that led to the arch under the King's bridge. He turned the corner and found Finlay standing at the top of the stairs blowing smoke into the air like a chimney, grinning at the mischief with the woman he'd just overheard.

"I dinna actually live there, ye ken." Finlay stood with the sole of one shiny shoe propped against the wall behind him.

"You and I need to talk," Ian said.

"Aye, all right." Finlay shoved off the wall and walked down the narrow passageway, cocking his head to the right as he passed Ian, suggesting they should do it somewhere else, where half the slum's windows weren't open onto the corridor.

Ian followed as the last rays of twilight evaporated. Again he had to take twice as many strides as the sprite to keep up, even though they walked side by side. Finlay hit the bustling section of Oxgate Road where the hawkers still crowded together, shouting about the few items they had left in their carts for sale.

A man covered in coal and filth grabbed Ian's arm. "A nip o' whisky?" he asked, gesturing to a tube protruding from his sleeve. He produced a small glass from his coat and added a wink to seal the deal.

"I'll pass." Ian brushed off his suit where the man had taken hold.

Finlay, though, gave an encouraging nudge of his chin and took the drink from the man without a word, handing over a full queen's head for the effort. "He's one of yours," he said to Ian before swallowing the whisky in one gulp. Finlay handed back the glass and let out a burning sigh as the alcohol did its work on his insides.

The supposed whisky witch held up the arm with the devious copper tubing peeking out of his sleeve and suggested there was more where that came from, but Ian still wasn't sold. He had his favorite distillery witches up on the high road, aye, but this fellow looked more like a potions witch than the sort who'd studied the craft of spirits. A higher art, if ever there was one.

"Suit yourself." Finlay darted through the crowd to get to the next street over, where a wrought-iron fence surrounded a high-steepled church. "We can talk in here," he said, leaning against the fence beneath the sprawling branches of a wych elm. "What's on your mind? Have you discovered something?"

"You were right about the portals," Ian said, tuning in to his intuition to better gauge the sprite's reaction. "There was someone at the loch just below the kirk wall. A dapper fella in a black frock coat."

The veneer of Finlay's nonchalance slipped off. "You saw someone? Who? When?"

Ian raised an eyebrow. "You, or so I thought until two seconds ago."

Finlay's bright eyes went flat as he sobered and stood up straight. "Was the gateway disturbed? Had they passed through?"

"You swear you weren't down by the loch this afternoon?" Ian had seen only a glimpse of the diminutive creature, but even from a distance there'd been no mistaking the otter-sleek hair, springy bowed legs, and long black coat. He was certain he was being played the fool by the sprite.

Finlay shook his head. He grew agitated, pacing as he tugged at his chin. "No, it wasn't me." He looked up, eyes flashing with curiosity. "What were you doing by the loch? Was the woman with you?"

"You mean Miss Blackwood?" Ian's instincts were buzzing like a hive. Something was very wrong. "Aye, she was there."

"Is she all right? Did he try to speak to her? Did you check the gateway?"

"She's fine. Said he was a real charmer." Ian recalled the scene after he'd had a look around. "A wee spider had built a web over the opening. Same for the crack in the rocks near my folks' place. If this fellow had come or gone recently, he couldn't have avoided the web, could he?"

Finlay shook his head. "His body could have slipped through in any form, but not the rest of him. That would have snagged on the threads. That's why the guardians use their loyal spiders to protect the openings."

"None of the others showed any sign of disturbance either. No one's been through. Whoever it is you're looking for, they must have been here already." Ian paused. "Someone like yourself."

"We've accounted for all the permanent residents." Finlay's agitation grew until his pale skin mottled from the rush of blood to his hands and face, lacing just beneath the surface. Ian had seen the reaction before in others. Men, women, and sometimes fair folk, whom he'd had to question after a brawl while working for the Northern Witches' Constabulary. Not only was their blood up but so was their inclination to hurl harmful magic. Spells and counterspells had flown back and forth with devastating accuracy in a few cases—arms lost, eyes gouged, the tips of ears singed beyond repair. But why was this sprite so upset over one possible trespasser? Ian had never been told the reason why he'd been asked to investigate the portals, only that there were certain parties who wanted to know if someone was sneaking through. He hadn't much cared. Getting paid so he could keep his flat above the river was the only motivation he'd needed to say yes. But now that Edwina was somehow in the mix, he took a keener interest.

"Where's the woman now?" Finlay asked suddenly.

Seeing the overwrought gleam in the sprite's eye, and not entirely sure he wasn't being lied to about who and what he had seen earlier, Ian wasn't inclined to fully answer. "Safe."

"Safe, aye." Finlay nodded, eyeing Ian as though sizing him up. "She's back at the old man's, then." The sprite fidgeted, drumming his fingers against his frock coat, and lit a cigarette. "Good, good. That's good."

Ian's witch and detective instincts were both flaring, but he couldn't account for it. "Are you going to tell me what this is all about?"

"So you allowed her talk to this fellow dressed like me?"

"It was nae a matter of letting her," Ian said. "She got ahead of me on the trail and he found her. She said it was all gibberish nonsense, what he said. Him going on about how she shouldn't be flying around just because she felt like it."

Finlay puffed hard on his cigarette, squinting at Ian. "Wait, you didn't tell me she'd changed form. In the middle of the city?" The sprite paced again, blowing out a stream of white smoke.

"Aye, well, there wasn't anyone around to see," Ian said, though he couldn't really be certain.

"*He* saw her. And you let him get away?"

Ian couldn't argue the point, so he simply nodded.

"Fair enough." The sprite seemed to be working something over in his mind. "Come with me," Finlay said at last and took off down the road, not bothering to look back to see if Ian followed.

Ian did follow, though, climbing the stairs of one narrow close and down another, working hard to keep up with Finlay as the sprite turned a corner and then two more. After more twists and turns through narrow passages, Ian became disoriented. He believed they were near the Queen's Mile, the great spine of road at the center of the oldest part of the city where multiple closes cut perpendicular between buildings, like ribs on a skeleton, to provide quick access to the next road over for the foot traveler. The sprite had led them into a narrow alley Ian didn't recognize, one enclosed by a stone roof two stories up. Without the open sky, the space had a dank, eerily calm feeling. Even the air didn't stir.

Finlay took another step and called a ball of crackling light into his hand. The narrow opening they'd entered through disappeared along with the daylight, as if a door closed behind them. Ian tried to get his bearings, but he'd never laid eyes on the place in all his time sleuthing in the city. He wondered briefly if it was a fairy passage he'd been unaware of, but the walls and steps were solid stone, and mortal-made black lanterns with the remnants of candle wax hung on the walls. Ian began to suspect the musty, damp space hadn't seen light in a very long time when something shifted in the shadows, sending a cold shiver to the base of his skull.

"What is this place?" he asked, barely raising his voice.

Finlay lifted the light in his hand, casting away the darkness before them to reveal a narrow lane that sloped steeply downward. Along the passageway, oak lintels set in the granite walls indicated doors to what he assumed might be homes or businesses, and yet no one was there. No man trudged up the steep slope on his way to work, no woman hung her washing from the rope lines overhead, and no child played with a stick and ball in the walkway. A ghost road.

"It's one of the touchstone places." Finlay looked over his shoulder at Ian. "Where havoc won the day."

"I don't understand. What happened here? Where is everyone? Why is it closed in?"

The sprite shivered and the light brightened in his palm. More doorways revealed themselves. Ian glanced inside the gloomy room on his right, which proved to be a pitiful place with a low ceiling and dirt floor. The proof of the last inhabitant's wretched life was evident by the rags hung on a wall peg, the wooden bucket still rimmed with the stain of human waste, and the apotropaic marks carved deep in the stone to ward off the unseen things that once scratched at the door at night.

"There are forces in the world, ye ken?" Finlay said. "They're constantly pushing on each other, back and forth in a great tug of war. Sometimes one side prevails, sometimes the other." The sprite walked down the first set of stairs and held up the light in his hand to a room on his left. Inside there was a single bed, hastily abandoned, with a moth-eaten blanket still crumpled in a pile above a thin and soiled mattress stuffed with straw. A child's leather shoe with a buckle and split toe rested beneath a toppled stool beside an upturned table. "This was the scene of one such battle."

Ian couldn't fit the pieces together in his mind. There was no battle he could recollect that had taken place in an abandoned lane of the city. Then again, he was with one of the fair folk and couldn't be certain he was still in his own city. For all he knew he was in some wicked underground fairyland, which made him cringe.

Finlay grinned that hideous smile of his, as though intuiting Ian's thoughts. "No, you've not been swept inside a fairy mound. This is a human shrine to failure, though it is our shame."

132

"Why do you call it a touchstone?" Ian asked.

"Life is mirth and misery," Finlay said with an odd starlike quality shining in his eyes as he looked around. "Even here in your city, where the forsaken were washed into the pits of the foulest streets by poverty, their prospects flowing to the sludgy bottom of the city along with the loo water, there was always hope. The people kept it bottled inside. A tonic one swallows when ill with despair. Hope has always been the bright light that fends off the darkness."

Finlay lowered his light until it glowed soft as moonshine, casting a blue shadow over the stone walls. "Our people lost this battle," he said. "Those who gain succor from pain and hunger and despair won that day. They struck hard until even that tiny spark of hope was extinguished."

Ian began to see a glimmer of the stakes Finlay was talking about. "The unseelie," he said. "They wreak havoc, then feed on the misery they create." He looked at the space again, visualizing the numbers of humans who must have inhabited the multiple houses and businesses that had once filled the filthy lane. "What happened to the people?"

"Plague. Poverty. Death for most. Later the mortals bricked up the space to hide the ugliness of it all." Finlay looked up at the darkness, where a sliver of a gray sky had once been visible. "The unseelie outsmarted the mirth-makers. They do love to toy with human lives above all else," he said, shaking his head, "especially when there are such depraved emotions to be sucked on like marrow bones after the feast."

As unsettling as the information was, the poverty and hardship Finlay had described were nothing unusual. Not in the slums, where those on the bottom rung barely clung to life by their fingernails. Not now, and not hundreds of years ago. "Why are you showing me this place?"

"Because *this* is why our adversaries have sent one of their creatures through." Finlay stretched his arms out and raised his voice until it filled the void as some sort of dare. "Because dishonor is all they know!"

Something scurried away in the dark at the bottom of the slope. Ian still didn't understand, but his neck suddenly tingled with vulnerability again, and he pressed his knuckles under his chin before he could stop the motion of checking for a gash. Naturally there was no blood there, only the lingering shadow fear of a dead man's memories. "You're making no sense, man." He hunched his shoulders against an imaginary chill breathing against the back of his neck as he thought of the shriveled vegetables in his mother's garden.

Finlay lowered his gaze. His spindly eyebrows bunched together. His thin lips twitched. He leaned forward and whispered, "We know the unseelie are coming for her on this very eve. And this time if they get her, you can be sure more misery like this will follow in heaps and bushels." Then he turned to Ian with his glittering eyes. "So you see, we have to stop this interloper. Because when we do, we free her to be what she's meant to be, and in return many innocent lives may be saved."

"Free who?"

Finlay reached for his tobacco with his free hand before having second thoughts and replacing the tin in his jacket. "The prophetess."

Ian finally grasped what this sprite had been trying to warn him about from the beginning. The queen's prophetess was who she relied on to help guide the course of the coming year and, he suspected, to chart relations between her court and those of the unseelie. The seer was said to be an old crone from the highlands who leaned on a staff made of yew. If the unseelie could somehow disrupt her effectiveness in the court, or steal her talents for themselves, chaos would be theirs to reap without the fair ones' ability to preempt their transgressions.

Ian glanced sideways at Finlay and cleared his throat. "But who would dare take the prophetess when the queen is expected in the earthly realm this very eve?"

"The world is in constant flux. Powers ebb and flow. Lies and truth mingle in the mist." The sprite blew out a stream of breath in the cold air. Tiny ice crystals sparkled as they floated like stars. "We understand the temptation. Ambition and reward are the gems the unseelie wrap their malicious intentions in before tossing the sparkling stones in the path of the uninitiated." The sprite paused and turned to Ian, the threat unmistakable in his eyes. "Those they may have already led astray to do their bidding."

Ian agreed the unseelie were notorious for manipulating mortals. But who had they recruited? He needed to get his hands on the guest list for Lady Everly's Midsummer party. It had to be one of the attendees, perhaps someone working with that black-coated fellow.

While Ian contemplated the difficulty of vetting the entire list, the sprite suddenly shifted position to stand in front of him. Blocking him, really.

"Had you been allowed to go ahead to the festivities," Finlay said, checking over Ian's suit with his eyes, "your reward would have tasted of ash in the mouth." Finlay's breath again crystallized as tiny shards of ice in the air between them. "As I mentioned, the unseelie know no honor."

What? Ian realized what he was being accused of.

"Now hold on," he said. "You've got the wrong end of the—"

Ian didn't have time to finish his objection. The ice crystals shot at his face, flying into his eyes and up his nose. The shards stung his throat and froze his brain until he couldn't speak or even stand. He sank to his knees and finally slumped onto his side.

Finlay doused the light in his palm and dragged the witch into the dirty hovel on the right. The sprite's eyes glowed purple in the dark as he jammed the door shut. "You'll be sorry you sullied your good name with the fair folk," he said before dissipating, leaving Ian trapped and alone in the dark of the underground.

Chapter Eighteen

Edwina stared at the paper-white moon rising in a blue sky outside her window as Mrs. Fletcher laced up the back of her borrowed black gown. Being invited to a party on such short notice, she'd had no choice but to accept an offer of a dress in storage from one of the wardrobes down the hall. Her choices, however, were limited. Edwina was still officially in mourning for her sister and would be for the next six months, if one were to strictly abide the custom. Black was naturally the only suitable color for a woman in her position to wear in public, even to a party as grand as the one Lady Everly had planned. She'd had a beautiful lavender ensemble tucked away in her trunk in the flat above the shop, the one her mother had made for a someday wedding. Given the circumstances, she couldn't have worn it, but such a color would have suited a summer party honoring the fair folk perfectly. Alas, it, too, had been devoured by the flames of their shop.

"It's nae a bad fit," Mrs. Fletcher said, standing back to gaze at Edwina's reflection in the mirror. She coughed softly into a handkerchief.

"I could make you some licorice root tea for that cough if you like," Edwina said. "I'm sure Sir Henry has a supply on hand."

"Oh, 'tis nothing." Mrs. Fletcher waved off her concern before asking, "What do you think? We could add a velvet bow and perhaps a feather to your hair? A lacy veil?"

Edwina had been informed that Lady Everly's party included a masquerade dance before the revelers gathered on the green to watch the trooping of the fair folk at midnight. The women would be dressed in elaborate costume gowns—this was a witches' ball, after all—and she would be expected to dress accordingly. And yet the gown Mrs. Fletcher provided was an old-fashioned cut—tight in the bodice with a bell-shaped flare for the skirt and puffy sleeves with ruffles around the shoulders. In its day, it would have made a decent gown for a fine lady, but now its fussy details would only draw looks of derision from the fashion-conscious crowd. Still, with its silk and velvet trimmings, it was finer than any dress Edwina had ever dreamed of wearing in her lifetime. "Perhaps if we tailored it a bit?" she asked. "Remove a few panels from the skirt and sleeves to narrow the silhouette?"

Mrs. Fletcher grimaced at the amount of work it would take to alter the gown. Edwina inwardly balked at the reaction, knowing her mother wouldn't have flinched at the effort. Lenora Blackwood was a seamstress witch so practiced at her craft that a needle and thread practically danced in her hands. Reworking the fabric would have been a huge undertaking, yes, but it was the sort of creative challenge her mother would have devoured.

"I'm not sure we've the time for anything too involved," Mrs. Fletcher said. "Mercy, I need to have you dressed and ready to go in two hours, and while I'm many things, I'm no fairy godmother." She tapped a finger against her lips, thinking while she looked up at the ceiling. "Hmm, there is another gown tucked away in a wardrobe upstairs that might do the trick. Sir will object, but of course he's still busy repairing the breach in the hedgerow." A spark of mischief lit in her eyes. "Never you mind. He charged me with finding you something suitable to wear, so unless he wants to see you go to the Midsummer celebration dressed in mourner's wool and crepe, he'll have to abide by this woman's prerogative."

Pleased to learn the housekeeper had a little pluck in her, Edwina slipped out of the old-fashioned gown and gladly set it aside while she awaited Mrs. Fletcher's return. She hadn't explored the house much beyond the main-floor library, the gardens, and the hallway leading to her room, but she knew there was another floor of bedchambers above. It hadn't been explained why there were women's dresses still housed in the wardrobes of various rooms. The grand house had once had a mistress, though. Elvanfoot's wife, or rather his former wife, was one of the fair folk, according to Ian. The woman had tried to kill him using a potion made from fly agaric, if she remembered the infamous incident correctly.

The housekeeper returned shortly, cradling the new gown as though it were a sleeping child. Piles of silk and lace cascaded over her arms as she laid the dress gently on the bed and spread the fabric out for Edwina to admire.

"Been in storage for a few years, wrapped up with lavender and thyme, but it's as fresh as the day . . ." Her thought trailed off and she smiled. "Never you mind that. 'Tis a lovely gown fit for a night of wonderment, is it not?"

"Exquisite." Truly, Edwina had never seen such fanciful lacework. Lacy flowers, vines, and feathery ferns had been stitched onto the chiffon layer to trail up from the hem, culminating in a bouquet across the scalloped bodice. The black silk undergown bled through from beneath with just enough contrast with the lace to spark interest, while long sleeves ended in a point above the wrist. The delicate chiffon had the silky feel of floss from a milkweed pod as she ran it through her fingers. It was almost too fine to contemplate wearing. "But is it proper?" she asked.

"I know you're grieving for your sister, dear, but it is Lady Everly's house you've been invited to. Anything less would be out of place for one of her Midsummer masques. And you canna be saying no to the lady's invitation. 'Twould be a tragic mistake you'd regret the rest of your life, in my opinion." Mrs. Fletcher spread the skirt out to its full length and nodded. "Shall we try it on?"

The gown was too extravagant, too fine for Edwina's rough skin and plain ways. Yet she slipped it over her head, persuaded by the beauty of the silk and the invitation to attend a once-in-a-lifetime affair. The dress went on like a second skin, an utterly familiar sensation, though one she usually experienced only after transforming into the bone-light body of a raven.

"Well, now, doesn't that look grand," Mrs. Fletcher commented, pointing Edwina toward the mirror. "I know a handsome young man who will be starry-eyed after seeing you in this dress tonight."

Edwina's ears grew hot at the mention of Ian. She did rather hope he would be pleased by the sight of her. He'd kissed her properly that afternoon, making her dizzy with desire. The taste of him lingered on her lips like a sweet cachou. "He is handsome, is he not?"

"Och aye, I'd fancy the lad myself if I were any younger." Mrs. Fletcher gave Edwina's shoulders a lighthearted squeeze before fussing with the lace at the back of the dress.

Edwina admired the fit of the gown in the mirror, imagining how it would move if she and Ian danced under the stars. "Why won't Elvanfoot approve?" she asked, seeing how the train rippled at her feet as though lifted by a spell.

"Oh, well, it belonged to his lady, then, didn't it?" Mrs. Fletcher clucked her tongue. "And if you dinna know the story there, then you haven't ever picked up a newspaper. Stars above, I thought he'd never live down the scandal. But, no, it only made him more of a celebrity in these parts."

Ah, of course. The touch of the silk, the fine threads of the lace and chiffon—now that she knew what she was looking at, the gown had the cut and shape of a fair one's sensibility. The way the fabric hugged the body yet flowed with the grace of tall grass swaying in the breeze when she walked was a dead giveaway. Edwina found the otherworldly quality of the gown alluring. Spellbinding, even. With her mood temporarily unfettered from the worries of her life, she shamelessly twirled before the cheval glass. The gown's train billowed and swept around her feet.

"'Tis a beauty," Mrs. Fletcher said, and in that instant, still light-headed from spinning before the mirror, Edwina got an image of the housekeeper with her third-eye vision. The woman rocked a baby in her arms, a tiny shriveled thing with a tuft of red hair that peeked out of the swaddling blanket. Mrs. Fletcher sat before a stone fireplace, cooing at the baby boy while a young woman in homespun plaid watched with worry from across the room of a crofter's humble cottage. The baby coughed up a wretched, sickly noise that the woman—the mother—claimed was no voice belonging to a human child. A changeling, she claimed, fretting and tearing at a thumbnail with her teeth while she watched from the darkened doorway as though she were on the edge of escaping. "Nothing but mischief out of the bairn since he was born two months ago," she said.

Mrs. Fletcher hummed a sweet tune to the child, the vibration resonating from her heart with the thrum of love and healing. "If changeling ye be, give us a sign, if babe ye were born, all will be fine." Mrs. Fletcher produced a small iron weight tied to the end of a string. She held the pendulum over the baby's head and directed the weight to swing in a circle above, warning that the iron would swing wider and wider away from the child if it were otherworldly. "Be ye sprite or pixie born of flame, we cast ye back whence ye came. If ye be flesh, blood, and bone all whole, we welcome you home, body and soul."

The pendulum swung over the child's head three times and then suddenly stopped directly over the boy's nose. He sneezed and smiled as he clutched at the swinging object above his head. Mrs. Fletcher proclaimed the boy "nae touched by the fairies" and returned him to his mother, who cried tears of relief at the proclamation.

The shadow of doubt receded from the mother's eyes, but it had never made itself known in Mrs. Fletcher's gaze. Edwina saw nothing transpire between the women to signal the housekeeper's opinion, yet she sensed her motives and knew them to be true. She hadn't come to heal the baby; she'd come to heal the mother.

Drawn down a well of trancelike thought by the vision, Edwina startled when she came out of her altered state, blinking up to find Mrs. Fletcher hovering beside her in the mirror, chattering on about veils and feathers and a small beaded purse.

"Yes, of course," Edwina said when the interlude broke. "Whatever you think best." She wondered briefly if the housekeeper had noticed her daydreamlike state, but the old woman kept on with her work as if nothing had happened.

Mrs. Fletcher nodded in approval and had her step out of the gown again. "We'll have you sorted and ready to travel by this evening," she said, coughing again into her handkerchief.

This time Edwina thought she spotted a speck of blood. "Are you sure you're all right?" she asked.

"Just some congestion," the housekeeper said, patting her chest. "Never you mind that. You've got a grand party to attend with a fetching young lad."

Edwina fidgeted a bit, wondering if the old woman was truly all right and feeling uncertain about having to maneuver the intricate rules of society. "But how will I know how to act in Lady Everly's company? How to speak or eat or even walk properly?"

"The upper class do have their peculiar ways, I grant ye. But if you've a keen eye, as I suspect ye have, you'll watch and learn, aye? That's how I managed my first ball at Lady Everly's."

Edwina swung around. "You've been to the party before?"

"Oh, many times over the years," the woman said with a wan smile. "But my time has passed for such things. When you get there, try to do as they do, and if that doesn't fit ye, then you just do what your heart tells you is proper. I have a feeling everything will turn out as it should." Mrs. Fletcher nodded at her own wisdom, then added she'd sew a calming charm on the inside of the dress, just a small one so Edwina would know it was there. Then she winked and whisked the dress away, scurrying off to wherever it was the housekeeper went during the day.

Somehow settled by Mrs. Fletcher's sage advice, Edwina reflected on the vision she'd had of her. Without more evidence, she couldn't be sure if she was seeing a person's indelible future or merely some possible version of events, and yet the vision she'd had of the housekeeper was undoubtedly real. She was certain it must be, after experiencing the woman's compassionate brand of magic firsthand. Instead of feeling confused or disconcerted after experiencing another episode, she embraced the pleasant afterglow left by the positive vision.

Edwina changed back into her mourning dress and returned to the main floor. The halls were unusually quiet for such an auspicious evening. She almost always came across Yates puttering around in the main hall, catering to Elvanfoot's needs, but neither he nor the wizard were to be found anywhere. She was just about to check the back stairs leading to the secluded workroom when the front doorbell rang, a terrible clanging thing that operated on an electrical current. No one stirred in the house in response to the bell. So, remembering that Elvanfoot was working on the hedgerow spells, with Yates likely there assisting him, Edwina didn't think anything of it when she opened the front door herself. She expected to find a postman or telegram delivery. Instead she found an empty stoop. She craned her neck to look over the tops of the rhododendrons growing beside the entryway but saw no one in the yard or driveway.

Baffled, she looked down, and there, placed on the center of the slate steps, sat a small white envelope addressed to her. The green ink glittered under the cloudy sky.

Edwina froze like a mouse hiding in the shadow of a hawk's wings. The handwriting. The ink. She knew without opening the envelope it was from *him*. He'd found her. But how? They'd removed the tracking spell. She wanted to stomp on the letter with her boot and kick the thing into the bushes, and yet curiosity made her bend to pick it up.

The envelope appeared to contain more than a mere missive from a madman. Something solid and weighty slid around inside. Her hand shook as she broke the seal and opened the envelope.

Inside was the expected scribbled note but also a shiny gold band. Edwina poured the ring into her palm and gasped. Grandfather Merlin old with twin gemstones set in a double bevel. There wasn't another like it in all the world that she knew of.

She and Mary had been girls walking along a rocky cove below the great serpent's head that jutted into the northern sea when they found it. As waves splashed at Edwina's bare feet, she'd spotted the ring half buried on a spit of sand. Mary saw it, too, but by then Edwina had already plucked the gold loose to study in her hand.

"A space for twin stones," Mary had said.

"Just like us," Edwina had replied.

Always fond of mischief, Mary had plucked a pair of berries from a wild cotoneaster growing in the cliffside and conjured two teardrop-shaped rubies from them. Edwina fastened them into the bevel with a metal-shaping spell, and then both girls carried the ring back to their mother, passing it gently back and forth between them every ten steps, as if they carried the crown jewels of the isle kingdom in their hands.

How could this ring—this precious one-of-a-kind ring—have found its way into an envelope sent by a maniac? Edwina sank to her knees. Her vision was partially obscured by welling tears, but she opened the envelope to see what the devil had written her this time. The pungent scent of vinegar wafted up as she unfolded the enclosed card.

Dear Miss Blackwood,

Perhaps a ring does not suffice as proof of life, but it will surely be her death if you deny me my request. You possess something I desire above all else. Meet me alone in Lady Everly's garden at midnight where the moonflowers grow. I shall await your presence there.

Yours Truly,

A Fond Admirer

Her first instinct was to run to Elvanfoot and show him the note so he might cast another protection spell around the house. Around her! Then she would call Hob from the land of the hobgoblins and let the little fellow warn Ian. But then her fingers began to tingle as if something were crawling on them. The pungent scent of vinegar rose up as the madman's note disintegrated in her hands, curling up at the edges until she held a small pile of pulp with green streaks running through it like a clump of moldy cheese. All that remained of the message was the ring—and its implied threat.

The ring had been the sisters' first valuable find. Their mother had vowed to never take it off. It was a reminder, always, of her oddly enchanted daughters and their unique gifts. Edwina closed her fingers over the ring and swore she could still detect the warmth of human flesh held within the gold. The echo of energy was so subtle she didn't think another being could detect the pulse, except perhaps Mary.

The madman's note had been wrong. The gold had whispered the proof of her mother's life to her as no other article could have. But how had he come to take it from her? If this man had their mother's ring, then he had their mother—there could be no other conclusion. Was she being held against her will? For how long? And what about her father? Was he there also? Was he, too, being threatened with death?

"Oh, Mary," she said out loud. "What if Mother didn't leave us? What if she was taken? What if they both were?"

The revelation that she and her sister hadn't been abandoned unlatched the door in her heart where she'd been keeping hope quietly alive. She pressed her palm to her mouth and sobbed at the prospect of someday seeing her parents alive again. Her mother, at least, was close. She could feel it.

Edwina considered the implied threat contained in the note again. The truth of the matter became clear, and she knew what she must do. Yes, she would meet this despicable man's demands and rendezvous in the garden at midnight. She'd give him anything he desired if it meant sparing her mother's life.

While she contemplated the challenge before her, all evidence of the note disappeared from her hands, scattering like sawdust in the breeze. The door behind her opened, and Mrs. Fletcher balked to see her on her knees.

"Good heavens, Miss Blackwood," she said. "What are ye doing on the ground? And with the spell wall in flux as it is?"

"I dropped something," Edwina said, quickly drying the tears from her cheeks as inconspicuously as she could. "I think it fell in the crack in the walkway."

The housekeeper eyed the pavement in front of the house suspiciously until Edwina assured her she was fine. "Well, you'd best be coming inside. Poor old Yates has taken a spill. Fell face-first in the hemlock out back after he tripped on that daft mechanical rat of Sir's. His face is all blistered in a rash. Mercy, you never saw a grown man moan so much."

"Not dead?" Edwina asked.

"Dead? Of course not. What a thing to say."

Edwina, dumbfounded by the revelation, managed to keep her face neutral as she gathered her skirt and rose from her awkward position on the ground. "Found it," she said, holding up the ring and slipping it on her finger. Her eyes scanned the road, the trees, and even the verge near the house. Whoever this madman was, he knew she would be at Lady Everly's party. And now, thanks to his note, she knew he would be there too.

What was it Ian liked to say? Forewarned was forearmed? Stars willing, she'd prove him right.

Chapter Nineteen

"The witch has put the ring on," Maligar said, nibbling on sweets.

"As I said she would." The man stared at himself in the mirror, admiring the cut of his suit, the shine on his shoes, and the flow of his silk cape while his feet remained firmly planted within his protective circle. "Like all women, she has the mind of a child. Manipulation is almost too easy."

"Of course." Maligar smirked as he slouched in the wingback chair with one pin-striped leg draped over the velvet arm. The man had learned to let the anger the insufferable demon provoked in him wash away until the accumulation of affronts pooled together at the bottom of a poisoned well. When all this was over, there would be a final reckoning when he would teach the upstart jackanapes his proper place.

"The hex embedded in the ring will have infused with her skin by now," he said, adjusting his bowtie. "Her mother's tainted blood will seal the binding spell, and then she'll have no choice but to do my bidding when we meet. See that the cage is ready when I return."

"Such complicated thoughts men are capable of." The demon's eyes gleamed in what the man could only interpret as the anticipation of witnessing advanced magic being done. And why not? He sat in the company of one who understood the intricacies of spellcasting better than almost anyone. Maligar had plenty of his own spells in his repertoire and a sharp and devious mind, but he didn't possess the intellect of one who'd mastered the art of higher magic.

"Indeed," the man said, straightening the circle pin with crescent horns on his lapel. It was the symbol of the Order of the Night Hunter and had to be worn proudly when in the company of so many esteemed witches. There was only one more thing he required before being presented at Lady Everly's. "Do you have the stone?" he asked, grabbing his top hat and gloves.

Maligar dug in his frock coat and produced the tiny round moonstone. The opalescent quality of the gem shimmered in the demon's hand as if it had been plucked from the night sky. "Swallow it just before you leave your cab. It will shine from within, giving you the aura you crave."

The demon tossed the moonstone in the air for him to catch, but he fumbled it and the stone skittered onto the wooden floor, where it rolled outside the circle. *Blast it!* He didn't dare leave the safety of the circle, not with that unnatural thing staring at him from the other side of the room with its clammy white skin and eyes so dark purple they nearly hypnotized with their depth.

"Very well," the man said with a wave. "Be gone until I summon thee again."

Maligar grinned and popped a black-and-white licorice allsort in his mouth before getting up from the chair. He straightened his frock coat, then casually walked over to where the stone had rolled against the hearth. The demon picked up the dropped moonstone, then returned to the circle, where he stepped just up to the line. The man held his ground, confident in the power of his magic and superiority. No harm could come to him inside the protective circle. It was noted in every book he'd ever read. So when Maligar, his face a contortion of pleasure and malice, shoved the moonstone between his lips and held it there with his ice-cold finger, the man rooted his feet to the floor while the demon whispered, "Until we meet again, sir."

Chapter Twenty

Ian sat up, stunned that he'd been outwitted by that bandy-legged sprite. He'd trusted Finlay, and now he found himself trying to exit a small hovel that had once been lived in by a family hundreds of years earlier, and probably a cow or two as well. He gave the wooden door a shove, but it didn't give way even when he heaved his shoulder against the wooden planks. The walls proved to be solid stone as he slammed his hand against their hard surfaces.

Ian cast a spell to test the strength of his stone prison. Lighting a flame on his fingers and holding his hand high, he focused on the weakest point of the wall—between the stones, where the fit wasn't precise. "Sticks, stone, rocks, and mud, yield the space, if ye would."

It was a simple and tepid incantation, but he dared not blast the place apart and bring a mountain of rubble down on his head. Still, he expected more than a single pebble to rattle loose from the mortar. He did manage to open up a small crack of light, so perhaps he just needed a little more heft to his spell. Ian pushed the flat of his hand against the wall and said, "Cleave and crack, smash and rumble. Break this wall and make it tumble."

A sprinkling of dust sifted down from the ceiling, but otherwise his spell had no effect. And lucky thing, as he suspected the walls were the very pillars supporting the establishment above. Some kind of enchantment surrounded the place besides the one that secured the door. It was a trap set by that bloody Finlay, and he'd walked straight into it.

He doused the flame on his fingertips and looked again for the sliver of light coming through the chink he'd created in the stones. It was faint, seeping through an opening too thin to offer much hope of escape. *Damn that Finlay!* He'd trusted the sprite, taken in by his humble appearance and clever talk. No, if he were honest, he was flattered that one of the fair folk had come to him for help in a matter they weren't capable of settling for themselves. He'd been pleased to be involved. It would have made a grand advertisement for his business, had he been able to boast about providing his detective skills to serve the fairy world. Instead he found himself outwitted, out-magicked, and sitting inside what amounted to a rotting cell.

Ian brushed the dust from his dinner jacket. The Everly party would be underway soon. The Midsummer sun would have put a golden glint on everything it touched by now, as the northern hemisphere leaned into its apex of light. He'd taken his home for granted, so often standing at the window in his flat and overlooking the river, the spires, and the distant fairy hill standing like a stalwart sentry on the other side of the city. He'd never once imagined there was such a hell buried beneath the busiest thoroughfare.

Uneasy from sitting too long in the dark, Ian brought the flame back to life on his fingers. Faint sounds of the city bled through the stone so that he began to feel like a ghost trapped within the veil between worlds as he listened to the familiar sounds of horses clomping by and a pair of men making a ballyhoo on the street, though he knew not what the ruckus was about. Life bustled outside, yet the cold nothingness of the dark where he stood chilled his innards with its silence and his inability to get through to the other side. He wasn't the sort to panic in an enclosed space, leastwise not in a cave or dark forest. Those sites were born in the gleam of Nature's eye, but man-made places underground had an altogether different energy to them. They were filled with the residue of emotions left behind by the mortals who'd built them—fear, loneliness, hate, jealousy, suspicion, reckless adventure, manic joy, and occasionally love. The sensations remained like a bad odor trapped in a rug that would not scrub clean. The deeper in the ground one went, the worse it got.

As proof, he took a closer look at a set of marks carved into the stone near the entrance to the room he'd been abandoned in. The symbols were familiar enough. The concentric circles, star, and triskele were a form of mortal magic meant to ward off evil, which he always found slightly offensive, since it was his kind they were aimed at. Yet he was not so naive as to believe there weren't witches who actively practiced magic from a standpoint of ill will. Some thrived on the false sense of power that magic gave them, inflating their perceived supremacy. He thought of Mary and her unnatural appetites then as his finger traced over a set of grooves that felt like the shape of a *W* on its side.

With his neck exposed to the cool, dark air behind him, Ian shivered, revisiting the stomach-churning fear of a dead man's memories. He flipped his collar up and cursed Finlay for the tenth time since he'd vanished. Why did the damned sprite believe him capable of conspiring with the unseelie? If anyone, it was Finlay who clung to the downtrodden quarters of the city, choosing to live amid the misery and depravity that thrived on Oxgate Road. Aye, maybe he could have done more to apprehend the sprite who'd talked to Edwina. He could see in retrospect how that might have looked suspicious on his part when he was tasked with finding a trespasser, but when the fey fellow disappeared, all he felt was relief that he'd left Edwina alone.

A noise skittered at the bottom of the abandoned lane. Ian traced the witch marks with his finger again. The people who'd once lived in these quarters had feared the unknown creeping in the dark. They likely didn't understand all of what they should fear, but they had an inkling of the danger that awaited them outside the glow of their torchlight.

He imagined they, too, could feel the cool breath on their necks from those who lurked in shadow, watching and waiting for vulnerability to show them its belly. Mortals dreaded the dark so badly they'd gone and invented a way to keep the lights on twenty-four hours a day with their electric fidgety bobs until there were nights Ian had lain awake in the glow of a streetlamp, forced to wonder if the old magic could survive human fear.

Flummoxed for the moment about how to escape, or even what Finlay hoped to achieve by locking him up, Ian took a cue from his frightened mortal forebearers and gathered an armful of straw from the abandoned bedding and piled it up at the base of the wooden door. With his enchanted flame, he lit a bonfire, tossing in the legs of a broken table to coax the door to burn quicker. Whatever spell had been cast to keep him locked up, it gave way quickly to ordinary fire. The wooden planks disintegrated in the flames, turning to ash as if they'd been pulped and pressed into paper.

Wasting no time, Ian made a torch of his own using the last leg from the broken table, a little burlap from the bedding, and a quick spell to keep the flame burning bright. With his torch held aloft, he escaped the room and searched the abandoned underground alleyway for a seam in the enchantment where he might make a wedge out of an incantation. He first inspected the top of the lane where he knew they'd entered through some sort of mist or illusion of a door, but there was no crack, no portal to pass through, or at least none he could detect without a member of the fair folk to open it for him.

With that option extinguished, he headed down the lane in the other direction as it dropped deeper into darkness. There had to be another way out. How could an entire alley of homes and businesses be sealed off from the rest of the city? He ducked his head into several cave-like rooms looking for escape, only to come away with a growing sense of dread that he truly was trapped beneath the city. "Finlay, you bastard," he muttered.

At the bottom of the close came four distinct clangs of something metal hitting the cobblestones, followed by a grunt. Ian removed his pocket watch. He took a reading of the space and wasn't surprised to learn something supernatural waited outside the glow of his torchlight. Who else was down here with him? He could hear quiet shuffling just outside the reach of his light. Footsteps. The rattle of metal. Heavy soles clanging on the cobblestones. Like someone walking in armor.

No sooner had he come to the conclusion than a stone the size of a cannonball came hurling up the lane at him from the shadows. A great round thing that rolled and bounced and would have hit him were it not for his experience with quick defensive spells. "With this charm, I disarm!" The stone veered around him, crashing into a set of crooked steps.

"Who's there?" Ian shouted. "Show yourself." He sounded braver than he felt. Not unlike primitive man, he stood there brandishing his torch against the dark, willing the thing he feared to show itself, while at the same time trusting his feet were ready to run in the opposite direction should the need arise.

An angry grunt answered his challenge, followed by footsteps that echoed off the narrow passage walls. A diminutive goblin emerged from the dark, his face wrinkled, his ears grotesquely pointed, and his nose grown so long and bulbous the tip drooped over his mouth. His hand bore a long pike, and on his head rested a red cap that slouched over one pointed ear. A pair of stub-footed sabbatons were responsible for all the stramash.

The creature narrowed his eyes and lowered his pike so the pointy end was aimed straight at Ian's heart. "Ye've been making a right ruckus down here."

Too stunned by the creature's appearance, Ian forgot to give in to his fear and run, though he suspected now he should have. "Have you lost your way, wee man?" he asked, taking his eye off the pike to glance at the narrow walls long enough to imply their humble surroundings.

The redcap fellow ought to be guarding the vestibule of some haunted castle, not defending the bowels of an abandoned pestilence-filled lane. *Aye, but these are odd days indeed,* thought Ian, gripping his torch a little tighter.

The goblin, whose red cap was said to come by its color from the many times the wool had been dipped in the blood of his victims, appeared momentarily muddled by the question. His pike dipped, and his mouth curved in a frown. "I'm nae lost. You're the one trespassing. And you'll pay for it in blood," he said, raising his weapon again.

"It's nae a castle keep, man," Ian said. "It's naught but a dirty lane where folks used to live and sell their goods. Hardly worth protecting, although it has its own strange magic, I'll grant you." The goblin bore a sallow complexion, and his eyes had gone yellow where they ought to be bright as stars. "How long have you been down here?" he asked.

The wee little man blinked as if dazed by the question. "I canna remember. It's been an age since . . . since . . . I remember slipping out of yon castle on the hill to have a wee nip of Margaret's whisky. She was a witch, aye, but she sold the best batch on the mile." He smacked his lips at the memory. "But when I got here she was gone. All of the inhabitants were gone. So I went looking for them up the lane, slow like, staying in the shadows, but every last room was empty and smelled of sickness. I wasna feeling too good myself and went to take a kip in the hay in yonder cowshed, when the bricks went up." The goblin shrugged. "I haven't stabbed anyone with this useless old thing in an age," he said, standing his pike up on the cobblestones to lean against the staff as though worn out from all the work of carrying it with him for so little reward.

"You've been down here by yourself all that time?" Ian swung his torch around, confounded by the place. "Have you never tried to leave?"

"Och aye, there's a way out." The goblin cocked his head toward the dark at the bottom of the sloped lane. "Down there, but where is there to go?"

"Could you show me?" Ian asked.

"Why should I?" The little goblin grimaced as his grip tightened on his weapon, showing a glimpse of his former fury. "You should already be skewered on the end of my pike, by rights."

"Fair enough." It was the grouchy fellow's job to protect his lair and kill those who invaded, even if he was misplaced. He needed other people's blood to sustain his own life force, after all. "But since you've been down here," Ian said, thinking out loud, "another fine witch on the Queen's Mile has taken up the art of distilling the whisky. I'd put her spirits up against anything you've drunk in the past. I'll take you there, if you like. Get that drink you've been waiting all this time for."

The redcap stamped his sabbaton on the cobblestones. "It's a trick."

Seeing the goblin needed more persuading, Ian mimed holding a glass in his hand. "You raise the glass to your nose first, aye? The smell rises and fills the inside of your head with a cloud of woodsmoke." The goblin's jaundiced eyes widened, and he leaned a pointed ear forward. "And that first sip? Heat on the tongue, a spark in the throat, and then a full fire in the belly to keep you warm on a night when the sky is nothing but *dreich*."

The goblin swallowed, making the Adam's apple in his skinny throat bob up and down.

"But if you'd rather stay here in the dark," Ian said, leaning his back against the wall to suggest he was willing to stay, too, "that's all right by me."

The wee fellow let out a frustrated growl. "Woodsmoke and a fire in the belly?"

"She enchants the hogshead with a bonding spell that joins the alcohol and the faint char in the wood together. 'Tis pure magic." He might have oversold it with the last bit, so he shrugged as if to say *you have to taste it to believe it.*

The goblin clenched his clawed fingers into a fist, clearly wishing he could have it both ways: kill Ian and then have his drink. But he'd have to do it in the other order, which Ian suspected was the source of his aggravation.

"No, I canna do it without taking yer life first," the goblin said, stomping his metal sabbaton against the stones and lowering his pike to run Ian through the heart. "'Tis the only way you'll leave this place."

Chapter Twenty-One

Edwina came down the stairs wearing the fairy gown beneath her shawl and her mother's ring on her finger. She'd worried the cloak was too plain for such a fine evening, but Mrs. Fletcher had assured her it would be better to have it than not for such a momentous occasion as the Midsummer party. Along with the calming charm the housekeeper had sewn into the gown, she suspected Mrs. Fletcher had enhanced the shawl with a small enchantment that gave it the slight illusion of a shimmer.

Sir Henry Elvanfoot, dressed in a tailored suit trimmed in silver embroidery along the lapel, waited by the door, checking his watch and patting his pockets to make sure he had everything. "Ah, Miss Blackwood, you look splendid. Shall we be off?"

"Isn't Ian meeting us here?" Edwina asked, searching the entryway.

"I'm sorry, my dear, something must have come up. Hob sent word Mr. Cameron went out earlier to attend to an investigation and hadn't returned. The poor imp couldn't seem to locate him anywhere."

"Has something happened? Is he all right?"

"I'm sure it's nothing to worry about. In his line of work, unforeseen incidents come up at the last minute. Something you should probably learn to accept sooner than later with our Mr. Cameron."

Elvanfoot had a point about detective work, but Edwina didn't think Ian would abandon her to attend an evening among the witchy elite on her own. Then again, he'd felt no remorse after allowing her to arrive on the threshold of Eidyn House alone on her first day in the city. If not for that, she might have insisted they wait for him to arrive. But as she'd apparently been left to fend for herself yet again, she gladly took Elvanfoot's arm as he escorted her outside to a horse-drawn carriage. The extravagantly posh interior boasted velvet seats and curtains, glass sconces filled with sweet-smelling posies, and glittering moons and stars painted on the midnight-blue ceiling.

"A little more suitable for an evening out than the dog cart," Elvanfoot said, assisting her inside.

The driver shut the carriage door and Edwina sat back against the velvet, knowing she'd likely never experience such luxury again. As they headed out of the city, she remarked that the ride was smooth enough she could embroider a silk scarf and never miss a stitch. She exhaled, marveling at her present circumstance, but after a brief exchange of polite conversation about the countryside and expectations for the Midsummer party, Elvanfoot drifted off into private thought while staring out the window at the passing countryside.

Edwina mimicked the wizard's gaze, though she set her concentration on Ian and his failure to show up. With Elvanfoot content to ride in silence, she decided to attempt an experiment. So far, her strange visions had been thrust upon her when she was least expecting them, but what if she tried to initiate one for herself? She began by visualizing the features of Ian's face: his crooked nose, the laugh lines around his mouth, and the look of surprise he got in his eye whenever she made an unexpected observation from what he perceived as her mysterious female mind. She rather thought that look on his face was what had made her fall in love with the rough-around-the-edges detective.

The easy motion of the carriage lulled Edwina into a meditative state. Since her first vision had occurred while soaring above, she thought it might help to watch outside her window, imagining herself on the wing above the moving landscape. The carriage rolled on, and soon she got a glimpse of Ian in her mind's eye—a strange image of him standing in a darkened lane holding a torch. A diminutive creature stood close by holding a wickedly sharp-looking spear at his side, but the little fellow wasn't like Hob. Instead, this imp looked to be hundreds of years older, with his long nose and hunched back. She didn't know what to make of the image once the pair began discussing the merits of whisky. Had he really stood her up so he could stay behind to drink with some sort of goblin?

She leaned toward the image to gather more information when she felt the shadows creep in, darkening the border of the vision. All around the edges, a thousand curious little eyes widened, watching her. *Expecting* something from her.

The carriage hit an unusually deep rut in the road, jostling Edwina. She sat up, startled out of her bizarre reverie. Had the faces been real or mere fanciful thinking under the influence of the Midsummer celebration? Wondering if she'd tapped into some strange energy floating in the ether, she decided that was enough experimental gazing for one night.

Edwina hated to think it, but if the vision *was* real and Ian was otherwise indisposed with the odd creature she'd seen, then in all likelihood she'd been left on her own for the entire evening. She felt a pinch of disappointment at the discovery. She'd been looking forward to getting the stoic detective to dance with her, but she'd also meant to confide in Ian so they might come up with a plan for confronting the miscreant who'd taken her mother. Now she'd have to meet the abductor alone. But things might still work out. She could always overwhelm the scoundrel with her voice. If he was as inferior a witch as Elvanfoot's ink experiment had made him out to be, a single spell sung in the man's ear ought to render him unconscious. Yes, the man had proved himself deceitful and treacherous, but when it came to magic, she was quite confident she could out-craft him. And then she would get her mum back.

She shrank in her seat, thinking about her mother. If he'd harmed her—violated her—in any way, Edwina would devise a hex to use on him so painful his grandchildren would feel the force of her magic.

Elvanfoot cleared his throat. "Everything all right? We're nearly there."

"Wonderful," she said, keeping her secret plans to herself as she looked outside the carriage window at what she could describe only as a fairy-tale castle.

"The first view of Albion House is always the most stunning," Elvanfoot said, pointing out Edwina's side of the window. "But don't tell Lady Everly I said so. She's already commandeered every spell at her disposal to make the place appear enchanted. She thinks it favors her with the fairy folk."

Elvanfoot proved a master of understatement. The house, set on a hill, had four medieval-looking spires that rose up above the surrounding trees. A golden halo crowned the castle towers from behind as the setting sun cast its fading influence over the evening horizon. The carriage rolled forward around a crescent-shaped driveway, and the enormous entryway came into view. Opposing unicorns, carved in stone, reared their hooves over the doorway. Below, a set of double oak doors with heavy iron hinges looked as though they could stave off an army at the threshold. And yet the magnificent gothic windows peeking out of the turrets, with leafy ivy growing up to their sills, softened the idea that this was any kind of fortress other than one for magic and whimsy.

The carriage came to a stop in the courtyard behind a line of other coaches. Edwina twisted her mother's ring on her finger to steady herself. That vile man who'd inserted himself into her life with violence and insolence would be somewhere inside, smiling and impersonating grace itself while in the company of others. She almost lost her nerve, but with a gentle nudge from Elvanfoot, she left the refuge of the carriage and stepped into the warm light of festive celebration.

The infamous wizard of the north escorted Edwina up the front stairs and into the reception room, where a young woman dressed as a sunflower was collecting women's shawls and men's hats for the evening. She paused, momentarily awestruck to see the bearded witch before her, and then gathered her wits. She took his top hat and gestured to a long mahogany table to the side. Spread out on top were rows of masks for the guests to wear for the masquerade. Edwina reluctantly handed over her cherished shawl to the young woman, revealing the borrowed gown beneath.

The old witch did a double take at her over the top of his glasses. "Good heavens," he said, recognizing the dress once her shawl was off. "How did you come by that gown?"

Edwina reflexively tried to cover the front of the dress with her arms, afraid she'd drawn the wizard's ire.

"I apologize," she said, accepting a black velvet mask from the attendant. "It was the only suitable black gown we could find on such short notice." She stepped out of the way as more guests entered the house and presented their invitations.

Elvanfoot took full notice of the dress, gazing at the gown from shoulder to floor with his brows drawn tightly together. He accepted a silver mask from the grinning sunflower girl and then shuffled Edwina along. After they'd moved far enough down the hallway, Elvanfoot rubbed his thumb and fingers together, testing the air around Edwina for spells. "Do you feel faint? Excessively hot or cold?"

"No, I don't think so," Edwina said. "Truly, I meant to go in my own clothes, it's just . . ." She fanned out the material of the skirt, feeling the fine silk. "Mrs. Fletcher wouldn't have me looking out of place."

Elvanfoot arched an eyebrow. "I'm not surprised. She's a golden-hearted hedge witch if ever there was one." He gave up testing the air for spells, concentrating instead on her complexion and pulse. "Which is why I'm sure she felt confident offering my former wife's gown for you to wear on this occasion."

Edwina looked down at the expensive silk in shame. "I do apologize. I should have known better than to put on anything so fine without your permission."

"No, no, it's quite all right, now that I'm over the shock of seeing it out of storage again." He seemed to recover from whatever distress the gown had stirred in him. "But how is your pulse? Does your heart race or your fingers feel tingly?"

"No, nothing like that." Truly, there was no denying the exquisite sensation that radiated over her skin from the touch of the fabric. "It's fairy made, is it not?"

"Quite so. My former wife, Clarissa, was . . . is . . . a Lady of the Woods. A guardian of the silver birch. She once taught me to make a delightful cordial from the sap," he added as an aside. "You must try it sometime."

Edwina's mind was a whirlwind of questions. How had he met a woman of the woods? Why had she tried to kill him? Where was she now? Would she be at the party? Alas, propriety wouldn't allow her curiosity to be sated.

"The silk slides across the skin feather soft," she said.

"That's very telling," Elvanfoot replied. "There is a reason I was so worried to see you in the gown at first. You see, if you were a mere mortal, the fabric might sting the skin as if it were made of nettles. Purely witch-born and the silk could give off a sulfurous odor. Clarissa was, is, notoriously vindictive and vain, and she quite often sabotages anything and everything she doesn't wish others, meaning mortals and witches, to have."

Edwina checked her arms for welts. "Yet none of those things appears true for me," she said, sniffing the dress for the scent of rotten eggs as discreetly as possible.

"I believe," he said, removing a pocket watch identical to the one Ian carried, "that is because even though you are a witch, you've been fey-touched." He watched the wheels go round, calculating the energy in their immediate radius. "I had suspected from the moment I met you that you were perhaps one of the fair folk, yet your aura suggested otherwise. A common witch, if the light spectrum and frequency humming away on my watch are to be believed." He snapped the device shut. "If I do say so myself, the magical mechanics of the device are beyond reproach. So what conclusion should we come to but that you are a witch who's been blessed by the fair folk in some way."

Edwina shook her head in frustrated ignorance. "Everyone keeps saying that, but how?"

Elvanfoot took the velvet mask from her. "Perhaps your father paid for a fairy blessing at a well when you and your sister were born? It's not an uncommon practice in the rural villages."

Edwina knew that couldn't be the case. Her parents had been as flummoxed about her and Mary's abilities as the rest of the witching world. But there was no denying the dress had little effect on her other than to make her feel grand.

Elvanfoot took the liberty of slipping the mask over her eyes and tying in place. The moment he let go, the gown tightened slightly over her chest, the fabric seeming to almost meld with her body. A moment later her back twitched and a pair of lacy black raven's wings sprouted, looking as though they were made of the same material as the black overlay of the gown. Mortified that she'd transformed as though she had no control over her own body, she recoiled, backing her wings against the wall.

"I don't know how that happened," she said, staring at her hands. She'd never grown wings without her arms also disappearing. "What magic is this?"

"No need for alarm," Elvanfoot said with a spark of mischief. "It's simply masquerade magic." He slipped his silver mask over his eyes, and a halo of stars encircled his head. "Lady Everly enchants the masks every year. The illusions are meant to coordinate with each guest's attire and mood. Something to that effect."

Edwina looked over her shoulder. "They're not real?"

"Not this time," he said and escorted her to the grand hall, where the sound of violins filled the air.

Self-conscious of her wings, Edwina worried people would stare and know who and what she truly was. Yet everyone seemed to be sporting strange and wondrous illusions. Unicorn-horned men, fish-skinned women, and cat-eared dancers twirled across the floor. Saturn rings encircled one man's body, while the woman in his arms had antlers growing out of her pompadour. No one even looked twice at a woman with black raven wings. To be so normal in a roomful of strange illusions gave her the same freeing sensation as soaring over a mountain valley from one updraft to another.

"This way, my dear. I'd like to introduce you to someone." The wizard handed her a glass of champagne and had her follow him to the veranda outside the double glass doors. The air was cool and slightly damp, but braziers burned all around the perimeter, keeping guests comfortable for outside conversation. There, a stone path cut through the grass to where an enormous green-and-white gazebo stood twinkling under flickering fairy lights. Elvanfoot led Edwina up the short steps. There, a small crowd, all costumed in masquerade illusions, laughed and chatted like old friends. At the center of the attention stood a woman with shimmering gold hair that fell in thick Godiva waves to the floor.

Edwina couldn't tell if the witch was old or young simply by looking. The woman's manner implied she held command over those around her, suggesting she was in her matronly years, yet her aura seemed to shine with the vibrance of youth and energy. And then the woman's eye met hers. A warm gaze fastened on Edwina, earnest in its curiosity. The crowd surrounding the woman watched everything she did and soon took notice of Edwina too. They stood back so that the woman might have an unobstructed view of the witch with raven wings.

Elvanfoot gently urged Edwina forward. "Lady Everly Frances, may I introduce Miss Edwina Blackwood. Miss Blackwood, I'd like you to meet our gracious hostess."

Caught in a web of ignorance about how to answer the introduction, Edwina did the only thing she could think to do. She curtsied and bowed her head slightly. Lady Everly bit back a smile and bowed her head in return.

"A pleasure to meet you, Miss Blackwood." The curious eyes tracked to the wings on Edwina's back. "I've heard such tales."

After kissing Lady Everly on each cheek in greeting and thanking her for the invitation, Elvanfoot drifted to his left to say hello to an old friend whose head was covered in hedgehog spikes. Edwina, left on her own to engage with the author of the eponymous grimoire and her minions, listened to their stories of spell mishaps involving volatile liquids, substitute ingredients one can use when out of mandrake root, and how to rid the home of pesky hexes that cause one to trip on the same rug every time. To her great surprise, Edwina grew bored of the conversation until she thought she might have to stifle a yawn.

Lady Everly seemed to take notice of her disinterested guest and quickly changed the subject. "Enough of that. Who'd like to take a turn around the garden now that the sun has gone down?"

A few guests waved and chose to go back inside the grand hall to dance, including Elvanfoot, but the rest followed onto the garden path, eager to be at the side of the celebrity witch. Edwina perked up. Anxious to spot the location of her impending rendezvous, she fell in line behind the others.

Their hostess wore a gown of silver and gold threads that glittered under the waxing moonlight when she walked. An enchantment perhaps, though it was just as likely the threads were divinely expensive, made to catch the light of a ballroom chandelier. By comparison, Edwina's gown greedily swallowed the starlight as she walked on the garden path beside the others, giving her a delicious feeling of invisibility.

As they wound through the path, she gawped at the suspended string of candlelight. Such expense to cover the entire grounds. But as the group passed a patch of lavender and foxglove, pixies tittered overhead on the branches of a rowan tree. The twinkling glow, she discovered, was from their Midsummer glimmering that flickered as they hopped from limb to limb to spy on the people below.

"Have you watched the trooping of the courtiers before?" Lady Everly asked. "They'll pass through the woods just there." She pointed toward a stand of silver birch that reflected the moonlight off their papery bark. "We'll dim the torches later so as not to disturb them."

Edwina thought of Elvanfoot's ex-wife, a guardian of the silver birch, and smoothed an uneasy hand over her borrowed dress. "No, never. I'm so looking forward to it," she answered. "Thank you for the opportunity."

"Oh, no, my good woman, it is I who should be thanking you." Lady Everly stopped before a formal garden filled with pale night-blooming flowers that opened their mouths to take in the moonlight.

"Whatever for?" Edwina asked.

"My sole dedication in life is the pursuit of magic in all its forms so that I might educate others." Lady Everly brushed her fingers tenderly beneath Edwina's chin as if to say *cheer up*. "Your gift, as I understand it, is the stuff of dreams for an academic like myself."

Whether it was the concealment magic floating in the masquerade air or the incandescent desire to understand her sister's intent, Edwina felt emboldened to broach a subject with Lady Everly that she hadn't felt comfortable discussing with her wizard host previously. "Might I ask a question on the subject of magical study?"

Lady Everly lit up, eager to help. "Of course."

"Someone left me a message. Coded, I believe. She marked a crescent moon above the sigil for Mercury and then wrote our initials beside each one. I can't make sense of it. Is there some relationship between the two beyond the obvious that I'm missing?"

"Why do you think it's a message?"

"My sister passed recently, but before she died, she made those marks in my grimoire."

Lady Everly tapped a finger to her lips, slightly intrigued. "Well, we have the moon, which represents silver. And also emotion, don't forget. Mercury, on the other hand, is associated with quicksilver and the intellect. They share a link through a loose affiliation with silver, but they are often in opposition."

"How so?"

Lady Everly gestured to the sky. "We understand that the moon rules over emotion, wrapping its arms around all it encounters, but Mercury rejects such foolishness, preferring thought, deliberation, and decision. Perhaps your sister meant it as an apology or explanation of some kind, understanding your anger over something when for her it was the perfectly logical thing to do."

"Yes, of course, that does make sense," Edwina lied. She was no more enlightened than before, as suicide was not the logical thing for anyone to do, but she smiled and thanked Lady Everly for entertaining her foolish question anyway.

Two ladies and a gentleman stared at Edwina with envious curiosity after the exchange. One, a Mr. Chalmers with pale skin to rival the midnight flowers and the illusion of a beetle shell on his back, leaned in very close—had he inhaled the scent of her hair?—and asked if the rumors were true about her ability to shape-shift. For a terrifying moment she thought she'd stumbled into the arms of her stalker, but then he admitted he'd never seen a moon garden before and vowed to plant one himself as Lady Everly resumed her tour, leading them over a maze of whitewashed stepping-stones. Edwina smiled politely without answering his question, letting the illusion of wings on her back speak for her. She dismissed the fellow as nothing more than a party guest who rarely ventured into the sunlight. Her stalker, however, was somewhere among the guests. Was he watching her this very moment? She glanced quickly at the ground to see that her footsteps weren't being tracked again, but all she saw were the paving stones they trod on.

The winding garden path led to a marble font in the center of the moon garden. A placid silvery liquid rested in its bowl. Lady Everly directed everyone to hold hands in a circle around the font. Chalmers sidled in beside Edwina, taking her hand in his clammy flesh as their host uttered her charm. "Moths and bats we do beseech thee, dip thy tongues in flowers sweetly. Celestial stars and moon so bright, illuminate their way tonight."

It was a simple charm meant to draw in nature, but the pale flowers, stones, and even the marble font shimmered a little brighter when they let go of each other's hands. Edwina casually slid her palm against the fabric of her dress to rid it of Mr. Chalmers's cold sweat.

"Oh, look! How delightful," said one of the women. A brown moth with feathery orange antennae fluttered near her hair before diving toward an exuberant gardenia yawning in full bloom.

So much ethereal white planted together produced an eerie glow under the moonlight, like a lighthouse in a fog. Edwina twisted the ring on her finger, hoping the illumination spell might linger. It would certainly make finding the garden on her own at midnight that much easier, she thought, as the group circled the back of the manor house to continue their guided tour.

Chapter Twenty-Two

He'd waited until the last moment to swallow the moonstone. Now, as he sat in the line of coaches outside Lady Everly's grand estate, he squeezed his eyes shut and felt the stone's luminosity release into his bloodstream. The horse team shifted their weight, slightly rocking the carriage. He opened his eyes and checked his reflection in the cab window. After a brief pause, a faint shimmer peeked out of his collar. He smiled at the secretive pleasure his deceptions gave him. If not for the taint of mortal blood in his veins, he would have been master of them all by now.

The Everly house shone with the luster of a harvest moon, inside and out. *Quaint, really, the way such a powerful witch draws people to her house to have them play silly games of masquerade.* But he would not let another's immature taste spoil his evening. Tonight he vowed to rejoice in all things, and so when he walked inside and was presented with a mask, he graciously tied it over his eyes. There was a slight tingle against his skin, but he relished the infusion of magic. The material, he determined, must be laced with traces of belladonna. *Ah, yes, an illusion spell,* he thought, as flames burst to life on his sleeves. He flinched for only a moment before it was plain there was no heat, merely the shadow of fire.

The man accepted a glass of champagne from a waiter bearing a tray and watched the crowd from the entryway to the grand ballroom. Dozens of witches mingled under an enchanted dome as violins played in the background. Idle chitchat was accompanied by posturing, aura gazing, and forced laughter by women remarking on dull observations made by dull men. He lifted his eyes to the ceiling in contempt and then entered the fray.

The man skirted the bulk of the crowd, circling the perimeter like the predator he'd become. His eyes surfed the sea of masked faces, searching for vulnerabilities, alliances, opportunities. He thought he'd mastered the anonymity of the invisible as he scanned the area near the orchestra, until he heard a startled intake of breath at his back.

"Carlin, is that you? Marvelous to see you here. I had no idea you'd made the trip north." He'd been spotted by that stiff Geoffrey Hipworth, a fellow member of the Order of the Night Hunter obviously up from the city. "Effy, this is Mr. Alistair Carlin of the Broadmoor Lane Carlins."

Forced into the obligatory pleasantries of idle society, he kissed the woman's hand, which was covered in an illusion of rainbow-colored fish scales. "Delighted to make your acquaintance, madam."

"Ah, yes," she said, eyeing him through her aquamarine mask. "Darling, wasn't he the one who came up with that delightful prank of freezing the river solid in front of Parliament last December?"

"The very same," Hipworth said. "Damn fine spellwork, Carlin. Hope to see more of that sort of thing from you in the future."

"Oh, I promise," Carlin said. He exchanged the required talk about the dreadful northern clime, then made his excuses so he might be parted from the pariah and his horse-toothed wife.

Circling the crowd again, he made his way through the double doors and pretended to show interest in the outside veranda, where couples danced to a waltz beside a gazebo. Pixies shimmered in the adjacent trees, where he imagined they plotted their revenge for being exploited in such a demeaning manner, as if the annoying creatures had any other purpose in life other than providing their superiors with soft ambient lighting.

Amused by the cutting righteousness of his thoughts, he sipped his champagne and congratulated himself for his arrival at this moment. Here he stood on the Midsummer, under the stars and pixie light of Lady Everly's grandest party, his false aura radiating as bright as any witch's. He'd persisted, and now he was a man transformed from mortal to witch in nearly every sense of the word through his own ingenuity and hard work. He'd spent hours, weeks, and years researching in musty old monks' cellars, scouring forbidden libraries buried in cliffsides on the brutal northern islands, and bribing government officials for access to confiscated grimoires saved from the ripe old days of relentless persecutions. Eventually, he'd mastered the occult. He, a mortal-born, had attained the highest goal: controlling magic at his fingertips. He'd become a witch.

Almost.

Maligar, of course, had been pivotal to his transformation so far. Until he'd conjured the demon on the previous Samhain, his powers had stagnated at an apprentice level—creating fire with a little flash paper, making objects disappear by sleight of hand, and casting moderately successful revenge spells by mixing fragrant oils and bits of dried animal parts together. The recipient almost always became ill. But once he'd mastered the summoning spell, everything fell into place. He'd finally tapped into the stream of power he'd craved his entire adult life. It did trouble him that Maligar had been able to breach the sacred circle of protection earlier, but after this evening, the demon would no longer matter. He would simply dismiss the beast and never summon him again.

Good riddance.

A raven-haired woman walked past on the arm of the old wizard. His predator instinct roused once more, tensing his muscles. He was certain it was her, even without the tracking spell to single her out in the crowd. Edwina Blackwood. She was smiling and enjoying herself, forgetting her mourning. The sister, of course, had been fated to die. She was an aberration. An affront to the rules of decency. But he hadn't yet deciphered the fate of this one. Once he got what he needed from her, what further use would there be?

Then he noticed the black lace wings fluttering on her back as she bowed out of her conversation with the old witch. The sight sent a thrill reverberating through him that he couldn't control, and he accidentally snapped the stem of his champagne glass. A tiny glass shard embedded itself in his finger. Unwilling to be distracted, he tossed the broken glass into the bushes and sucked the finger dry. What difference did a little spilled blood make when the holy grail of transformative magic had just walked past?

He followed the dark-haired woman back inside, where she was greeted by Lady Everly herself! He hadn't yet approached the mistress of the house to express his gratitude for the invitation, yet Miss Blackwood chatted with her as if they were old friends.

But wait, what's this?

Miss Blackwood blushed and shook her head, as if to refuse a request of Lady Everly. The matron of the house would not be put off, holding on to the dear girl's hand and smiling. She led Edwina to the stage in front of the string quartet and asked for everyone's attention after silencing the musicians. The Blackwood woman turned a delightful shade of mottled pink, like a fiery newt freshly emerged from under a mossy stone.

"Ladies and gentlemen, we are nearing the hour when the fair folk will grant us the honor of observing their procession as they return to traverse their ancient lands." Lady Everly raised her arms in a grand welcoming gesture, as though she were appointed host of Midsummer itself. The guests from the veranda gathered nearer, crowding the double-door entry. Henry Elvanfoot joined them, a circle of stars spinning over his head. Carlin wondered briefly, as a matter of convenience, if he ought to have eliminated the wizard in the south when he had the chance. To do it now would be risky but not impossible. The old man still possessed enviable skills and could prove a problem otherwise.

Carlin had no doubt it was Elvanfoot who'd abolished the tracking spell. As a precaution he moved along the back of the crowd slowly, pretending to find a better view of Lady Everly, all the while inching closer to the old graybeard. He also kept an eye out for that brute of a man, Cameron, who insisted on escorting Miss Blackwood everywhere she went. Curious, he wasn't at the woman's side now, but perhaps he'd proved too coarse to be invited to such a grand event.

"We will soon gather on the green facing the silver woods to watch the entrance," Lady Everly continued. "But first we will have an invocation to call our friends out from their fairy mounds. And I have it on good authority," she said with a nod toward Elvanfoot, "that our newest guest, Miss Edwina Blackwood, possesses the perfect scintillating voice for attracting the fair folk on such a night as this. If you please."

Lady Everly retreated from the stage while clapping her hands in welcome. The guests looked up expectantly through their masks at the young woman. She presented herself as a woman of means in her fine gown, though he knew she came from plain country stock. Another upstart reaching beyond her station.

Edwina cleared her throat. "Goblin, pixie, fairy, sprite, we welcome all this summer night. Sing, dance, and we'll make merry, 'neath the moon our luminary. We'll eat, drink, and make amends, and next we wake we'll part as friends."

Curious how the young woman had resisted when she was in full possession of a remarkably fine voice. Once she'd accepted the challenge and begun to sing, he thought she'd proved her right to take the stage. She bowed and thanked the guests, blushing as she exited the spotlight. Naturally, hers was not a formally trained voice like those he paid a fortune to listen to at the opera house during the height of the summer season. Instead, Miss Blackwood had a mystical quality with an enchanted vibrato, but the words she chose to sing suited her rustic and quaint style. Yes, quite lovely. He couldn't wait to extract all her best-kept secrets from that sweet mouth. Whether by charm or by force, it mattered not.

Chapter Twenty-Three

For all his diminutive stature and rotten disposition, the goblin held true to who and what he was. Ian could hardly fault him for that, but he also couldn't stay a moment longer, knowing Edwina and Elvanfoot might be in serious danger from those hiding behind false faces.

"You require my life, you say?" Ian eyed the goblin with a dose of resignation. There was no way around the debt to be paid, as the goblin had set his feet in a fighting stance. "Let's strike the bargain, then."

The goblin had already got the scent of blood in his nostrils. His nose flared as he breathed in the anticipation of a long-awaited kill. "Every man tries to bargain with death." He spit on the ground. "Pitifully predictable."

Ian held his torch aloft while he searched his pocket. He'd carried the orb with him ever since it had been fished out of the river and dropped in Mary's casket. He'd never truly doubted the memories contained within were his. Elvanfoot had shown him how to expand the orb to see the shadows inside. He'd spun them around his first night back home, watching his memories play out as if they belonged to another version of himself. One he wasn't sure he recognized anymore. And anyway, he'd long decided he wanted a future with Edwina, not a past he suspected at times held regrets.

"A life," he said and held the orb out in his palm for the goblin.

"What's this? More trickery?" The creature hesitated, thinking Ian's offer a trap, until the orb expanded and the memories danced inside.

"What is a man's life, if not the moments he's experienced?" Ian said. "It's all in here. My entire life. Take it. And in exchange you show me the way out."

The goblin stared transfixed at the orb until a thought occurred to him. "Blood. There must be blood." He removed his red cap and shook the dirty thing at Ian as though it ought to be obvious enough he needed more.

Seeing there was no way around the demand, Ian poked his thumb against the end of the goblin's pike. The blade was sharp and did the job neatly. Blood pooled on the end of his thumb until a drop fell and landed on the cobblestones. The creature's jaundiced eye spied the red stuff and he soaked it up with his cap, which turned a brilliant shade of vermillion.

With his hat back on his scalp, the goblin grew spry and almost cheerful. He snatched the orb from Ian and held it up against the torch-light. "Aye, a man's life is a wonder," he said, staring at the shadows inside.

"So we have a bargain?" Ian asked.

Still agitated that he might have to adjust his standards, the goblin made a show of thinking about it, but so mesmerized was he by the contents of the orb, Ian could hardly draw his attention.

"Aye, aye, aye, but I want the whisky too," the goblin said, shoving the orb in his pocket.

And with that there was nothing left but to show Ian the way out. And just in time. His watch read nearly eleven. The trooping of the fairies would commence soon. If what he believed about Edwina was true, she was in danger from the unseelie. He had to get to her before midnight.

The goblin's exit from the bricked-in lane proved to be a grate at the bottom where water drained into the main runoff of Cocklebur Road.

Ian gave only a brief thought to his borrowed clothing before squeezing his shoulders through. He scraped by under the grate, emerging wet and reeking of soiled rainwater, while streaks of mud covered the front of his suit. *So much for returning the jacket in decent shape.* After pointing the goblin in the direction of his favorite pub one lane over, he stood on the pavement and hailed the only hansom cab to approach in either direction. The driver took one look at his drenched appearance and kept going. Recalculating, Ian walked up to the Queen's Mile, and after the third driver there ignored him, he stepped into the lane and raised his hand in the path of the next cab-for-hire. Being on the public road, he had the presence of mind to temper his spell with an incantation incognito.

"By a route obscure and lonely, haunted by ill angels only," he called out. "Where an eidolon named Night, on a black throne reigns upright." He pointed to the driver atop his black hansom. "I have reached these lands but newly, from an ultimate dim Thule—from a wild clime that lieth, sublime, out of space, out of time." He brushed the muck off his coat from the drainage grate as the driver pulled up on the reins. The few night stragglers on the street who'd heard his recitation laughed in drunken solidarity. "Halt forthwith!" he commanded from the middle of the road.

The horse reared and shook its mane. The driver cursed. The cab came to a stop, and while the driver knew something was amiss, he gestured with his thumb for Ian to get in. Under the influence of Ian's incantation, it did not matter the hour, it did not matter the miles, it did not matter the Midsummer moon above was as ripe as a woman in her ninth month. The driver, compelled by the spell, prodded the horse with the reins to ride through the city and into the hinterland. Ian rubbed his palms together inside the cabriolet and blew the heat toward the lanterns to make them shine brighter on the road. The horse sped up, spurred on by the mortal atop his rolling throne.

"The horse can see as well as you or me in the dark, you know." Hob popped his head through the window. "Lanterns won't help."

Ian slid over on the seat. "Where've you been?"

"I've been looking for you for hours." Hob climbed in, then wrinkled his nose on the seat beside Ian. "The horse can smell too," he added after a quick sniff.

"Aye, I'm covered in it." Ian did an inventory of the damage done to his suit. "You canna help me out, can you?"

Hob removed a gold whisk from his jacket and whispered "spot out, spot out, spot out" as he worked his hearth magic on the ruined suit.

"How did you get in this state?" he asked when he was done.

"Finlay," Ian answered. "He's a two-faced liar. He tried to have me killed by locking me up with a redcap." He ground his teeth together, thinking of the revenge he'd exact when he caught up to the bowlegged sprite again. "He thinks I'm working with the unseelie to kidnap the prophetess tonight."

Hob's puggish nose scrunched up as if something still didn't smell right. "But didn't he hire *you* to find out who was sneaking through to cause the mischief?"

"Aye, he did, and then he accused me of lying when I told him what I'd found."

"The unseelie are always trying to cause trouble," Hob said. "Turmoil is a tasty hors d'oeuvre for them."

"We have to get to Lady Everly's before the trooping of the fairy court. Curse this slow horse!"

"The party has already begun," Hob said. "Milady is dressed in silk and lace. She's begun to sing. Such a lilting voice."

"You were there?" Ian checked his jacket, giving it a sniff. The elf was an absolute magician at repairing such things, but he seemed to have left behind a hint of a foul odor. "Did you notice anything out of the ordinary?"

"Milady was wearing a ring with two stones."

"Damn it, Hob, that's not what I mean. Was there anyone there who shouldn't have been?"

"Everyone is veiled in spells and illusions." The elf shrugged. "Who can say what is out of the ordinary in such conditions?"

Ian shook his head in frustration and pounded his fist against the roof of the cab for the driver to go faster.

The Everly manor house was located outside the city at the base of one of the seven hills, the one that sat two miles east of his folks' place. At last the ghostly green glow of spellfire burning in braziers at the estate's entrance came into focus. Ian patiently waited for the cab to pull through the half-moon driveway, then jumped out before the wheels had even had a chance to come to a stop. He flicked a queen's head coin up to the driver, who grabbed it in his beefy fist. Still under Ian's spell, he turned the cab toward the road and never looked back, even as the first of the heather pixies began to dance in the grass with their seedpod lanterns held over their heads.

Ian ran up the steps and tried to enter the party but was stopped by some sort of energy force that refused to let him pass through. "I'm invited," he said to an attendant dressed as a sunflower.

"All guests have to wear one to enter," the young woman said, waving a gold mask.

"*A dhia!*" Ian trudged back and tied the eye covering on. When he was done, Hob snickered beside him. "What're you on about?" he asked.

"Lady Everly has such fine illusions!"

Ian spotted his reflection in the mirror hung outside the ballroom and saw that he'd grown a lion's mane. "Never mind that," he said, unamused by his appearance. "Help me find Edwina."

Inside the main hall, couples danced to quartet music at the far end, while a man in a silver cape seemed to be reciting a poem near the doors leading to the outdoor pavilion. There were perhaps one hundred people gathered, each sporting a different illusion—horse tails, dragon scales, flames on sleeves, rainbow headdresses, and there in the far corner beyond the heads of two dozen people, with wings on her back, stood Edwina. Though she, too, wore a mask, her eyes watched the room as she pretended to carry on a conversation with a woman covered in fish scales. She nodded and smiled, but she was checking the face of everyone who walked or danced within three feet of where she stood. Who was she looking for?

"Maybe she's looking for you," Hob said, attuned to Ian's emotions. "You're very late." The hearth elf climbed atop a chair beside an oversize potted palm tree. "She's finished her song, and now everyone is going outside to await the queen."

"No, it's something else," Ian said. He retreated beside Hob and the potted palm. "She's wary. See how she looks over her shoulder the moment she senses someone near. And then studies them when they walk away as though she's anticipating finding a sign in a stranger's eye, even while she pretends to listen to what the woman beside her is saying."

Hob furrowed his shaggy brow. "She's very tense, now that you mention it."

A woman with swan feathers for hair walked past and pointed out Hob to her male companion, whose dinner jacket was covered in ivy. "Oh, isn't he charming. What a brilliant disguise. I want that mask next year!" The pair laughed, slightly tipsy on champagne.

"Everyone's heading outside," Ian said once the couple stumbled by with their hands pressed to their noses after catching a whiff of his suit. "Hold on. Where's Elvanfoot? He isn't with Edwina." As soon as he took his eyes off her to search for the wizard, he lost her in the shuffling crowd again. He raised his head, but half the crowd had already dispersed through the double doors to the veranda. "We need to get out there."

"The Midsummer moon is rising. I'm obliged to join my kind."

179

Ian halted. "Right," he said, hit by an attack of guilt for forgetting the solemnity of the special night for his friend and guardian. "Off you go. I'll find Edwina and join you later."

"Milady will be drawn to the moonlight like a moth," Hob said and dove into the urn holding the potted palm.

"Daft numbskull." Ian gave his head a quick thought-clearing shake after the elf had gone. Outside, he scanned the sward from the house to the side of the veranda but didn't see Edwina or Elvanfoot among the guests. The grassy area where everyone had gathered faced a silvery copse of birch. The crowd stood in anticipation like an uncorked bottle of champagne, full of energy and excitement. The eager faces were all turned toward the arrival point of the queen's procession.

All but one, that was. A man dressed in a dinner jacket with flames dancing on his sleeves walked up from behind the gazebo, straightening his hair with his fingers before checking his pocket watch for the time. When the man joined the others at the back of the crowd, his attention turned not to the silvery woods like everyone else's but toward the gardens at the rear of the house.

Ian had never seen the gentleman before, yet his detective instinct flared. Why would a man attend the Midsummer party and then show no interest in the main event? The behavior struck Ian as out of character for a guest. The man's aura was odd as well. The energy seemed to seep out the back of his collar in an unnatural way, as if it floated like mist instead of radiating strongly from his being. When the man retreated from the group five minutes before midnight, just as the first of the fairy creatures crept out of the woods, Ian listened to his instincts and followed.

The gentleman walked toward the rear of the house, where the evergreen bones of a formal garden were arranged in a maze. It was possible the man meant only to relieve himself out of view of the other guests. A normal-enough reason to sneak off in the dark, but then he kept going, walking stealthily away from the festivities. Ahead, a misty light rose in the night air like a puff of warm breath exhaled from the earth. Ian didn't know if it was a Midsummer illusion, a witch's spell, or a will-o'-the-wisp hovering on the green. It was only after the man turned a corner and disappeared around the back of the house that he ventured a little closer and saw the glow was coming from a garden filled with night-blooming flowers whose petals reflected the light from the moon.

And there, standing in the center, was Edwina.

She could have passed for one of the fair folk in her flowing gown and the illusion of wings beating softly on her back. But what was she doing out there alone and away from everyone else? He worried some lusty sprite would pick her out of the garden and carry her away to the Otherworld. Midsummer was a lark, aye, and a great time to commune with the All Knowing, but it was no time for a woman to be caught under the stars alone.

Ian had just taken a step forward to go persuade her to return to the group with him when the man he'd followed returned and walked straight toward Edwina while her head was turned the other way. Something was wrong. Ian had to get to her. Protect her. He broke free of the shadows, ready to run, an incantation forming in his mouth. And then all he could see was white-hot sparks inside the darkness as a sharp pain in his head exploded and he hit the ground with a thud.

Chapter Twenty-Four

The scents of jasmine flower and gardenia left a heavy perfume in the air. Even without the soft glow of the moon garden, Edwina could have found the meeting place by sense of smell alone. She lifted the chin of a moonflower. A fat moth sucked the nectar from the flower like a little vampire, she thought, though she supposed the exchange was entirely consensual.

Edwina twisted the ruby ring on her finger. She was nervous. What if he demanded money? Or expected her to find gold for him? Or perhaps this "admirer" expected his own consensual exchange? She nearly backed away, chiding herself for being a fool for ever thinking she could handle this confrontation on her own. Then the shape and shadow of a man approached, and she stiffened her resolve. She could always peck his eyes out if his bargaining price was too high.

"Miss Blackwood, how good of you to meet me." A masked man emerged from the dark, lit by the overspill of moonlight from Lady Everly's celestial incantation. His speech, his manner, his appearance—he was a gentleman, in the strictest meaning of the word. A posh from the inside out, with his slicked-back hair, polished shoes, and exceedingly expensive suit that rippled with false flame. He took a step toward the marble font, where the illumination gave his pale skin a bloodless appearance. His forced half smile did nothing to warm his cold demeanor.

"Who are you?" she asked.

He circled the font so that he stood opposite her. A gold lapel pin with a familiar circle and crescent horn insignia—not so different from the symbol for Mercury her sister had made—showed briefly when it caught the light. The last time Edwina had seen the insignia, everything she owned turned to ash.

"A man in search of knowledge," he answered with an air of nonchalance.

"You tracked my movements through the city and burned down my shop."

"Oh, that was just so we might become better acquainted sooner rather than later." He smiled, then dipped a finger in the marble basin, where an image of a woman in a ragged gray dress emerged. She was curled up on her side atop a straw mat in what appeared to be some sort of prison with iron bars. An aura of enchantment glowed from the space between the metal. "I'm capable of much worse, believe me."

Edwina's breath caught in her chest at the veiled threat. "Is that her?" She leaned forward, not quite believing. Then she saw the face, the hair, and the same dress her mother wore the day she'd never returned home. She could barely hold back a wall of tears. "What have you done to her? She looks ill." Edwina reached out as if she could touch her mother, but the image rippled and faded from view. "If you've hurt her, I swear I'll curse you and your descendants for eternity."

"She's been well taken care of," the man assured her, though it was obvious her mother wasn't well at all. The hem of her dress was in tatters, and her hair had frazzled and turned gray. Dark circles rimmed her tear-swollen eyes.

"You want something in exchange for her safety, so what is it?"

"Straight to business." The man gave a small laugh. "How charming. Yes, let's talk about that. Might we continue our conversation while we walk?" He gestured to the lightly trod path that cut away from the garden.

However limited the moonlight spell on the flowers gleamed, it was a beacon compared to the sprawling dark woods looming behind the manor house. Besides, there was something unusual about the man's aura that set her intuition on edge. While it radiated in the expected manner, the color had a counterfeit quality. Everything about him gave her pause, as well it should, but she still maintained she could evade him easily enough should their present civility deteriorate.

Edwina agreed and trailed behind the man as he led her toward a trio of towering oak trees fifty yards away. The trunks formed a perfect equilateral triangle on the ground. Embedded in the center sat a boulder large enough to serve as a seat. Or altar. He led her to the stone, then gawped at its side in awe as though it were a pilgrimage site. She followed the direction of his gaze, wondering what had brought the dreadful smile back to his face. There on the stone's side facing the northern tip of the triangle was a faint carved spiral dotted with lichen, ancient looking and consecrated with the patina of old magic.

"I have it on good authority Lady Everly built her house on this site because of the presence of this stone and the trio of surrounding oaks. It's the last remaining portion of a stone circle that once stood here." He took his eye off the boulder and looked directly at Edwina once again. She saw then what it was about his aura that disturbed her. None of the light shone through his eyes. They were flat, like a mortal's. Ian and Elvanfoot had been right about who and what he was. A drab so unaware of his own shortcomings as a witch he had the audacity to be arrogant.

"The trees are only a hundred years old at best," she said, keeping the conversation going. "Surely the stone carving is much older than that."

"Of course it is," he snapped, showing an intolerance for one stating the obvious. "The carving is well over a thousand years old." He bent to trace the spiral with his fingers. "This was made by some of the first custodians of magic to express their reverence for what had been bestowed upon them. The trees are the sacred guardians of the last remaining stone."

His assertion brought to mind Ian's story of the acolytes who had served the fair folk in their ceremonies and in return were given the gift of magic. The first witches. But what did a drab know of such things when she herself had never been acquainted with the history?

"The people were mystics, and this space was once a place of worship," he said before she could utter any inferior hypothesis on the setting. "Mortals who had obtained the power of incantation. Enchantment. And transformation." The man formed a white-knuckled fist as though attempting to grip the things he spoke of.

"And why have you brought me here?" Edwina asked. "I appreciate an origin story as much as the next witch, but I thought our business was about an exchange. What do you want?"

"Oh, you are direct, aren't you." Any hint of posh manners evaporated from the man. "Very well, we'll do it your way, Miss Blackwood."

He circled the stone, keeping his eye on Edwina, while the strain of artificial geniality fell from his face. Charm was this one's false face, and she'd had enough. Believing he was the drab Ian and Elvanfoot had made him out to be, she readied an incantation. Nothing too harmful—just something to knock him out until she could figure out what to do with him. He stepped to his left, and she countered his circular motion, maintaining the distance between them. All she needed was the location of her mother, and then she would incapacitate him.

"You need not fear me." The man took off his masquerade mask. "Your life is precious to me. Others, however, are quite expendable. Including the owner of that ring you're wearing, so I suggest you cooperate and hold still." The flames on his suit extinguished, revealing him to be even less remarkable than she'd first assumed.

"I ask you again, what is it you want for her safety?"

The odd aura that had seeped out of him faded, and he stood before her with no more light radiating about him than the stone between them. "Do you know how exceptional your talents are?" He did not expect her to answer, only to listen. "I first heard about you and your peculiar sister five years ago. I was in the border marshes researching the effects of alcohol on foxglove in the course of creating an anticoagulation potion. You see, the pursuit of knowledge of the occult has become my sole devotion in life, particularly where it concerns the art of transformation."

Edwina backed up a step, ready to give him an up-close lesson in the art of shape-shifting if he didn't stop advancing. "What did you hear about my sister and me?"

He genuinely smiled then. "Oh, what a day that was. The men in the ghastly little pub I'd ducked into to get out of the rain were telling tales of a pair of young women who were half-human, half-bird. As I eavesdropped on their dull-witted take of this phenomenal event, I began to believe there might be a hint of truth in the account. Without realizing it, I'd stumbled into a pub that catered to witches. Though, of course, I know now it was providence that led me there."

"You didn't know it was a witches' pub because you're nothing more than a drab," Edwina said, mustering enough derision in her voice to make a glancing blow without a spell.

"No, not a drab, Miss Blackwood. A mortal." He slid a finger in his shirt collar to show her the lack of even a faint aura buried beneath his dinner jacket.

"A mortal? But how? You had an aura earlier. I saw it."

"A moonstone enchanted by a demon to dissolve after swallowing. The shimmering quality of the gemstone seeps through the throat to create the false aura."

No demon would consort with a mortal. The man was as mad as she'd first believed him to be. Fed up, she saw little reason to continue standing in the oak triangle in the middle of the night listening to a fool spew on about his deficiencies. All she needed to do was sing a spell to make him lead her to her mother. She formed the opening notes of her incantation to make him speak and cleared her throat. "A truth on the tongue is—"

"I wouldn't do that if I were you." He muttered a foreign phrase under his breath, and her voice locked up on her mid-spell. "I'm aware of what that voice of yours is capable of," he said as he watched emotionless while she coughed and spewed up an oak leaf that had lodged in her throat. "I am mortal-born, I don't deny it, but one who has unlocked that which was forbidden to me through sheer determination, skill, and, I'll allow, a dash of luck. Do not doubt I now possess every molecule of magic within me as a witch-born like yourself."

"Impossible," she said with a voice that was hoarse and foreign to her.

"For most men, I would agree." He paused and then raised his voice to recite a brief yet archaic incantation. "*Da mihi ignem.*" A flame appeared on his fingertips.

Deprived of her power to sing, Edwina tried bargaining again. "If it's gold, money, or jewels you want, I can find those things for you. That isn't something you can do for yourself. Please, just release my mother and let us be."

"Don't be vulgar," he said. A breeze extinguished the flame on his fingers. He sat on the stone and crossed his legs so the crease of his trousers came to a perfect point over his spats. "Allow me to explain myself more thoroughly, Miss Blackwood. While I was not born with magic, I was born with money. I can buy anything or anyone I like. That is not what motivates me. Dominion, however, is an elixir I would kill for. And that is where you become very useful to me. The transformation code swimming in your blood is what has value. I believe that component is the key to my own transformation. Don't you see? With the Midsummer moon nearing its apogee, we are both on the verge of becoming all we were meant to be in this world."

Edwina couldn't outrun him, but she could fly. Before he realized what was happening, she would claw his eyes out and warn the others of who and what he was. "I'm afraid this is where we'll have to agree to disagree," she said and shifted into her raven form, ready to take to the air. She felt the twitch in her bones, the feather-light change in her body, then flapped her wings, ready to soar above the trees.

But something was wrong. The air felt as heavy as water. Edwina flapped and fought but could not rise. Something held her by the leg. A chain. A gold chain attached to a gold ring with two rubies wrapped around her ankle! She tried to change back, but her magic failed her. It had to be an enchantment. A hex. A trap.

The man grabbed the chain in his fist and held her there as though she were a kite, refusing to let her rise into the sky.

"I warned you to cooperate," he said and reeled the chain in, wrapping it around his forearm as she frantically flapped her wings. "Now we'll do things my way."

Edwina cursed her foolishness as the man tucked her under his arm and stole away into the forest, far from the fair ones and their Midsummer revelries.

Chapter Twenty-Five

Ian blinked until his eyes focused, and then he pushed himself up. His temple throbbed and his mouth tasted of turf. Finlay crouched in front of him, his sharp-edged smile gleaming like a steel dagger.

"Finlay, you bastard, what did you do to me?" Ian stretched his arm out to shake off the numbness in his elbow. He was sitting in damp grass beside the Everly house, while in the distance halos of light frolicked on the green between the stands of silver birch. The fair folk had begun their revelries.

"That thump on the head isn't even half of what you deserve." The sprite lost his grin. "Now you'll learn what we really do to traitors," he said and flicked open a knife with a scrolled blade.

"Me? I'm trying to help you, and you locked me in a hole under the city with a redcap."

"I locked you up to keep you from interfering."

"For all I know, *you're* the traitor," Ian said. "Maybe it's no coincidence the fellow I saw by the gateway could pass for your double. Maybe it's you who's turned on his own kind."

Finlay growled deep in his throat. "I'm the one protecting them. Now tell me what the unseelie are planning to do with her."

"Who?"

"The Blackwood woman."

"Edwina!" Ian sat forward with sudden urgency. He craned his neck to see the moon garden. "Where is she? That man was following her. Get out of my way!"

Finlay laid his blade against Ian's neck when he tried to stand. A shiver of déjà vu froze him to the spot as the memory of choking on his own blood at the hands of a serial killer washed over him. It wasn't his memory, but he owned the experience as sure as the man who'd died thanks to Mary Blackwood. He swallowed gently against the knife. "He's taken her. I have to find her."

"Why are you so willing to let them kidnap the woman and embarrass the queen on her affirmation day?"

"Are you off yer head, man? I'm trying to stop that from happening."

Finlay pressed the blade tighter against Ian's throat as a creature dressed in a gauzy gray robe approached him from behind. She glowed like a moonbeam with white hair that floated in the air above her head.

"It isn't him," the creature said.

"It is!" Finlay twisted around to look the gray fairy in the eye. "He's been working with the unseelie from the beginning."

"I haven't," Ian cried.

"Do not mock me!"

"The witch-born is telling the truth." The creature gazed wide-eyed at the faint glow of moonshine rising off the garden. "It was another. A mortal man. I saw them talking while I inspected the petals of a gardenia."

"That's not possible." Finlay fell back on his haunches, lowering the knife. "There are no mortals on the grounds except that arrogant Hipworth's wife. We checked."

Ian rubbed his neck and exhaled with relief, though he didn't dare move. Not yet.

Finlay squinted at him. "If you're not helping the unseelie, then who did you let through the portal?"

"I told you, I never let anyone through. The gateway was nae disturbed when I checked." Ian looked the sprite over, wondering what was really going on.

"But you saw someone."

"I thought he was you," Ian said with a chin nudge toward the sprite's attire. "Same dark hair, same long black frock coat. Only he dinna fidget like you do. He was perfectly calm when he spoke to Edwina."

"I dinna fidget." Finlay folded his knife and tucked it away.

Ian got to his feet. "I have to find Edwina."

The fairy creature with the moon eyes fluttered her wings. "They left the garden for the oaks," she said. "The mortal has the most terrible thoughts."

Ian tore off his mask. "Show me where you saw them."

"Wait," Finlay said, looking away sheepishly. "There's something you should know first. The Blackwood woman . . . She's ours."

A stone dropped in Ian's stomach. "Aye, I'm beginning to figure that out."

"The Gathering has started, ye ken?" The sprite looked over his shoulder to where the pixie lights floated over the grass. Party guests oohed and aahed at the edge of the green in soft whispers of delight. The first of the trooping fairies had arrived. A female fairy in a green cloak embroidered with silver flowers sat atop a dapple-gray horse. The tiny bells affixed to her pointed shoes rang out when her horse leaped into the air to prance with the elves on the ground. Finlay reluctantly tore his eyes away from the spectacle. "She doesn't know yet. They never do, but she's been expected. Everyone has taken great care to make sure she arrived here tonight."

"She's truly got the mark of the fey on her?" Ian asked, even though he'd suspected from the moment he'd first witnessed Edwina transform that she was touched by the fair folk. But until Finlay had said it out loud, he hadn't truly acknowledged that a gift like hers would require a tithe. If the fair folk claimed her, the privilege had to come with a price.

"Half the debt has already been paid, but there is yet a balance due." Finlay nudged his head toward the garden. "Come, let's find her and this reckless mortal who thinks he can take what is not his."

The fairy creature led them back to the place she'd last seen Edwina with the man. From there, she pointed toward the towering trees whose crowns were yet silhouetted against the sky by the moonlit night. The forest was vast and silent save for the birds and squirrels they disturbed with their passing. Finlay's fey instincts led them to the site of an ancient rock embedded in a triangle of oaks. There were impressions in the soil near the boulder suggesting someone had recently walked around it, but no sign of Edwina and the strange mortal man who'd lured her away. Ian called on all his senses to find their trail, but he heard no voices, detected no trace of Edwina's hair pomade in the air. Nor did he see the faint trace of her footsteps when he conjured a thin fog on the ground. He'd arrived too late.

"A mortal can't have got far," Finlay said.

And yet Ian already feared he'd well and truly lost her.

Chapter Twenty-Six

Carlin had seen her change once before, high on the tower bridge overlooking the river at midnight, but the transformation still took his breath away. To shape-shift without use of an incantation relied on an altogether different source of magic. When he'd first heard the rumors about the strange sisters, he thought it had to have been an exaggeration or a hoax.

The young man, Eddie or Neddie or Freddie, had just downed his third pint when he'd been induced to tell the story again for the crowd at the witches' pub. Carlin, naturally, had remained alone at his table with his scarf tied high around his neck, afraid to be found out as a mortal. So while the others gathered around the drunk young lad with the feathery black hair and sharp blue eyes, he'd pretended to concentrate on his cold soup while he kept one ear attuned to the details. Was the lad making the story up? Had he really been kissed by one of the sisters; had his memory been taken, then replaced; and could he have seen the sister change into a bird? It seemed impossible, but he'd heard the tale twice, and the elements remained the same each time.

The part Carlin had bungled, of course, was believing the shawls were the source of the sisters' magic. That's what Eddie-Neddie-Freddie, Edwina's one-time fiancé, had believed, but Freddie Dankworth had been an idiot. Carlin had found that out the painfully long and hard way. A mistake he was still dealing with in his cellar.

At first it seemed plausible. A textile witch with ample skill could infuse woven fibers with a spell strong enough to create the transformation. His research had indicated there was a limit to how much magic could be retained in the material, though. Most often after a spell had been spent, the fabric lost its potency and the incantation had to be repeated. Yet the Blackwood sisters were rumored to have the ability to change at will under their shawls. The mother seemed the likeliest person to know the truth, so he'd taken her. He plucked her off the street in broad daylight after inducing her into his cab by asking for a woman's opinion about a bonnet he was thinking of buying for a nonexistent fiancée. He'd set two hats out on the seat, and she'd gullibly leaned in to see them, happy to be of assistance. One airborne sleeping potion later and she was held behind a spell wall of his making with everything she needed to produce a shawl like those she'd woven for her daughters. But of course, aside from serving as bait to capture her daughter, she'd turned out to be as useless as a bucket with a hole in it.

He put the horrible woman out of his thoughts and entered the cottage with the enchanted key, making sure to keep a firm grip on the golden chain lest the raven try yet again to struggle free while his other hand was engaged.

Carlin drew the curtains in the sitting room and then put the raven in the brass cage he'd had the demon conjure especially for this moment. It was large enough that she could transform should the need arise later—after all, he wasn't sure which form would be optimal for drawing her blood—though he'd already decided it was best to have her remain a raven for now. He sighed. Perhaps he should have asked that the cage be made smaller. When he did allow her to change back, it would have been a nice touch to have it squeeze her just a bit. Pain was a great motivator for encouraging others to give you what you wanted.

Below the stairs, the woman banged her dinner plate against the cellar wall again. He stomped his foot against the floorboards, but it only made the bird jump, so he refrained from cursing at the woman.

Calm was needed now, he reminded himself, if only to garner an inkling of trust from his newest captive.

"There, now, Miss Blackwood, there's no need to be nervous." The reassuring words felt foreign in his mouth, and he had to remember how to adjust his face so it conveyed a pleasant demeanor when he spoke. "I've taken good care of her, just as I said."

"You'll pay for this." She'd spoken as a raven would so that her voice hadn't quite enunciated the words perfectly. Still, it did make him wonder if he'd overlooked something. Could she work out an incantation in this form? None of the ancient texts he'd studied had indicated it was possible among the fair folk shifters, yet hearing the witch speak gave him pause.

The raven cawed and scratched at him from behind the bars with its foot. He shut the door to the cage a little harder than needed, fastened the golden chain around the latch, then secured it with a lock and spell. "Be quiet now while I go and prepare," he said. "You'll be tempted to change form while I'm away, but you'll only find disappointment and wear yourself out. As long as the chain is attached, you will remain under my control. Do you understand?" He paused and watched her for a moment, making sure she took his message to heart. The raven screeched, clucked, and called him a misanthrope, but she remained a bird. When he was satisfied she understood the parameters of her confinement, he removed himself from the room.

Carlin entered the back bedroom and changed into his ceremonial robe and hat, satisfied with his evening's efforts so far. She was a pretty-enough thing, he thought, remembering how she appeared in her winged gown under the moonlight. He slipped the silk robe over his head, letting it slide over his bare skin. He'd not yet taken a wife. The pursuit of the occult had long been his only mistress, but that could change. His body's healthy response to thoughts of her in that gown told him there was ample reason to consider her for a life partner. When the matter was done, of course, and if she were still alive. Naturally, the chain would have to remain in place even in marriage.

He returned to the sitting room and set out his ritual items. He needed to call Maligar one last time, and then he'd be done with the jumped-up demon. The Blackwood woman made a vulgar noise in that guttural raven speech of hers, and he shushed her harshly. "I must concentrate and draw my energy," he said. Once she quieted, he arranged his candle and gemstones on the floor, then set the last of the licorice allsorts on the northern point of his pentagram. The raven stayed silent and watchful, backed up against the rear of her cage.

"And now we shall begin the final stage of my transformation," he said, raising his ceremonial knife above his head as an offering to the All Powerful. "Doorway deep I knock on thee, call thy spirit willingly. Summoned here to do my will, be it good or be it ill. From your hellish depths afar, rise before me, Maligar."

He used the normal chant to summon his demon, yet he had to repeat it three times in front of the raven woman before Maligar showed himself. Smarmy as always, the demon materialized from behind the window curtains and snatched up the bag of sweets. The raven cackled from her cage, as unimpressed with the demon as he was. *Yes, she might just make the perfect wife with a little encouragement,* he thought.

Chapter Twenty-Seven

Ian and Finlay stood in what appeared to be a sacred space surrounded by oaks. Faint lights flickered in the higher branches, followed by the chitter of small voices. At first Ian thought they were squirrels making all the noise, but then he saw the puggish faces, wispy wings, and pointed ears of those on the limb nearest. A band of pixies hovered above their heads, taking advantage of their short time on earth to laugh and dance and, as Ian discovered, fornicate, as evidenced by a particularly nimble pair coupled in impressive midair acrobatics.

"I don't understand what would induce her to go into the woods with a mortal man," Ian said, turning from the display.

Finlay pointed up as if the answer were obvious. "A tryst on such a night as this is not uncommon," the sprite said, casting his eyes upward to the copulating pixies, but when he read the growing fury in Ian's face, he took the words back. "Or maybe he forced her, in which case we should probably expedite our search."

Ian was about to suggest they split up to cover more ground when a silver sylph glided over the meadow grass toward them beyond the trees. Behind her walked Lady Everly, her aura glowing hot beneath the illusion of her glamorous tresses.

"Where is she?" Lady Everly directed her fury at Finlay. "What are you playing at? She was due promptly at midnight."

"They are already preparing for the final ride to the spiral of stones to affirm the queen," said the Lady of the Woods.

Finlay held his palms out to the women. "We're searching now."

"Searching?" Lady Everly was a woman obviously accustomed to having her every whim fulfilled on the spot. "Produce her this instant. We've coordinated together on this event for months. The time is upon us!"

Ian cleared his throat. "If it's Edwina Blackwood you're talking about, she seems to have arranged to meet someone in the garden, and now we don't know if she left of her own free will or was taken by force."

"And who, in the name of the All Knowing, are *you*? And what are you doing at these festivities?"

"He's the one I hired to help with the glitch in the veil," Finlay said, as if the three of them had already had conversations about him. "The one the prophetess saw."

Lady Everly's aura cooled. "The detective," she said, nodding. "My apologies. So where is our girl? Can you find her?"

Ian wanted to tell her to go stuff herself. Neither she nor the sylph nor the Queen of Elfhame could have Edwina. If she belonged to anyone, it was him, because he loved her. But he wasn't naive enough to believe that what he desired made any difference to those standing before him, not when Edwina's destiny was somehow entangled with the fair folk.

"No," he said. "I dinna know which way she's gone."

"This won't do," Lady Everly said. "This won't do at all. Do you have any idea how this catastrophe will damage my reputation? The fair folk will never trust me again. Find her. Both of you. Now!"

The Lady of the Woods pivoted to stand toe to toe with Finlay, whom she towered over by a few inches. "Find her. Do not return if you value your freedom. One way or another, there will be a tithe paid on this Midsummer."

"We'll find her," Ian said. "And tell Elvanfoot where we've gone. Might be something he can do to help."

"I haven't seen him since we left to watch the parade on the green. I'd assumed he'd left early to avoid"—Lady Everly glanced at the Lady of the Woods beside her—"bumping into Clarissa."

"I thought he'd walked outside the ballroom with the rest of you," Ian said. "But now that you mention it, I never did spot him among the partygoers."

Lady Everly exchanged a concerned look with the Lady of the Woods. "I'll have the staff search the grounds," she said. "Meanwhile, bring me that young woman!"

"We'll ask every creature we pass," Finlay assured her. "Someone must have seen her." He nudged Ian by his arm, and the pair stalked into the forest.

A few paces on Finlay held up his hand, tipping his ear toward a sound. Ian stopped. His night vision was as good as any and his hearing still keen, but he neither saw nor heard anything. Yet his intuition bristled. "What is it?"

"Shhh." Finlay held a finger over his mouth. Ahead, in the branches of an ash tree, sat a young boy. Or was it a woman? They wore about them a cloth made of a band of wispy, cloudlike light that hid their shape. "Merry Midsummer," Finlay called.

"And to you," said the dryad, who was using the point of a knife to carve holes into a hollow bird bone.

The creature moved so that their back relaxed against the tree, and one leg dangled over the side of the branch. Ian couldn't remember if he should make eye contact or not, so he made only fleeting glances at the creature, enough to say he hadn't looked away but not enough to offend if he ought to have kept his gaze on the ground. On the third such avoidance, their eyes met and held. Immediately a sense of calm permeated Ian's aura. The dryad smiled before holding the bird bone to its mouth and blowing. An eerie whistling flute sound floated over them, calming their anxious nerves.

"We're looking for a witch woman and a mortal man who may have come this way," Finlay said when the dryad finished the long, fluttering note. "Did you happen to observe them passing through?"

"I've not seen a woman walking in the woods who ought not to be here," the dryad said. "But a man as you describe tromped through the ferns that way several moments ago." The creature aimed a finger east toward the forest below Hare Hill. "He had a bird tucked under his arm with a beautiful gold chain attached. I was quite envious."

"Edwina." On a hunch, Ian checked the ferns on the path where the dryad had pointed. He half expected to find them blackened and shriveled like the carrots in his parents' garden, but all he saw was a broken frond as green as the day it first unfurled in the spring.

Finlay bid the dryad farewell, and he and Ian broke through the bracken at a run. It was two miles to Hare Hill as the crow flies. But it could be two miles as the man ran, too, if he knew the shortcuts, which Ian had learned from the time he was a boy whooping wild on the open moors.

"This way," Ian said as they left the trees behind. "There's only a handful of places he could be headed in the middle of the night. And one of them is my folks' place."

Finlay could have easily run ahead on his springy legs for a short way, but between the cigarettes and the whisky, the sprite had to pace himself beside Ian for the long distance. They leaped over hidden rivulets and clumps of heather and gorse full of golden pixies who tried to poke them with their thistle wands. It was not twenty minutes later when, out of breath and heaving from the exertion, Ian pointed to his folks' cottage. All the lights were out except the one fire left burning in the pit. He knew his mother would be on the hill dancing under the moonlight on this auspicious Midsummer night. His father, too, would be laying out a blessing on the ground of bannocks, a bowl of fresh cream, and a wee glass of whisky for the fair folk wishing to refresh themselves during their merrymaking.

"Your folks are good people," Finlay said. "And a large part of why I was asked to hire you for this jaunt we're on."

"Aye, and I can't wait to have a word with your employer when we're done." Ian checked the house quickly to make sure no one was inside. When he found nothing disturbed, he took a breath and said, "This way."

Running again, he and Finlay cut back through the trees, hurdling over the knee-high ferns that sprang up between. A quarter of a mile away, they came to a clearing where a small white cottage with a thatched roof sat alone in a grassy clearing. A thin trail of smoke rose from the chimney.

"What is this place?" Finlay asked, catching his breath.

Ian held the sprite back behind the cover of trees. "An old haunted house that had been sitting empty for the last twenty or more years."

"And now?"

"My father told me someone bought it recently," Ian said. "Some fellow who likes to keep to himself."

"Witch or mortal?"

"I've only ever known witches to frequent the place. Summer holidays and such, but now I dinna know. You see the mortals in the south, they're fascinated with the occult, having their séances and whatnot. They would nae be put off by a place with an unsettling reputation."

A light moved in front of the curtain. Someone carrying a candle or an oil lamp. The pair ducked behind the tree trunks.

Ian removed his watch and fiddled with the settings. He could account for himself and Finlay, but there were two other beings in the vicinity too. Whoever they were, he'd stake his reputation they were witch-born. So either both cottage occupants were witches and they'd come to the wrong place, or the owner was the mortal they sought and he had Edwina in there with someone else. "If Hob were with us, I'd send him inside to see who's there, but he's off with the fairies now."

"Aye, he's a braw wee smout," Finlay said. "But he's nae the only one with skills to see what's going on inside."

They sidled closer to the house until the sprite held his hand up for them to stop. He pointed to what he described as a slight shimmer emanating from the front door of the house and the edge of the roof. Evidence of static magic. Ian couldn't make out anything until, on a hunch, he held his scrying stone up to get a different perspective. All around the cottage there were lines of spell energy interlocking like a protective net that he could see only through his astral lens. Fairy magic.

"What's a man need all of that protection for?" Ian asked, lowering the stone.

Finlay nudged his chin toward the side of the house. "Nothing good."

They crept around the wooded perimeter of the yard, watching for signs of a gap in the spells, when they found what appeared to be a rip in the energy near a window just big enough for a man to slip through. Curious to know how much of a breach it was, they stole to within fifteen feet of the house when a shiver overtook Ian. His core turned ice cold as some sort of storm cloud passed over him. He fell back on his haunches, then turned to check with Finlay to see if he felt it, too, but the sprite had gone pale and quiet as he ducked behind a fern, eyes on the house. There, creeping up to the window of the cottage to slip through the seam in the magical barrier, was the creature in the long frock coat Ian had seen talking to Edwina.

"It's him," Ian whispered. "The one I thought was you."

Finlay held a finger to his lips and shook his head. They watched the creature dissipate and slip through the rip in the protective magic, only to reanimate on the other side of the window. Inside, he pushed back the curtain and stepped into a room lit with soft candlelight.

"Who is he?"

"Trouble," Finlay replied.

Chapter Twenty-Eight

The metal cage reeked of linseed oil and male perspiration. In her altered form, Edwina's senses also picked up the slightly charred tinge of spent magic near the cage door. She pecked at the lock, but the man's spell held firm, as did the chain and cuff enclosed around her leg. She tried again without luck to change form and slip the chain while her mercurial body was in flux, but neither the metal nor the spell relented.

A woman cried out somewhere below the house. Her mother! It must be. Edwina tilted her head to listen. The voice was angry, defiant, and full of the will to survive whatever this man had inflicted on her. But her mother was weary, too, as she wailed again for someone to hear her. The man stomped his foot on the floor, making Edwina jump. She would scratch his eyes out for that, but first she had to get free.

Exhausted from her attempts to transform, Edwina sank to the bottom of the cage, tucking in her wings. Her captor had blessedly left the room, leaving her alone to contemplate her predicament. Curious, she nudged the gold chain with her beak. There was nothing extraordinary about the way the metal rattled when moved. If there was an enchantment embedded within the gold as there was with the bars of the cage, it was too subtle for her to detect. Yet she knew some kind of spell had to run through the chain and ring to control her the way it did. Her mother, too, must be guarded by such a spell for the man to have kept her as long as he had. But what spell had he used? And how could a mortal attain such powerful magic?

Ian was right. She hadn't given the origins of magic enough thought. For her, witches had simply always existed, the power passed on from parent to child, from one generation to the next, in the same manner as red hair or brown eyes. But Ian had long understood the source of their craft had been granted from a higher power. A sort of parting gift from the fair folk, which they'd bestowed upon select mortals for their dedicated service. Had this fool found a way to gain favor for himself? Could a mortal truly attain the power of spellcasting?

The mortal returned, and she slunk back to the far edge of the cage. He was wearing a robe with moons and stars on it and a hat with that same symbol she'd seen before of a circle and crescent horns. His bare white feet stuck out of the bottom of the robe. She could see the little hairs curling up from atop his toes. She cawed at him in short clucks, knowing the guttural noise grated like derisive laughter.

He shushed her harshly, so Edwina watched as he approached a pentagram painted on the floor and prepared to enter the circle. She understood what he was about with the stones and candle, but what was he doing in those ridiculous clothes? And why set a bag of sweets on the northern point? An offering of some kind? The scent of licorice wafted up to her sensitive nostrils, confusing her even more.

The daft mortal raised his arms and spoke his invocation, calling upon a demon named Maligar. Thrice he had to repeat his spell and still nothing happened. How had she been taken captive by this absurd man?

But then the energy in the room shifted. A cold chill brushed the tips of her feathers. The curtains ruffled before the window. She didn't dare look, yet she couldn't turn away. A shimmering cloud materialized in the room, and then there, standing in a frock coat and silk waistcoat, stood the quirky fellow she'd spoken to by the loch.

"I have summoned thee," said the mortal, as though it weren't obvious to everyone in the room. "You are bound and must do my bidding."

The being summoned was no demon, so what was the quirky fellow doing by answering the dolt's call? Edwina noticed the mortal constantly checked that his hairy toes remained inside the circle. He was afraid of the supposed demon he'd called up. Almost like someone being frightened of the flash of lightning yet still conjuring up a thundercloud because they liked the smell of rain. All she could do was laugh at the absurdity.

"I see you've successfully secured her." The creature in the frock coat stepped toward the cage. His sparkling indigo eyes fell on Edwina, sending a chill through her hollow bones. He picked up the gold chain attached to the lock and hefted the weight in his marble-white hand. "Shall we have her change back briefly? She can be somewhat charming . . . for a witch." He grinned at her, revealing a disturbing mouth full of pointed teeth.

"Not now. I am nearly ready." The mortal pulled a boline from the cavernous sleeve of his robe. The ritual knife had a curved steel blade that looked sharp enough to disembowel an elephant.

The fey creature rattled the chain against the cage, reeling it in toward him until Edwina had no choice but to fly to the perch near the middle of the cage. She flapped her wings and struck her claws at the creature through the bars. He didn't even flinch.

"You see that," he said, dusting a loose downy feather off his shoulder. "She's already proven herself twice as spirited as yourself."

The mortal lifted his head indignantly. "I beg your pardon!"

"Let's face it, Carlin. You're an overstuffed, overly indulged turnip of a man."

The man took a bold step forward, still holding the knife, then checked his position within the circle. "You impudent beau-nasty! You'll pay for your cheek."

Without bothering to look away from Edwina, the frock-coated fellow wagged a finger at the mortal. The man's feet lifted off the floor. His body spun around three times in the air so that his robe twisted tight around his legs; then he crashed atop his pentagram, hitting the back of his head. The candle on the eastern point sputtered and fell over, sending a cascade of molten wax across the man's ear. A muted scream escaped from his mouth, which had been gagged with the pointy end of his ridiculous hat.

"My apologies, Miss Blackwood," said the creature. He freed the golden chain from the lock and attached it to a ring fastened to his waistcoat, as though she were an added accessory like a pocket watch or key chain. "The mortal was long overdue for a correction."

Edwina cowered on her perch. She'd never seen anyone raise another off their feet with a mere flick of their finger. She blinked at the man on the floor, still whimpering over his blistered ear. "Who are you?" she asked in her harsh bird voice.

The creature grinned his awful smile again. "You can speak in this form. How delightful. I was afraid it would all be bird gibberish." He bent to swipe the sack of sweets off the floor before the writhing man accidentally kicked them with his foot. The creature popped one in his mouth. "Now, as to your question," he said and rolled the sweet on his tongue. "For the moment, however brief, I appear to be your savior." He finally spared a glance at the mortal on the floor. "You have no idea the terrible things that man had planned for you. His corrupt energy fed me for months."

Edwina struggled against the chain. She flapped her wings and willed herself to change, but the same terrible spell still held her captive. The creature seemed to take pleasure in the distress it caused her, inhaling the scent of her discomfort.

"It will do you no good," he said. "I devised the spell myself." He leaned his head closer to the cage and whispered, "They were all my spells, if you must know." He nudged Carlin with his pointed shoe until the man shivered and turned a grim shade of gray as his body went rigid with cold. "You certainly didn't think he was capable of fishing a lost memory orb out of the river. I had to call the thing to me, focusing on the veins of grief and misery it contained inside. Such a lot of pain too. It's a wonder I hadn't discovered your man for myself earlier." He shook free of his deep diving thoughts with a sigh. "The roses dipped in spellfire were also mine. Well, as long as I'm bragging, I might as well admit that every single incantation that came out of that man's mouth was mine." He swung around to catch Edwina's eye. "Do you know how exhausting it is chasing an imbecile mortal from one end of the city to another to keep him afloat on the belief that he's traversed the laws of logic to become a semi-empowered witch?"

The man on the floor moaned and shivered. The fey creature knelt beside him, taking in a deep breath. "Just know that your pain is my reward," he said.

The length of chain linking her to the creature slinked out of the cage and rattled onto the floor, reminding her she was now at his mercy, though she suspected he possessed none. He was mad as a hare. A maniac set loose for the Midsummer after the lunacy of the moon had taken residence inside his rotting brain. A sob escaped her, though it sounded like a soft coo from the vibrato of her bird voice.

A whimper to echo her own came from beneath the floorboards. The creature heard it, too, tilting his head to listen.

"What are you going to do with me?" Edwina quickly asked to get his attention back on her. It didn't work. Maligar pounded on the end of a floorboard with his fist so that the plank seesawed and flipped over, landing nails-up across the room. The clattering noise made her mother jump. Edwina could just see the shape of her through the hole he'd made in the floor. Her heart sank at the pitiful sight, and she tugged and tugged against the chain until she nearly suffocated herself in the effort of flapping inside the cage.

"I'll have you know," Maligar said, standing again, "the feeble-minded mortal actually believed for a time this woman held the secret to your shape-shifting ability." He waggled his fingers at Edwina's mother in a bizarre greeting, knowing he terrified her. "Carlin stuck her down there in the cellar with a loom and a mountain of yarn and fiber and expected her to produce a cloak that would bestow him with the same gift of the ancients that was given to you. What an arrogant fool. No earthbound woman could have given you that gift," he said, tempering his exuberant voice with a measure of disgust.

Edwina's mother spotted her in the cage through the gap in the floorboards. The hopelessness in her mother's eyes changed to recognition with a single blink. Fear transformed into courage. She sat forward with her straggly gray hair falling down around her face. "I'm here," she called, her voice raspy from screaming into the void of her captivity. "I'm here!"

"Mother!" Edwina flew to the top of the cage, gripping her claws on the metal bars to get a better view of the cellar.

"He, of course, was going to have her killed, once she proved herself a useless nuisance, but I always knew it would be beneficial to keep her alive, at least until I had you in my grasp." Maligar bent to pick up the mortal's knife. "And now here we are."

"Is Father with you?" Edwina called to her mother, ignoring the fey creature as she inched closer to the top. She stuck her beak between the bars to see her mother better.

"I thought I heard his voice in the kitchen. Days or weeks ago. I don't know." Her mother shook her head as her words dissolved into tears. "He never came back."

Maligar laughed. "Oh, he's still around, if you don't mind doing a little digging. About three feet below the pumpkin patch."

Both women gasped. Her mother cursed the sprite with a string of incantations that had no effect. When that didn't work, she threw her dinner plate at him, missing her target and shattering the dish against the wall. Edwina trembled at the cruelty of the creature's flip-pant remark. If her father were dead and if this beast had caused it, she would scratch out his eyes, cut open his belly, and pluck out his liver and heart. If his kind had a heart.

Maligar slunk by her, nostrils flared, as she thought her terrible thoughts, and not for the first time. After each malicious thing he said and each horrible action done, Maligar had a habit of leaning in to gauge the reaction of her and her mother. As if measuring their emotions. No, *absorbing* their emotions. His threats and innuendo caused the air to fill with the static electricity of their despair and fear, and then . . . and then he'd somehow consumed it for himself. Yes, he'd said he fed off the mortal's energy. Was he feeding on their pain and distress now? Had his eyes brightened each time his emotional cruelty hit its mark? Did his skin shimmer at the sight of a tear? What kind of creature subsisted on the emotional anguish of others?

Chapter Twenty-Nine

"He's one of the unseelie," Finlay said as he and Ian stared at the glittering wake left behind by the creature at the back of the house. "A sprite like myself, only fey-touched. Grim. He devours the bleak and dismal emotions of people. But to get them in that state, aye, he first inflicts the damage."

"We have to get in there," Ian said, rising from behind a fern. "He's got Edwina with him."

Finlay gripped his hand hard against Ian's forearm, stopping his momentum with enormous strength. Ian couldn't have rushed forward if he'd wanted to.

"No, we canna go rushing in like fools. Not with an unseelie involved. He's a wisp of dark cloud now, aye, but he can turn to a deadly storm if provoked by a flash of lightning."

"I take it you think I'm the lightning bolt."

Finlay cocked an eyebrow and tilted his head as if to say it were obvious which one was being levelheaded. "Whatever they're up to in there, we canna go in by ourselves. His power, it's the kind that feeds on emotions like I said. Fear, anger, and depression, ye ken?" Ian tried to jerk free, but Finlay stopped him again. "We're going to need help. Promise me you'll stay put. I'll alert Lady Everly and Clarissa and be back as quick as I can. Between us we ought to be able to surround him and take control."

Before Ian could object, Finlay dissipated. In his place sat a stoat with a white breast and glossy ginger back. The stoat stood on his hind legs and sniffed the air, twitching his whiskers. Ian offered his hand, but the animal jumped through the bracken and ran in the direction from which they'd come.

Ian waited in the ferns, watching the window where the unseelie creature had entered and cursing the day he'd ever agreed to do business with the fair folk. "Flighty, fidgety, and self-absorbed, that's what they are," he muttered to himself.

"Are we not also at times gracious and forgiving?" a voice called out.

"Hob, where the devil have you been?"

"Enjoying the festivities." The little elf parted the ferns and peeked out at the cottage. "You used to play in these woods when you were but a wee bairn. I remember the old man who lived here was odd even for a human."

"You remember Old Man Osborne?" But of course he did. The only reason Ian had any memory of the cottage at all was because Hob had held on to the recollection for him. "We used to dare each other to look inside the windows, afraid we'd see some weird ritual with skulls or a fiend of some kind."

"Just like now," Hob said. "By the way, the celebrations are boundless tonight!" He took a small meat pie out of his pocket as evidence and nibbled on the crust.

"The lads from yonder MacTavish's place once claimed they saw a woman in a long cape walk past the house and into the trees as if she were floating on air. Thought she was a ghost." Ian wished then he hadn't recalled that particular memory, sitting in the dark and chill of the night with naught but an elf beside him.

"What was she, do you think?"

Ian had no answer. He'd been too young to know who or what might be lurking in the woods near the old man's place.

A bang sounded from inside the cottage like a plank of wood splitting. Ian sprang to his feet. "Bloody Finlay." He'd been warned not to move, not to rush in. "The hell with that," he said. If Edwina was in there with some malevolent cloud of mood-sucking unseelie and his mortal lackey, Ian wasn't going to sit in the damp ferns waiting to help her.

He paused only briefly as he formed the words of a defensive spell powerful enough to deflect a fairy attack. He'd have to go through the protection defenses on the cottage and knew he'd lose the element of surprise. He took a deep breath.

"If you're going inside, you should take this." Hob held up a skeleton key. "I found it in the mortal's trousers. Methinks, by the way it shines, the key might bypass the spells."

"What are you playing at, Hob? You've been inside already?"

"Och aye," the elf said. "I had to make sure milady wasn't seriously hurt."

Ian swiped the key out of the elf's hand and charged for the front door.

"Have you any baccy for the pipe?" Hob called, but Ian was already on the threshold.

He had no idea what kind of spells might be holding the place together. Curses? Hexes? Ian slipped the key in the lock and turned the bolt. No jolt or shiver of magic trailed over his skin. He carefully pushed the door open, pleading with the All Knowing for well-oiled hinges. The door made no sound, so he blessedly slipped inside the entryway, pausing beside the partition wall to spy on those inside.

The fey sprite knelt in the sitting room, waving his fingers at someone through a hole in the floorboards. He was ghastly pale with skin so translucent it had a tinge of blue, like the inside of an oyster shell. The same creature Ian had seen at the loch, he'd wager. Except for the peely-wally complexion, he could have been Finlay's doppelgänger in his frock coat, springy legs, and shiny shoes. Only Finlay had called this

212

one an unseelie. A shadow. A late frost to kill the spring blooms. The creature's murky energy was palpable from across the room, skimming over his skin like cold air rolling in from the sea on a winter morning.

Ian dared to peek around the edge of the wall another inch. Behind the unseelie stood a giant birdcage with a raven sitting on a perch in the middle with a long golden chain trailing from its leg to the fey creature's waistcoat. *Edwina!* She appeared frightened but steady. *Bricky lass.* There at the foot of the cage lay a man. The mortal they'd been chasing? But instead of being the one holding Edwina hostage, he seemed to be confined by some invisible binding that left him wound up tight inside his robe with his arms firm at his sides. His lips and bare toes were slightly blue.

Recognition hit hard when Ian caught the full profile of the mortal's face. His detective training had taught him to remember defining details about the people he'd encountered. When he was standing in the miserable cold, conducting surveillance in the middle of the night, it helped to have a physical feature of his subject he could recognize from a distance. And this man had "posh dandy" written all over him, from his oiled hair to his finely groomed sideburns and angular nose. Looking for confirmation, Ian's eye traveled over the entryway until he found the gray homburg tossed atop a wicker settee. He knew the encounter in the marketplace had been no coincidence. Without a doubt he was looking at the man who'd burned down Edwina's shop and stolen their train tickets. But if he was the instigator, why was he incapacitated on the floor?

The raven, or rather Edwina, spoke the word "mother" from the sitting room.

Mother?

A woman cursed the unseelie and threw something at him, but it wasn't Edwina. The voice had come from the hole in the floorboards. There was someone else in the cellar. Ian's heart thumped at the implication. He stretched his body, lifting his head to try and get a glimpse inside the hole, but all he saw was the top of some metal bars like the ones the banks used on their teller windows.

The unseelie opened the birdcage, drawing Ian's attention back upstairs. Edwina screamed bloody murder.

"Settle down," the creature said. "You've no need to squawk so. Not yet, anyway." He lifted her out of the cage while she scratched and clawed.

Bloody Finlay! Where are you?

Ian withdrew and pressed his back against the wall. He'd rushed in without a plan, and now he needed to do something . . . anything. He sucked in two quick breaths, then came around the corner hurling a spell of blinding white light aimed at the unseelie. "Moon and starlight shining bright, find your mark against the wight."

He'd reasoned the flash of light might counteract the creature's stormier nature long enough to stun him so he could free Edwina, but the unseelie absorbed it like a cold, gloaming cloud, dousing the spell light. The only effect his quick incantation had was to alert the *dreich*-hearted fellow to his presence.

Shit.

"Ian!" Edwina cried out in her bird voice.

Maligar secured her under his arm and walked toward Ian. "With so much angst in the room, it would be an utter delight to stay and take it all in, but I'm afraid I have other plans," he said, raising his open palm.

The scent of licorice breath hit Ian in the face just before a freezing-cold zap struck his chest. He toppled backward, hitting his head on the wicker settee. A cold shiver passed over and through him, freezing his limbs so he couldn't move as Maligar stole into the night with Edwina held in his grasp.

Chapter Thirty

Carlin feared his blood had frozen stiff inside his veins. Needle-sharp pain stung the tips of his fingers, the inside of his nose, and the arch of his foot. He hadn't been able to move a muscle after Maligar cowardly ambushed him, but now that the demon had gone, he could blink his eyes again and swore his big toe moved. Still, the injury done to him plunged straight to his core. Had that insolent demon truly been deceiving him the entire time?

A muscle in his neck thawed enough that he could turn his head a few inches. Yes, whatever spell that monstrosity had used against him was starting to wear off. There'd been a witch in the room momentarily who'd tried to come to his aid. The man had hurled a bright light at Maligar before being thrown against the floor the same way he had been. If he strained, Carlin could just see the soles of the man's shoes in the entryway. There was no movement, so he refrained from calling out for assistance.

How had he misjudged Maligar so disastrously? The demon had made wild accusations about the legitimacy of his magical accomplishments, claiming *he* was the one responsible for the spells. And then he did harm to his one true summoner! If there weren't already a pestilence-ridden niche in the netherworld for such an impudent creature, Carlin would create one for him. *If* his body continued to thaw from this revolting demon magic.

A few moments later Carlin was able to move his arms enough to prop himself up on one elbow. Something scurried in the house in reaction to him moving. Rats in the cellar perhaps, drawn by the state of the filthy woman. Thank goodness he had his faculties back.

Finding his voice, Carlin called to the man in the entryway. "I say there, old chap, are you alive?" Still no movement from the fellow, but the woman shouted her usual obscenities. Perhaps it was the aftereffect of the spell on his ear canal, but he swore her voice grated louder than usual. Then he recalled the demon had pulled up a plank of the floor, leaving a gap for her voice to carry through.

"Shut up, you weary old hag!" he shouted over his shoulder. "Enough of you and your blathering." For good measure he pounded his fist on the wooden floor. The blow sent a shattering pain to his still-thawing wrist, but the expression of anger felt reliably good again. As soon as he could stand, he would smite her with a death spell and be done with her for good.

"Shut your gob, you weasel-faced impostor," the woman said.

Carlin caught the stench of her then and determined to get on his feet so he could be rid of her posthaste. He got balanced on one knee when the ragged hem of her dress came into view on the floor. He looked up to see the woman standing before him. Her gray hair hung lank around her face, her skin sagged from months of living in the cellar, and her nails were torn and bloody from all the times he'd caught her clawing at the walls to escape.

"Fancy that," she said with a spiteful grin. "Somebody removed their binding spell before they stole away with my daughter."

He raised a defensive hand, ready to plead his case with the loathsome woman, when she brought an iron skillet down on his head.

Chapter Thirty-One

It was nae a killing frost, thank the All Knowing, but Ian swore he could feel the ice in his veins melt inch by painful inch. He sat up on the floor and found himself nose to nose with Hob, who stood beside him, dropping crumbs from his meat pie while he chewed with his mouth open.

"What the devil happened?"

"Fey sprite," Hob said.

"Come again."

"One of the unseelie, according to your hairy friend here," said a woman in a ragged gray dress who stood holding a frying pan in her hand like a weapon.

Hob stopped chewing. "His ilk is about as welcome at these festivities as a potato blight, ye ken?"

"Aye, I ken," Ian said, wishing now he'd abided Finlay's warning. "I can still feel the ice rattling inside my bones." He struggled to his feet.

The woman backed away, clutching the pan in her bloodied fist. He remembered then that Edwina had called out "mother" before she was taken away. He tried not to stare, but aside from her ragged condition, the resemblance between the woman and her daughter was uncanny.

"You're Lenora Blackwood," he said, quickly putting together a story of what might have happened to the missing woman based on her current state. "Are you all right? Are you hurt?"

The woman nodded. "I'll do, though I'm not sure how long I've been here. Months, I think." Her hand covered her mouth as a sob burst to the surface.

"Quick, Hob. Can you do something for her?"

"Aye, can do." The elf brought out his broom and the length of string he'd saved from the suit delivery to Ian's flat. He laid the string in the woman's hand and told her to concentrate on stitching up the rents in her dress. She appeared skeptical, but being a witch, she was inclined to trust the elf's magic. Hob said his short spell to clean her up and her sobbing stopped, so shocked was she at the transformation of her clothes from filthy and torn to fresh as new again.

"How?" she asked, but Hob wasn't finished. He offered her a fairy cake he'd saved from the celebrations and told her to eat it. She hesitated, uncertain as anyone would be to accept food offered by one of the fair folk, but with a nod of encouragement from Ian, she took a bite. By the time she finished chewing, soft, golden starlight sprinkled over her skin. She smiled with childlike wonder as Hob did a little jig at her feet. "Meddle feddle, middle fiddle, thumpty scrumpty dee. Strong health for you, good deed for thee, and a lock of hair for me."

Before she could argue, he snipped a length of hair from her head with a tiny pair of golden scissors and tucked the lock in his pocket. "Heavens," she said, bewildered by what had just happened to her.

"It's the Midsummer," Ian said. "He gets a little balmy from all the celebrating." Ian shook off the last of the chill, stretching his fingers and arms. His muscles were stiff, but all seemed to be in working order.

"Midsummer!" Lenora pressed her palm to her cheek as though shocked by the news. "Have I been here that long?"

"You've been missed for quite some time, aye," he said. The woman looked on the verge of tears again, so he averted his eyes. "And what happened to him?" Ian approached the man on the floor. A pool of blood had congealed on the back of the mortal's head, though he didn't appear dead. Not yet.

"No less than he deserved." She sobered and relinquished the frying pan, which fell to the floor with a heavy thud.

"I'll not argue with you there." Ian scanned the room and the man's effects for clues to his identity. "Any idea who he is? Or what he was up to? The other one has taken Edwina."

"My daughter Edwina. I saw her briefly, but not Mary." The woman took a breath to steady herself and clear her thoughts. "I don't know who he is. A mortal who called himself a master of the occult. But it was the other one performing all the spells. He said so. I used to hear the two of them talking about my daughters. About their . . . gifts." She paused as though not sure how much Ian knew about the Blackwood sisters.

"About the shape-shifting?"

She nodded. "The fool thought I'd woven the magic into their shawls. He kidnapped me off the street, thinking I could do the same for him. Made me weave a dozen different cloaks for him. First in the city, and then later he brought me here. I thought he was going to kill me, but then the other one talked him out of it." She peered into the kitchen at the back of the cottage. "I think my husband is dead."

Lenora moved around the room as if trying to compare the things she'd experienced with the reality she now found herself in. "I know this place," she said. "My husband and I came here after we were married. Before the twins were born. I'm sure of it. I recognize the inglenook."

Ian didn't have the heart to tell her about Mary. And, anyway, he didn't think it his place to deliver such news to the poor woman. "Do you have any idea where the unseelie might have taken Edwina?" he asked.

"The mortal thought he'd summoned a demon," Lenora said, standing over the man. She let out a derisive laugh, looking at the pentagram he'd painted on the floor. "I overheard him ask the fey fellow once what the passage was like traveling from hell. He laughed and said it was as easy as slipping through a crack between two stones."

Hob and Ian looked at each other and said in unison, "Hare Hill."

Chapter Thirty-Two

Edwina found herself tucked under some brute's arm yet again. Forced to remain in her bird form by the binding spell attached to her leg, she squawked and complained, drawing blood on his hand with the rough edge of her beak. Maligar merely chilled her blood with a brush of a finger against her feathers. She'd seen him do much worse to the mortal, so she took heart that his plans for her included keeping her alive, at least for the moment.

The fey sprite walked with purpose through the trees and then the open moor. He seemed fretful at times, glancing over his shoulder as if he were a thief who'd just made off with a farmer's prized chicken. Edwina had no idea where they were headed until the outline of a rugged hill emerged against the backdrop of midnight-blue sky. The creature, who smelled strongly of licorice, took his bearings and adjusted her weight under his arm. Tired of being jostled, she pecked at his ribs through his waistcoat, testing his resolve. Again, he froze her blood just enough to immobilize her so that she was forced to rest her head against the crook of his arm.

She'd begun to despair when her keen eyesight spotted something shiny sticking out of the top of Maligar's shallow waistcoat pocket. She nudged her beak against the paisley silk in rhythm with the natural motion of his gait, and soon she was rewarded with the sight of a key tucked in his pocket. It was gold colored, and the teeth were small enough they might fit in a lock attached to a fine gold chain. With so many unknowns, and not wishing to have her blood turned to ice yet again, she nudged the key back in the pocket for safekeeping, holding firm to the hope that being free of the chain meant being free of the binding spell.

Maligar stopped beside a shallow creek, exhaling a cloud of cold breath as he eyed a cottage ahead. Even at this late hour, there was a light on inside the house and a thin stream of smoke curling up from its chimney. If he meant to carry her inside for a rendezvous with another mad mortal, she'd scream for all she was worth. *Surely there must be other beings about on this Midsummer night.* But Maligar proved as apprehensive about going too near the house as she did. He backed out of the moonlight and kept to the shadows.

"Stay quiet," he said, "or I'll not be as gentle as I have been."

Edwina's wings were bruised and battered from being toted roughly under his arm, and her beak was tender from striking the skin on his hands. She squirmed slightly to test the sprite's grip one last time, then remained silent when she could find no escape, knowing he was inclined to follow through on his threats.

Maligar veered to his right, where an outcropping of granite sheltered the house and garden from the harsh northern wind. Instead of skirting around the formation, he walked straight toward where a crack had split open in the rocks. A delicate spiderweb hung over the foot-wide opening, glittering with dewdrops in the dark. In its center sat the maker.

Maligar, whispering a series of clucking noises, encouraged the pudgy gray spider to climb onto his shoulder. "That's my precious girl," he cooed at the spider before tearing the webbing aside. The arachnid climbed under the lapel of his frock coat, where it watched Edwina while tapping one leg meditatively against the fey creature's shoulder.

Fearing he meant to squeeze them all through the space between the rocks and disappear from the earth, Edwina panicked. "Where are you taking me?" she cried, trying yet again without luck to transform.

"Oh, I have plans for you, my pet." He grabbed her by the feet and held her out at arm's length, giving her just enough room for hope that she might escape. She flapped her wings and struggled against his grip, thinking of Ian, her mother, of all the things she had yet to do in life, but it wasn't enough to set her free. After all she'd been through, she tired quickly and had no choice but to settle on his hands while he positioned her before the fissure in the rocks. "Do you see?" he asked. "Your future belongs to me now. Just through there."

"Why are you doing this?" she squawked.

He took a licorice from his coat pocket and stuck it in his mouth. "Reward and recompense and all that," he said with a shrug. "But mostly for the tasty morsels of distress and anguish so many will feel when I steal you right out from under their self-righteous seelie noses." He stroked her feathers, filling her with cold dread. "And since your presence here tonight will bring the queen pleasure and accomplishment, stealing you away from her is practically a duty of mine. Now, have a look, pet, before we go through."

He held her up to the fissure in the stones. Edwina wished to look away, but he held her head forcefully so she had no choice but to gaze into the gateway. She cast her raven eye on the space between the rocks and saw a vague swirling energy backlit by a shine akin to a witch's aura. The churning motion reminded her of the feeling of liminal space she briefly experienced while shifting from one body to another, when her bones, skin, hair, and feathers metamorphosed in defiance of logic and biology.

Maligar caressed the feathers under her chin and she recoiled. "The Otherworld," he said, "where you shall serve the empress. She has marvelous designs to exploit the inherent ills of this appalling earthen realm to our advantage using your talents."

"Why do something so cruel?"

"Because he is unseelie and that is what they do." Hob leaped out of an old slop bucket that had been thrown aside at the back of the garden. "Because misery is mother's milk for him."

Maligar gathered Edwina's chain in, clutching the leash tight in his fist. "You've no business here, imp. Go back inside and serve your master." He nudged his chin toward the cottage, dismissing Hob as little more than a toady, then turned his back on him.

"We all serve someone," Hob said, jumping to the ground. "Give me the witch woman and you may return safely to those who rule over *you*."

Edwina had never seen such a fierce look on the little elf's face. Stern eyes burned bright with conviction as he waited for the fey creature to twist back around.

"Go away, you contemptible, bare-footed, hairy dog before I bring this hillside down on you." Maligar pointed toward the cottage again, where two curious faces peered out the front window. "And them."

Ian's parents. They have to be. Edwina knew where she was now. Hare Hill and the cottage Ian had grown up in with Hob as his guardian. But where was Ian?

"You will not leave this realm with milady," Hob said.

Maligar gave no warning. He thrust out a hand and grabbed Hob by the ear, lifting him off the ground. The little fellow's legs dangled in midair as he fought against the sprite's grip. "The age of elves is over," Maligar said, and with little more effort than tossing away a hulled-out walnut shell, he flung Hob against the rocks. The elf whimpered and tumbled to the ground.

Edwina screamed and dug her claws into Maligar's side, searching for the key. He flinched at the needle-sharp pain and smacked her hard across the beak in return. She saw the pleasure in his eye as he grabbed her by the neck with terrifying speed. He sucked in her fear as she trembled uncontrollably, gaining sustenance as she weakened in his grip. He shoved her headfirst toward the gateway, and she feared she would be lost from this world forever once they passed through the crack in the stones.

Resisting with all the energy she had left, Edwina strained against the chain, ready to tear her own leg off to get free, when the man from the house came around the garden and tapped the unseelie on the shoulder.

"Dinna be forgetting this," the man said.

When Maligar turned around, he was met with a headbutt to the face. The sprite stumbled backward before falling to the ground, scattering his licorice allsorts on the grass. Edwina bounced free of his grip when he landed but was still bound by the chain.

Ian's father held his hand out palm first. "Stand back, ye wee corbie," he said and sent a flash of fire hurling toward the sprite's head the second she flapped her wings.

Maligar rolled out of the way at the last second, springing to his feet with incredible speed. The tension in the gold chain between them tightened. Edwina, summoning one last ounce of strength, took to the air just as the fey sprite cocked his arm back, ready to inflict his brand of freezing pain on the old man. She pulled away, flapping as hard as she could. The effort was enough to stretch the chain even tighter and unbalance the sprite.

His magic went astray, hitting the cabbages in the garden instead. Ian's mother, who'd run out behind her husband, shrieked at the damage to her vegetables as they shriveled and turned black. She picked up a shovel and pulled back, ready to swing it at the sprite. Afraid of what Maligar would do to the woman, Edwina dove and made a circle, wrapping the chain around him. While the sprite fought off her claw strikes and the chain biting into his neck, the woman smacked him on the back of the head. He teetered on his feet momentarily before his eyes rolled up in his head and he toppled over, landing on his back.

"Aye, and that's for Hob," Ian's mother said and threw the shovel aside when the sprite didn't get up again.

Chapter Thirty-Three

Ian closed the distance from the trees to the rock outcropping behind his parents' cottage at a full-out run. Hob had insisted on traveling ahead through his system of tunnels, and now he'd had to fight to catch up before his friend did anything foolish. He stumbled into the yard out of breath, only to find the fey sprite lying on the ground with a blue welt rising on his forehead and sticky blood oozing from the back. His father stood wiping his nose with a handkerchief, while Edwina, still in the shape of a raven, pecked at the unseelie's waistcoat pocket before plucking loose a gold key.

"Bloody hell, are you off your head, man?" Ian checked his father to see if he was seriously hurt but was pushed aside by his mother, who was eager to get to her injured husband.

Edwina shook out her feathers. "Help me," she squawked, stomping her feet and rattling the chain. She nudged the key toward Ian and he fitted it in the lock. The chain fell away from her ankle, and she shape-shifted back into her womanly form, gasping with relief. Her dress was torn, her hair hung in loose strands around her face, and her neck was bruised.

Ian's parents both sucked in a breath of surprise at her transformation and gaped at her. "Mercy, the rumors are true," said his mother.

"Are you all right?" Ian asked. Edwina wrapped her arms tight around his neck, as if she'd never let go, and swore she was fine now that he was there with her, but then she spotted Hob on the ground. They both rushed to the little fellow.

"He's not breathing," Edwina said, kneeling beside the elf.

Ian bent down and put his hand on Hob's chest. "No, no, no, no, no." He listened for a distressing moment but felt no movement.

"Poor wee lad," his father said. "He was trying to stop that unseelie fella from going through the gateway with that great big bird. No offense, lass," he said, eyeing Edwina. "I came out to help as soon as I heard the commotion."

Ian smoothed the hair away from Hob's face to check his half-shut eyes. There was still a flicker of light in them. "Ma, quick. Have you any rosemary?"

"Never mind that." His mother ran to the house and returned with a hip flask filled with whisky. "We were up on the hill setting out our offering for the passing," she said, handing Ian the container. "We only just got back home. Poor fellow. He stood up to that unseelie all by himself."

"Aye, he's a braw one." Ian offered the whisky flask to Edwina. "You do it. Sing him back if you can. He'll hear you."

There was no time for doubt. Edwina poured a handful of whisky in her palm and dabbed a taste on the elf's lips as she sang a spell to call him back. "Pixie, fairy, goblin, sprite, this one's heart is true and bright. Hither, thither on your flight, we call you stand before our sight. Hallo, hallo, old Tom Hob. Hallo, hallo, old Tom Hob."

The little elf didn't stir. Ian lifted him in his arms, cradling the imp like a bairn to get him to gently rouse. "Come on, old one, you're nae leaving me now."

Behind him, his mother rested a hand on his shoulder. "He's already gone, Ian."

He shook his head. "No, he's still got a light." But even as he said it, he saw the flicker go out in his friend's eyes. Ian hugged his lifeless body closer. The wee elf had been by his side since he was a babe. He couldn't imagine letting him go. Not yet.

"Mind if I try?"

Behind them, silent as the dead, stood a host of fairies mounted on horses. An auburn-haired woman on a white steed dropped out of her saddle, landing on the ground soft as an owl. She wore a green velvet cloak with a bejeweled gold band on her head. Her horse shook out his mane, rattling the silver bells on his harness. She patted him on the nose and approached the fallen elf as the fairies formed a circle around them, still on their mounts.

"He's been hurt," Ian said. "There's no blood, but he won't wake up."

The woman pulled off her calfskin gloves. "Give him to me."

Ian relinquished the little fellow to the woman. She cradled him in one arm and whispered, "Tom Hob. My, my, it's been an age." A youth dressed in a green tunic with ermine trim emerged from the troop of fairies to bring her a sprig of mistletoe. She waved the leaves over the elf's body in a sweeping motion, cleansing him of some unseen grime. A second youth then brought her a glass vial with the flowers of a wood betony etched on the side. She poured a wee drop of the liquid on Hob's tongue and sprinkled him with golden dust from her fingertips.

And still the elf's body didn't stir. Ian batted away a tear on his lashes as Edwina gripped his hand and leaned her chin against his shoulder.

The woman leaned close to his face and sniffed. "More whisky, please." Mild concern showed on her face as she studied the elf. Ian's father handed her the flask with a slight bow. "The trick," she said as she poured a nip in Hob's mouth, "is to get it past the lips and onto the tongue for the spark to ignite inside." With a stern tone, she bellowed, "Wake up, little one, you've work to do yet."

Hob's eyes opened at her command, and he sputtered awake to the taste of whisky in his mouth. He blinked, smacked his lips, and sat up in the woman's arms. "*Ban-draoidh?*"

"Welcome back, *mo charaid*," she said with some relief before setting the hearth elf down on the soft grass.

"*Mo charaid.*" Ian leaned down and kissed the top of Hob's hairy head, thinking he'd just lost his oldest and truest friend. His father and mother did the same, as did Edwina.

But as soon as Hob shook off the disorienting effect of having been knocked unconscious, Maligar stirred on the ground. Hearing him groan, the woman placed her slippered foot on his chest and waited for him to open his eyes. "Now, what to do with this thief who would take what isn't his."

"Is she . . ." Edwina asked in Ian's ear.

"The *Ban-draoidh*. Annag, Queen of Elfhame, aye."

A disturbance broke the ranks of the fairies on horseback. Finlay, Lady Everly, and Lenora Blackwood pressed their way into the circle, creating a ruckus. The Lady of the Woods followed with a battered Sir Henry Elvanfoot on her arm, explaining he'd been attacked by the mortal man. The old wizard held a white handkerchief against his bloodied head but waved off Ian, as if to say he would be fine.

"Edwina!"

"Mother!"

Daughter found mother and they embraced, holding on to each other as tears of relief gushed out. The overwhelming emotion of their reunion was palpable in the air as they caressed each other's cheeks and hair and hugged again, vowing they'd never stopped thinking about the other in all the time they'd been apart.

Still restrained underfoot, Maligar groaned as though the joyful reunion on display pained him. Queen Annag sighed and stepped away. "Up," she said to him.

Maligar got to his feet slowly, dabbing at the blood on the back of his head and bracing for a renewed attack from all sides. Finlay stepped forward and gave him a long, leering look of disgust as he bound the sprite's wrists with a length of rope. "So this is the unseelie who kept slipping through," he said. "I should have known it was him, your majesty. I take full responsibility for not discovering him sooner." Finlay's guilt-heavy eyes landed on Ian, though there was no apology in them, only acknowledgment, which was the fair folk's way.

"Our friend here went to great pains to cover his tracks while he went about his earthly subterfuge." Queen Annag held out an open hand, and the spider crawled out from under Maligar's lapel. It tapped its front legs tentatively before walking onto her palm. She studied the spider at eye level, whispered a word of advice about weaving tangled webs, and released the creature into the garden with a warning to behave. "And now," she said, "I should like to know why you've been coming and going between worlds when it's strictly forbidden on non-feast days."

Maligar smirked and shrugged as if to say he was within his rights to do what he did. "It's an unfair advantage, is it not?" he asked. "Having someone in *your* court to see what is coming." The fey sprite cast his eye at the circle of fair folk surrounding him. "By the way, where is your old crone? Has she seen a bad end to the day and hotfooted it to the Otherworld already?"

The fair folk hissed and stomped their heels against the ground in protest of the sprite's rudeness. He merely grinned at them, taking pleasure in their offense.

Queen Annag held up a finger to silence her troop. "I confess, Gavina has had a vision of this day." She took a threatening step nearer, daring him to disrespect her again in front of her own people. "But how did you, a lowly errand boy for the Unseelie Court, learn about my designs?"

The fey sprite held his tongue, unwilling to cooperate. The queen narrowed her eyes at the stubborn fool and nodded. "You should know I have little time for obstinance on this hallowed evening." She searched the faces around her until she found Sir Henry Elvanfoot. "Good sir, if you are recovered well enough, would you bring me the potion tucked away in your pocket?"

Maligar straightened as the bloodied wizard approached. Elvanfoot produced a small green vial, which he uncorked with a pop. The queen accepted the bottle, took a quick whiff, then advanced on the uncooperative sprite.

The unseelie tried to maintain his nonchalance, but the presence of the fairy queen so near to him seemed to cool his defiance. He attempted to retreat a step but was met by his seelie twin, who stood at his back, keeping him put. "Hold still and it won't hurt a bit," Finlay said before restraining the fey sprite and grabbing him by the jaw while the queen poured the contents of the vial in his mouth. She pinched his nose shut until he swallowed.

They released him and Maligar spat on the ground, trying to clear the taste of the potion from his tongue. "What was that?"

Elvanfoot took back the vial and replaced the cork. "A simple truth serum made from valerian root. Quite fast acting, you'll find. And effective."

Queen Annag repeated her question. "Now, how did you learn about the raven sisters?"

"It was the mortal," he admitted, slumping in defeat.

"Ah." The queen curled a finger at a lad on horseback. He walked his horse forward, cutting through the crowd to reveal a sled attached to the back. A semiconscious man lay strapped to the bed, moaning incoherently while holding a bandage of fern leaves and spiderwebs to his head. "You mean this wretched thing?"

The unseelie sprite nodded, doing a poor job of hiding his pleasure at the sight of the mortal with a knot the size of a goose egg on the back of his head. "It were only a bit of fun. He'd barricaded himself inside that cottage on Samhain and started calling up demons loud enough for every creature in the seven hills to hear him. I thought it would be a lark to answer him. A jape to scare the little mortal so he wouldn't venture into realms he had no business dealing with. A favor to us all, really."

"A good deed, was it?" Finlay gave the unseelie a small shove in the back with the front of his shoulder. "You're a regular bawcock, you are."

"What purpose did this man have in calling up demons?" Queen Annag asked.

"He'd heard a tale about a pair of witch sisters," Maligar said, still compelled by the potion. "Shape-shifters who could turn into birds." He made eye contact with Edwina and licked his cracked lips. "Naturally that caught my attention."

"Why would a mortal care about, let alone believe, rumors of magic? Most scoff at such news and ridicule those who do take an interest."

The fey sprite grinned as if impressed with his own mischief. "I may have led him to believe he was capable of doing a few spells himself, chiefly by answering his summons. Once he got the taste, he wanted more. He set off to study the great manuscripts on magic, all authored by mortals of course, and read some dusty tome in an old cellar that mayhap suggested a shape-shifter could help him transform permanently into a witch. Who was I to say no? Not when his goals could serve my own in meeting a witch touched by a fairy spell. Unique combination, wouldn't you say?"

"This was no jape," the queen replied. "You deliberately used the mortal man for your own selfish ends. There's no such book that claims a mortal can be transformed into a witch. None but the one you planted for him to find." Queen Annag unbuttoned her cloak at the throat and tossed it to her valet to catch. A sparkling gown of green and gold shimmered on her ethereal form as she paced before the unrepentant sprite. "What did you tell him was the purpose of the raven sisters and their magic?"

Maligar fought the serum, grinding his teeth to remain silent. The queen's patience wore thin. She held out her hand and motioned to her valet to fetch her riding crop.

Edwina intervened, stepping forward. "The mortal believed there was a ritual he could perform using my blood that would allow him to complete his transformation into a true witch. It's why he took me hostage. He had already begun preparations within his circle for the ritual when this one showed up," she said, pointing at Maligar. "And then *he* stole me, too, and would have whisked me off through that crack in the stones if it hadn't been for Hob and Mr. Cameron."

"Aye, I did give him a wee northern kiss, your majesty," Ian's father said with a tone that suggested he was prepared to do it again.

"As did I, your majesty," said Ian's mother, drawing a mortified look from her son.

The Queen of Elfhame gazed at Maligar. "So, you went through the elaborate charade of misleading the mortal into believing he could attain magic for himself, when all the while you wanted to keep her for yourself."

"The aim was to take her from you," he said. "We know who and what she is."

Edwina crossed her arms as if reaching for the comfort of her shawl, but it was not there. Instead, she hugged her arms as if overcome by a chill.

"He dinna mean to take her for a wife in the Otherworld, did he?" Ian wore a scowl to match his father's.

Maligar mocked the notion with a chirp of laughter. "I hadn't thought of that, but now that you mention it, she does look like she could use a good plucking."

Ian balled his hand into a fist, ready to wipe the smile off the fey sprite's face, but Finlay and Hob held him back. "Rein in your anger, man." Finlay patted him on the arm, then pointed.

Behind the sprite, a host of otherworldly creatures misted through the gateway in the rocks—three straw-haired males dressed in black velvet frock coats and a woman adorned in a burgundy cloak that trailed past her feet. The hem seemingly floated above the ground as she walked, becharmed by some fairy magic. Each had deep indigo eyes that had the effect of absorbing light. They circled Maligar, who acknowledged them with a sheepish grin. The woman swept her cloak back and acknowledged Queen Annag with a bow, one disrespectful in its shallowness. "Happy Midsummer," she said. Her tone suggested she meant nothing of the kind.

"Una, what an unexpected surprise to have you join us in our mirth-making," Queen Annag replied, her displeasure dipped in sweetness.

"Is that what you call this?" Una checked the faces of those nearest, including Ian and Maligar, who continued to glare at each other. "Perhaps I've misjudged the frolicking class of folk. I thought all your kind ever did was drink wine and fornicate on this sweltering day. Imagine my delight at discovering a brewing quarrel."

"Your man was caught stealing a protected ward of the Seelie Court. A bit more than a quarrel, Una."

"*Attempting* to steal," Una said with a sidelong look at Maligar. "If he'd actually done it, we wouldn't all be standing here."

Queen Annag's eyes flashed with irritation, which only made Una radiate with wicked pleasure.

The tension of so many supernatural creatures on edge created a cloud of sparking energy that threatened to ignite if tempers weren't quelled. Ian unclenched his fists, as did Finlay and Hob.

"Who are they?" Edwina whispered in Ian's ear.

"Unseelie. Una is their queen."

Annag's sharp ears overheard. "No, not a queen. Our Una is the self-proclaimed Empress of the Empty-Hearted." The fairies on horseback tittered, causing the unseelie to shrink back a step. "Yes, my darlings," the queen said, raising a hand in encouragement and smiling again. "You're meant to be enjoying yourselves on this celebratory occasion. After all, we are the mirth-makers. Let yourselves be merry. Sing. Dance. Partake of the wine."

An elf rattled a tambourine and a dryad played a tune on his pipe from the branch of a rowan tree. A band of pixies held hands midair and made a circle, spinning round and round until they fell dizzy with laughter. The sounds and scenes unsettled the unseelie until they huddled together near Maligar.

"Yield!" Una shouted, putting her fingers to her ears. The frenzy slowed to a stop. "What recompense do you demand for the lad's . . . mischief?"

The Queen of Elfhame contemplated the request, calculating the intention against the damage. "He shall find himself banned from entering this realm from any of the gateways for one hundred earth years," said the queen.

Una checked with her companions. "We acknowledge the punishment, but we also request the right to take the mortal with us for one year. As compensation for our loss."

"Your loss?" Queen Annag shook her head at the unseelies' cheekiness, then casually assessed the mortal as he moaned and came to life on the sled. "He's got a nasty lump on the head. Are you sure you want him?"

"All the better," Una said, bending to inhale as Alistair Carlin opened his eyes and shrieked at the vision before him.

"Done."

"Wait, that's it?" Ian asked. "You canna be serious. They nearly got away with stealing Edwina and taking her to the Otherworld."

"As is their right." Queen Annag's eyes sparkled in the moonlight as they turned on Ian.

His sense of justice was appalled. "But to cause so much harm and all he gets is a door slammed in his face?"

"It is not my place to cast eternal judgment on one abiding by his nature," she replied. "Wolves bite, wasps sting, and the unseelie steal. Our duty is to staunch the blood, daub the welt, and recover what we can so we might turn our cheek again to the sun's warmth." She laid a

235

finger alongside Ian's jaw, turning his head so he faced Edwina. "And when it suits, I gaze into the ether to see which of my sheep the wolf will attack before it strikes. But I do not punish the wolf for having a taste for lamb."

The queen's touch warmed Ian's skin, reminding him of when he was a lad sleeping in the hay when he should be doing chores. He smiled, overwhelmed by the tutelary stroke of her magic, yet he also understood the troubling implication of what she'd meant by turning him to face Edwina. Finlay had said she was theirs. With a single touch of her finger, Queen Annag had made clear her mark was on Edwina.

Finlay undid the binding on Maligar's wrists, setting him free. Both sprites appraised the other with a parting glance, seeing and unseeing the similarities, before returning to stand with their own people. The unseelie gathered before the split in the rocks, dragging the frightened Carlin, who screamed in protest, with them. Una produced a seedcake from her cloak and slipped it in his mouth to silence him. He tried to refuse, but after the first bite, he eagerly ate the rest, begging for more as the unseelie creatures lured him forward. Together they dissipated through the gateway to the Otherworld.

Maligar lingered, pausing to touch the torn threads of the spider-web with his finger. "It is a wonder, though, why a queen is allowed to interfere in the births of witches as if they were no more consequential than a litter of kittens," he said. He grinned at the fair ones, then turned into a cloud of mist that seeped between the stones.

Chapter Thirty-Four

In the wake of the unseelies' departure, a whirlwind of emotions caught up to Edwina. She felt unsteady on her feet as she thought of how she, too, had nearly been dragged through the portal to who knew what hellish existence that mortal now found himself in. Ian had suggested the unseelie would keep the man in confinement and torment him over and over again with visits from some of the more terrifying denizens of the Otherworld. Then Maligar and his ilk would feast on the anguish of human emotion until Carlin's mind grew so feeble it no longer responded to fear. She was distressed to hear it, knowing that the fair folk, with their grinning faces and curious stares, were not done with her. She'd not missed the revelation earlier that the queen had "designs" for this day, plans that included her. But to what end?

Having only just reunited with her mother, Edwina wanted nothing more than to be invited inside the warm cottage on the other side of the garden and sit with a cup of hot tea. There was so much they needed to discuss about what had happened in their time apart. Her fingers trembled at the thought of telling her mother about Mary's sad, disgraceful end.

Ian took her hand in his, and she reclaimed a measure of calm.

"Whatever did that appalling sprite mean about interfering in the birth of witches?" Lady Everly asked after the fair folk resumed their celebrations. She removed her mask to reveal a middle-aged woman with sparkling green eyes and a streak of gray in her otherwise wavy brown hair, which she wore loose for the festivities.

Elvanfoot's eyebrow twitched in response to the question. Curious, Edwina thought, that Queen Annag had known he'd have the valerian root extract on him and for the purpose it was intended. A conspicuous flicker of conspiratorial knowledge snapped in the air between the witch and fairy queen, now that she looked from face to face.

"Yes, what did he mean?" An uncomfortable welling pressed up against Edwina's intuition. Her mother tried to shush her, but she was the one the fey sprite had looked in the eye when he spoke his parting words. "Have I been touched by some fairy spell?"

The fair ones sucked in their breath to hear their queen addressed so directly.

Her mother placed a hand on her back. "Edwina, darling, you're out of turn."

"No, she's quite right to be curious." Queen Annag waved off Lenora's concern. "When the truth has been left in the dark too long, its cousins rumor and innuendo are allowed to grow into hideous shapes." She signaled for her courtiers to dismount. "Let us feast on wine and cakes, and we will bring the matter into the light."

In the time it took the night owl to call to his mate and hear her reply, the queen's entourage assembled a table from the branches of a pair of ash trees. A cloth of green moss was laid atop, and then came the cakes and puddings, gingerbreads and mallow fruits, bread with butter and honey, piles of apples, pears, and fat green grapes, and bowls overflowing with hazelnuts and walnuts. Cups were filled with wine and beer, and wee saucers of milk were set out for all to partake. After a flurry of action, a dozen chairs, woven together from the stalks of willow branches, appeared around the table. The tiniest pixies floated overhead, giving the scene a candlelit feel as a soft mist fell down around them.

"Please, sit and eat." Queen Annag took the host's chair at the end of the table while her guests filled all the seats but the one opposite her.

"You'll find all is to your liking," she said, acknowledging their apprehension about enchanted edibles.

Edwina and her mother were directed to sit on either side of the queen, only reinforcing the younger witch's creeping dread that she was tangled up with the fair folk in ways she'd never imagined a mere two weeks ago. The onset of visions, the omens of death, her near abduction to an Otherworld hell—there was more to her shape-shifting ability than merely having an ancient relative who'd passed on the trait after being seduced by a fairy.

Plates were passed and glasses filled as the queen addressed the women on her left and right. "This will be my fifth affirmation as queen," she said. "In all that time, I've been fortunate to have at my side a trusted prophetess to help me steer the course of the coming cycle after hearing her speak at the Telling." She nibbled on a slice of buttered bread, then swept the crumbs off her fingers. "Gavina also served my mother, Brigid, before her passing. The prophetess's visions have guided many of our most important decisions. But Gavina's health is sadly failing, which is why the unseelie took an unusual interest in our Midsummer celebrations this year. They recognized we are in a moment of flux. They have an appetite for such things, as you might imagine."

Edwina's heart began to thump inside her chest. She wasn't having one of her visions, but she knew without a doubt she and this prophetess were of a pair.

Queen Annag reached out to Edwina's mother and patted her hand. "Dear woman, I have an unseemly confession I must make to you before I go on."

"Oh heavens." Lenora looked up, bewildered. "To me?"

Annag filled both their cups with wine as a gray hare with long upright ears jumped on the empty chair at the opposite end of the table. There it remained, to the astonishment of none of the fair folk. "It was just over half a century ago," she began. "Earth years, mind you. Yes, I remember it well. I was walking through the trees yonder, which surround a quaint whitewashed cottage with a thatched roof. Similar to the Camerons', though at the time it was occupied by a bachelor fellow who preferred his own company." The queen sighed and sipped her wine. "We had a lovely series of trysts for decades."

Elvanfoot and Lady Everly cleared their throats loud enough to make a show of being shocked by such a statement, but they both leaned in eager to hear more. Ian's parents raised their eyebrows and commented they didn't think Old Man Osborne had it in him, but the queen didn't seem to mind their mild aspersion of the man's character.

"He was a lonely, decent man who had me enchanted by his warm spirit and gentle heart," she said. "I missed him terribly after he died, and so I wandered by the cottage from time to time to reminisce on all that had been. That, my dear, is when I spotted you and your new husband. You were making love in the shade of an oak tree."

Lenora covered her mouth with her hand and blinked back at the queen with owl eyes. Edwina stared down at her plate, too embarrassed to continue looking at her mother's face while the queen went on.

"I'd just been given some disturbing news from my prophetess, but I also saw an opportunity. More wine?" she asked. The hare shifted its weight at the other end of the table and twitched an ear.

"Yes, please," Lenora said and took a long drink from her cup.

"As I was saying, Gavina had come to me with a vision, as was our arrangement. Only this time what she'd foreseen was her own demise."

"How dreadful," Lady Everly said.

"Gavina has proven extremely reliable over the years, and so my heart was once again broken by sad news."

"She is still with you, then?"

"Oh yes." The queen tapped her fingers on the table. "She'd only wanted to apprise me of the vision to make me aware it was time to arrange for a new seer. And yet one does not simply go out to the garden and pluck one off the vine."

The fair folk burst into laughter, and several pixies reenacted a scene of Queen Annag looking under cabbage leaves and foraging among the squash for a new prophetess. Edwina believed them to be drunk on nectar.

Summoning her courage, Edwina asked, "What did you do then? About finding the replacement?" Beside her, Ian squeezed her hand beneath the table as if he might never let go again.

"As Queen of Elfhame I do occasionally have my own hazy visions, but they're more like inklings, not nearly as reliable as a true prophetess." She reached for a slice of pear and took a bite. "So when I spied on your parents entwined on the cusp of your conception, my intuition recognized the timing was no coincidence. Two witches in the midst of creating a new magically endowed being? I knew I'd been brought to that moment for a reason." She turned to Lenora again and topped off her cup of wine. "I added a spell to your lovemaking, one that would impart to your child the gift of the shape-shifter. A fairy gift bequeathed to your family, if you will," she said with a humble bow of the head.

Edwina's mother sat in stunned silence, her mouth slightly open, her eyes focused on some faraway time and place. "All those years," Lenora said at last, shaking her head. "We never understood how or why the girls were so different from everyone we ever knew."

While perhaps blush-inducing for her to listen to a conversation about her own conception, Edwina carried enough understanding of the fair folk's ways to recognize the queen wasn't being deliberately vulgar in mentioning such things in mixed company. She'd sussed out Queen Annag's candidness was merely a means to an end, of explaining the unexplainable. And yet the fairy queen didn't seem to have the entire truth, not when it came to her sister. Edwina dared to meet her mother's eye, wondering yet again how she would tell her about Mary on such a night as this one.

"Of course, I couldn't have anticipated you would carry twins," Queen Annag said. "Something Gavina forgot to mention, isn't that right?"

The large hare, which had been sitting and watching the feasting in the most unusual manner for an animal, ruffled its fur and used its back foot to scratch behind its ear. There was no flash of light or even a wrenching sound as the hare's furry body silently shifted from animal to woman. The spectacle was more like watching light bend in a carnival mirror, Edwina marveled from her strange new perspective.

"I'm not an automaton," Mrs. Fletcher said, shaking out her napkin at the end of the table beside Elvanfoot. The wizard showed absolutely no surprise in the revelation that his housekeeper served as the queen's prophetess or that she had seconds before been a hare, though Edwina and Ian both dropped their meat pies at the discovery. "I take it the unseelie have departed the grounds and I'm free to mingle again?" Gavina Fletcher said to each of her employers with a slight tone of resentment at being excluded from much of the celebrations.

"Scattered to the four winds," said the queen triumphantly. "And without my prophetess in tow, I might add."

Mrs. Fletcher helped herself to a serving of bread and jam. "Go on, then. Tell Edwina why you've made her into a great squawking bird."

"I'm getting to that."

"And Mary too," Lenora said, nodding, not wanting to leave her other daughter out.

"Aye, and Mary too," said the queen, sobering.

The table went silent at the mention of Mary. The worry lines between Lenora's eyes deepened with a mother's intuition that something was wrong. She glanced across the table at her daughter. "Where is our Mary?"

The vying emotions of wanting to tell her mother the sad news yet needing desperately to hear the truth about who and what she was had Edwina's heart and head spinning until she believed she would succumb to a form of vertigo. "She's . . . she . . ." She tried to say the words, but they melted in her mouth.

"She'll be along by and by," Gavina said, seeing Edwina couldn't find the words to explain to her mother the shocking demise of her only other daughter across a fairy feast table.

Queen Annag blanched at her prophetess's remark.

"It's nae what you think," Gavina said with a wry smile.

To cover up her open-mouthed reaction, the queen ordered another round of food and music. A pair of dryads blew softly on their flutes, while a team of hearth elves, still young enough to bear only one or two gray hairs in their beards, carried out plates of fresh oatcakes and mince pies, only slightly annoyed at having to serve a fellow elf at the queen's table. In the time it took to set out the new food, both the queen and Edwina seemed to have recovered their equilibrium enough to continue.

Queen Annag raised her glass. "Gavina, perhaps you're better equipped to address Miss Blackwood on the matter of her shape-shifting ability. If you're feeling up to it, that is?"

"Of course I am. I'm not dead yet." Mrs. Fletcher set aside her bread and wiped her fingers on her apron. "You see, dear, being a shape-shifter means you're a vessel for some of the oldest magic in the world. It's through our kind that the torch remains lit, so to speak, from one age to the next. Sometimes as a bird like yourself, sometimes a hare," she said. "Before me it was Fiona, who crept about as a wee black cat with white paws. She was married to a blacksmith, as I recall. Or maybe it was a fisherman. Anyway, you must think of your shape-shifting as a privilege. You've got equal parts witches' spells and fairy magic in your blood. That elixir of mixed blood is how you're able to see what's brewing on the horizon. Your visions come from the energy of the Otherworld. At times you can feel it settling on your skin soft as fresh snow. It's the same with all omens, even of death, ye ken?"

Edwina blinked at the housekeeper, still dumbfounded to see who and what she really was. "You helped me try on two gowns and never said a word."

"You were too busy having a vision," the housekeeper said. "One of me, if I intercepted correctly." Mrs. Fletcher clucked her tongue in a slight admonishment. "By the way, you've got a strong talent for the sight, but it isn't quite developed. You missed the mark with our Mr. Yates. That's something I can help you with. Truth is, there are so many factors that can affect the clarity and interpretation of what you're seeing. It isn't as straightforward as simply watching a play and reporting what you've seen. No, the magic from the Otherworld comes to us through a sort of prism, and you have to learn to read the bending light." She held up her finger. "If you're to advise the Queen of Elfhame on important matters, you've got to learn to be a braw observer of the plants, animals, stars . . . weather too." She held her hand out against the mist, letting the droplets collect on her palm. "Fortunately, I have just enough time left in this realm to guide you so you can develop the skills for yourself."

"But even though it is what you were born to do, it is not exactly a calling," Queen Annag added after sipping her wine. "It's more like a niche that only you can fill."

Gavina nodded, agreeing that was how she felt about her service to the queen.

Edwina fell back in her chair with her hands pressed against her cheeks. "I've searched my whole life to understand how and why I came to be this creature that no one recognizes." A gear clicked in her chest. A key turned in a lock. Pin tumblers aligned and sighed open with relief. A heart was freed to be what it was meant to be.

"You may refuse," the queen said. "I do not wish to draw contempt to my court from the discontented. That is for others to invite inside their circle."

"Will she have to go away to the other side?" Ian asked, nudging his chin toward the crack in the stones. "I've only just found her, ye ken."

Edwina froze, thinking of the man who'd just been sucked through the narrow space between rocks with the unseelie.

"For a brief time," the queen answered. "So she may understand our ways. But her place is here in the earth realm. This is where I need her eyes to see for me. To intercept certain harmful intentions stirred up by the unseelie before they can rise to action and destruction. Such designs aren't foolproof, mind you, but we tend to preserve the status quo more often than not."

"You're only required to report on feast days, dear," Mrs. Fletcher said. "But if you've got something more immediate that you want to share before a celebration, dinna fash. You just look up Finlay there on the Oxgate Road, and he'll get word to her majesty you've a prophecy for her to ponder."

"Would be my pleasure to assist you," said the sprite.

"You see, it's nae a bother at all. When I was married to Mr. Fletcher, he hardly noticed the times I was gone from the house. 'Twere the same after he died and I went to work in Sir Henry Elvanfoot's grand house."

"There were a few times I feared the fox might find you out when you scampered off in the middle of the night in your other form, but we've managed just fine," Elvanfoot said.

"We will need to start soon, dear, so do think about your answer and let us know," Gavina said, but of course she likely already knew Edwina's answer.

It was all too much. *Such a responsibility!* But an honor, too, one unmatched by any dreams she might have secretly held for herself. Edwina found herself smiling from the revelation. And yet she couldn't help thinking about her twin.

"What about our Mary?" her mother asked before Edwina could form an answer. "Was she not born with the same gift? The same visions? Will she not also serve in some way?"

Again the question of Mary stilled the talk around the table.

"As I confessed earlier," Queen Annag said, delicately breaking the silence, "I didn't know you would bear twins at the spell's inception. My ignorance seemed to have created a schism in the magic. A possible reason for why they developed into ravens, considering the bird's reputation for embodying both thought and memory. What one child ought to have been endowed with in whole seems to have been split in two. But not necessarily in equal parts. One child developed an inclination toward prophecy and the other the gift of collecting the memories of the dead."

Lenora deflated, slumping in her chair, as if remembering all the times Mary's strange ways had been too odd to fathom, even for those who loved her.

"Both talents are of equal value in our world, of course," Queen Annag said. "Each in their own way."

"So Mary's knack for seeing the corpse lights has a place with you as well?" her mother asked, reaching for hope.

The queen set her wine cup down. "My dear woman, you must know—"

"Mum." Edwina couldn't stand another moment of deceit. She reached across the table to take her mother's hand. She appreciated the queen's willingness to be honest, but the words needed to come from her. "Mary is—"

Before she could find the words to finish, a whoosh sounded from the crack in the rock between worlds, followed by a heavy thump. Finlay and Ian left their chairs to investigate the disruption while the rest of the fair folk craned their necks in curiosity.

"A mortal," Finlay said.

Ian rolled the man onto his back and did a double take. "It's Edwina's stalker."

It seemed impossible. The man was as gaunt and shriveled as a dried bean pod. His hair and beard were streaked white, his moon-and-stars robe was worn to tatters, and his bare feet were covered in filth.

"What happened to him?" Ian asked. "He was only gone an hour."

"In earth time, perhaps, but not necessarily in Elfhame." The queen rose from her chair. "Is he alive?"

"Nae for long," Finlay answered, pressing a finger to the man's neck. "The unseelie have sucked him dry, then tossed him back here for us to deal with the body."

"In that case, we should make way." The queen stepped aside as a carriage approached on the road. Drawn by four black horses, whose heads were adorned with plumes of raven feathers, the coach made no noise as the wheels floated above the ground.

Edwina gripped her mother's hand as the silent carriage rolled to a stop beside the unconscious mortal. Black velvet swags covered the windows of the death coach, obscuring their view of the passenger inside. They wished they could say the same for the driver—a headless corpse dressed in pinstripes and a morning coat who held the reins in an iron grip.

Ian and Finlay instinctively backed away from the mortal on the ground as the coach door opened. From the cab stepped a tiny female figure, no bigger than a child. She was clad in mourning silk and a veil, with tufts of black hair that poked out from behind the lace. On her back was a pair of insect-like wings, gray yet translucent, that unfurled when she cleared the steps of the coach. Once on the ground, she appeared a dainty yet fierce creature. One that was best to avoid, like a wasp or dragonfly.

On a night of odd goings-on, the coach-and-four stood out as the strangest of them all, and yet Edwina wasn't necessarily afraid. There was something weirdly compelling about the creature as she watched her approach the man on the ground.

"Be careful with your words until she's finished or she may take more than one soul with her on this Midsummer evening," the queen warned.

The creature ignored the wary spectators as if unaware of their presence while she knelt beside the man. A last rattling breath shook loose from the mortal. The creature spread her knobby hand over his mouth. Edwina gasped when a blue light rose out of the man and the creature snatched it in her hand, quick as a bird catching a moth.

"Mary?" she whispered.

"Mary Blackwood?" Ian and Hob both backed away to stand protectively nearer to his parents.

"Our Mary?" Lenora studied the creature, shaking her head. "No, it's not possible."

The creature looked up from her work at the sound of Lenora's voice, tilting her head as though to listen. She lifted the veil, revealing a face so like Mary's but with black holes for eyes and chalk-white skin.

Lenora shrieked and covered her mouth with the back of her forearm. "What's happened to her?" she asked, shrinking away.

"As I said, your daughters inherited different aspects of the gift." The Queen of Elfhame pursed her lips. "When Mary passed over, the magic cleaved her talent for communing with the dead from Edwina's emerging skill for envisioning the future. What once was shared was now separate." To Edwina she said, "You may have noticed your gift intensified after the separation, as did Mary's when she died and became a *ban-sìth*."

"*Ban-sìth*?" Lenora shook her head in confusion. "My Mary is dead?"

Edwina put her arm around her mother's shoulders and whispered it was true as Lenora wept at the news. She told her how Mary had died in the river after confessing to abetting the murders of several men so she might collect their corpse lights and own their memories forever. "I think the compulsion to be who and what she was always destined to be was too strong to keep her in this world for long," Edwina said as her mother sank to her knees.

The *ban-sìth* finished collecting the blue light from the mortal man's body. She didn't seem to recognize the living around her, having only eyes for the dead, but Edwina thought she caught a flicker of empathy in the death fairy's puckered mouth when their mother's crying turned to sobs—sobs for her husband, her daughter, and the months she'd lost to the fiend now dead on the ground.

"Take him!" Lenora said, risking the wrath of the creature. "Take him to hell and take me, too, and spare your mother another moment of grief."

The creature's head turned toward the voice and sniffed the air. Her lip snarled but then softened into a confused pout. The *ban-sith* lowered her veil again, then lifted the mortal's body off the ground by pumping her wings. The man was floated into the death coach, and the fairy signaled to her driver with a wail. The crack of the whip against the horses startled the fair folk and witches alike so that they jumped back in unison. The coach rolled forward in silence and took to the air. Then, just before the carriage pulled out of sight, the curtain lifted on the back window and a tiny, knobby hand waved. And there on the ground, where the creature had stood beside the body, were the tracks of a small narrow foot with a pointed toe.

Chapter Thirty-Five

The death coach's absence left a wash of cool air in its wake. Edwina winced at the sight of her mother on her knees crying out in pain. Still absorbing the revelation of her daughter's transformation in the afterlife, Lenora sobbed, her body shaking. Edwina wished she had her shawl to drape over her mother's shoulders to settle her. Instead she made do with a firm arm and gentle words, comforting Lenora until she was able to coax her to her feet again.

Hob brought a warm mug of tea, offering to add a nip of whisky. "If milady thinks it would help."

"Just this once," Edwina agreed and then held the mug to her mother's lips until she drank.

Behind them, Queen Annag ordered the procession to regroup, as it was nearly dawn and they needed to arrive at the stone spiral with the rising sun for the Telling. On her cue, the fair folk dismantled the moss-covered table and willow chairs, removing all evidence that the Queen of Elfhame and several witches had just feasted on cakes and wine outside the cottage where Ian had grown up. Finished before Edwina's mother could even swallow her tea, the trooping fairies mounted their caparisoned horses, ready to parade toward a grove of trees to the east. The queen sat atop her white horse and motioned the procession forward, sparing a brief glance at Edwina before she rode on.

Mrs. Fletcher quietly encouraged Edwina to let Maggie Cameron escort her mother inside the cottage, where she could rest and recover from her terrible ordeal.

"The lad's parents will watch after your mother," Mrs. Fletcher said as Maggie hooked her arm in Lenora's to support her.

"But I can't leave her now," Edwina said.

"She needs the comfort of a warm fire and a tender hand," Ian said. "She'll be well taken care of here." He shook his father's hand and thanked his mother. "I'll stay with Edwina," he told them.

Mrs. Fletcher coughed into her handkerchief. "You and I need to follow the procession," she said to Edwina. She waved to one of the queen's wards, who brought over a pair of horses. "And there are still matters we should discuss before we get to the Telling."

Feeling the tug of curiosity pull her away from her mother and the cottage, Edwina nodded and mounted the dapple-gray horse presented to her. Together, she and Mrs. Fletcher followed in line behind the parade of fair folk. Ian, Hob, and Finlay took up the rear on foot as they all walked through the morning mist toward the dawn.

"It's true what Queen Annag said." Gavina Fletcher coughed, then tucked her handkerchief away and cleared her throat. "I never foresaw your mother delivering twins. It was only after you were birthed into the world that we witnessed the schism in the magic. I was always curious, of course, how your individual talents would manifest as time went on and your shape-shifting developed."

"Did no one ever think to visit when we were younger?" Edwina shook her head. "To explain to us what was happening? My parents spent years trying to get us help to figure out why we were so different. Do you have any idea the strain it put on our family?"

"Of course I do, dear. My own family was run out of every village we ever settled in when I was a lass. But that's how these things are done. The identity of the new prophetess must be kept secret until she's presented at the Telling. You saw what might happen otherwise. Believe me, your life would have been much more difficult if the Unseelie Court had found you first."

The image of the ruined mortal's body chilled Edwina's blood and cooled her ire, only to be replaced by the vision of the unearthly creature her sister had become.

"What happened to Mary?" she asked, unable to shake the memory of her riding away in the coach, waving her tiny hand. "She died a week ago. I buried her myself, and yet she lives on as that creature."

"She passed in this realm, aye, but there is another world beyond the veil for some." Mrs. Fletcher held her arm out to allow a pixie to land. The creature, no bigger than a sparrow, shook out its wings, spit out a seed, and hopped back in the air, chittering and laughing.

"And you foresaw even that?" Edwina asked, trying to understand. "Does that mean there was never any hope for Mary? Was she always doomed to die young?" The question of whether there was more she could have done to save her sister would haunt her for the rest of her life.

The procession rode along a narrow stream, waking birds in their nests and stirring the vixens in their dens. Mrs. Fletcher seemed to take it all in as if it were the first time she'd laid eyes on such a beautiful morning. At last she shook her head. "Mary was never hopeless," she said. "Because her destiny was no more determined than yours appears now. Our choices still dictate our fate, for the most part. Though some are more easily influenced than others to choose the ill-begotten path."

"I don't understand any of this."

"No, of course you don't. Fairy logic follows its own course. Always has." Mrs. Fletcher lifted the hood on her cloak as a fine mist made halos around their hair. "I will say Mary had a better grasp of the fundamentals than yourself. Because her talent developed the way it did, I think she took more of an interest in the nature of change. No offense, dear, but many was the time I believed she was the one who'd be making this ride with me instead of yourself."

"But Mary never had visions that I'm aware of."

"Oh, she had a fair talent for it. She was as attuned to visions of the future as you are at seeing the dead."

Edwina thought of the ghost boy in the lane who'd taunted her with his rhymes and teasing faces. He'd seemed as real as any other person on the street, but most witches had the ability to see the recently departed, at least for a short time. "I could never see the corpse lights like my sister," she said. "It was always just a faint haze for me."

"Her visions of the future were likely just as hazy and not worth pursuing without tutoring, but she could have been a braw prophetess with some guidance."

Knowing her prophetic visions had fully manifested only after her sister's death, Edwina couldn't help but wonder if it would have been the same for Mary if she'd survived. She shivered at the mystery of fate. "One of us had to die," she said. "That was always going to be the outcome, wasn't it? We couldn't both be a prophetess with visions of the future. Not with the magic mingled between us."

"As Queen Annag said, we were not expecting twins."

Edwina's stomach lurched when her suspicions were confirmed. She pulled up on the reins and dismounted, landing in the wet grass. She didn't know which way to go, which direction was home, but she wanted to be done with this mad-as-a-hatter business.

"What's wrong?" Ian asked, walking up beside her. He patted the horse's neck and checked that the animal wasn't lame.

"No, lad, the horse is fine," Mrs. Fletcher said. "Edwina is merely in flux."

"In flux?" Edwina spun around. "You've just told me my sister died because she wasn't good enough at second sight to merit becoming the queen's prophetess."

"I dinna say that." Mrs. Fletcher gathered her cloak around her and slipped out of the saddle. "And that isn't what happened. Mary told you so herself."

"What? When?" Edwina shivered again, but it wasn't the weather giving her a chill. Nonetheless, Ian told Hob to go and fetch her shawl from Lady Everly's house.

"The message she left in your grimoire, dear. She explained herself as best she could." Mrs. Fletcher bowed her head, then sheepishly looked up at Edwina again. "I had a wee gander at your grimoire when you were out with your young man yesterday. It's there plain as day in her own hand."

"That means nothing," Edwina said, exasperated with all the secrets and nonsense. "It's just gibberish. Mary liked to play games, that's all."

"There's nae a witch 'twould mark in another's Book of Shadows on a whim. Not even Mary in her last desperate state."

"Desperate?" Edwina thought back to that horrible night when she'd had to identify her sister's body in the riverside morgue. Mary had drowned after filling her shawl with stones and strapping it around her neck. "Yes, I suppose she was terribly desperate in those final hours, but I can't be sure what she was trying to tell me."

The procession slowed as the horses veered into a mixed woodland of oak, ash, and hazel trees. Primroses and wood anemones leaned their flower heads toward the riders as they passed. Mrs. Fletcher watched anxiously as the fair folk moved on without them. "Of course you do. Just think on it a moment."

"Mary left you a note?" Ian asked. Hob returned, popping out of a fox den with Edwina's shawl. Ian slipped it over her shoulders, then kept his arm there. "What did it say?"

"She'd made the mark of silver for me with the crescent moon," Edwina said, happy to have the comfort of his arm around her again. "Quicksilver for herself, using the symbol for Mercury. One above the other. I understand that part. She was always quick to temper. Quick to change moods. I thought she was trying to say she did what she did because she was angry with me."

Mrs. Fletcher reached a hand in her cloak, brought out a small pouch, and took a quick peek inside. "No, dear, you're not going deep enough. As I said, Mary had the rare ability to see on both sides of the veil. She had a keen understanding of transmutation from childhood, isn't that right?"

Edwina thought of the other mark in her grimoire, the symbol for Gemini that Mary had written nearly ten years ago. She'd boasted then of finally grasping the term that explained what she was able to do with her magic by turning wisps of ether-fine memories into orbs and bits of leaf and ribbon into precious gems.

Mrs. Fletcher sighed as the procession of fair folk stalled, clearly waiting for them. Edwina felt a sense of urgency, as though she couldn't move forward until she understood what her sister had wanted her to know.

"Your sister assigned you the crescent moon because it represents intuition, ye ken?" Mrs. Fletcher said.

"Feminine wisdom," Edwina said, tracking a trail of thought like a wisp of light moving through the fog. "A higher attainment of the psychic power. Visions."

"Aye."

"But then why choose Mercury for herself? Unless . . ." Edwina reconsidered the alchemy books she'd browsed in Elvanfoot's library, holding up the information she'd gleaned against the mirror of knowledge she already understood. "Like the moon, Mercury also involves the mind. She knew she was capable of visions."

Mrs. Fletcher nodded. "Aye."

"But in alchemy the symbol represents the mercurial component of quicksilver," Edwina continued. "An element that can change form without altering its internal makeup. It also represents the ability to slip between life and death." She looked up at the prophetess, startled by her own epiphany. Edwina paced over the grassy ground, following the trail of thought to wherever it may lead. "Mary chose to end her life because she grasped the fundamentals of her gift better than anyone. She knew between the both of us her visions weren't as strong, but that she had the ability to transform in a way I never could survive. Because of her gift, she was able to change from one state to another through death to become the *ban-sìth* she is now. Like some sort of metaphysical quicksilver."

"Are you saying your sister killed herself because she discovered the pair of you were fairy-touched?" Ian asked, unconvinced. "Are you sure it wasn't because she was going to hang for her crimes?"

The host of fairies had turned around. They nudged their impatient horses nearer, gathering around those on the ground, staring with curious eyes. Queen Annag, too, watched and listened from her mount as pixies fluttered over her head in perfect silence.

Mrs. Fletcher looked to her side, squinting slightly as though trying to recall the fine details of a faraway dream. "No, Mary made her choice knowing Edwina would serve as prophetess should she be the one to remain," she said, tightening the string on the small purse she held.

"But how could she have known about the queen's spell?" Edwina asked. "I only just learned about it today."

Queen Annag adjusted her posture in her saddle. "Mary was not alone when she died," she said. "Maligar appears to have been by her side at the river, whispering in her ear about what I'd done, eager to create more chaos by insisting she challenge you for the right to be my prophetess. Apparently he'd heard your argument on the tower bridge and thought he could pit her against you. The unseelie never take into account all the good that has passed before."

"He killed her?"

"No, but I dare say he influenced Mary to reflect on matters more deeply. But rather than serve his bleak designs, she chose to embrace what had always served her well—a final transmutation. Not because she had any desire to end her life, but because she wanted yours to shine here if hers could not. Do you see? She sacrificed for love in the end, knowing you could not survive such a transition as she has done. Call it amends, if you will."

The queen's description of Mary's final moments sank like an anchor inside Edwina, fixing the image of her sister's selfless choice forever. Grief and anger still dwelled within her, but it no longer filled her. She could see a way forward. A way to forgive. A way to reclaim what they'd once been together as sisters. Twins with the ability to transform and take wing. To sing a spell to the living or sit with the dead at the moment of gentle passing. Raven sisters born to perch aside an elven queen—one in the earthy realm and one in the Other.

"Come, dear," Mrs. Fletcher said, mounting her horse as the parade of fair folk trotted off toward the trees once more. "We must make it to the clearing by sunrise so we might impart our vision of the coming year on the foot of the old stone spiral. The world, as ever, carries on." The old woman coughed. "But there is another matter of business before we get to the Telling."

Edwina and Ian looked up, preparing themselves for more revelations.

Mrs. Fletcher tossed the small purse she'd been holding to Ian. "For your work, Detective."

"That was you?" he asked, accepting the coins. "You're Finlay's employer?"

"Even my visions aren't always perfect. The shadowy nature of the unseelie kept me from seeing who it was coming through the portals. Between the two of you, though, we flushed him out."

Ian pocketed the purse and pulled Edwina to him, kissing her forehead.

"Oh, and one more word of advice, dear." The prophetess tapped a finger to her temple as she looked at Edwina. "Say yes to the lad when he asks," she said with a wink before kicking her horse into a trot.

"It doesn't take a prophecy to see the wisdom in that," Edwina said, enfolding Ian with her shawl, thankful for the solid warmth of his body tethering her against the ethereal pull of the fairy realm.

Hob did a little jig around them while they kissed, then skipped into the woods singing, "Meddle and mell wi' the fiends o' hell, an' a weirdless wicht ye'll be; but tak' an' len' wi' the fairy men, ye'll thrive until ye dee."

ACKNOWLEDGMENTS

I've had the pleasure of working with basically the same team of people for all my novels with 47North thus far. The continued relationship lends both familiarity and consistency to the work, making my job as an author that much easier. There were moments during the writing and revising stages of creating this novel that demanded more from the people around me than normal. Their efforts did not go unnoticed by me, and I wish to thank them for their continued dedication to making the words shine so we could get the right story told. Thanks to Marlene, Adrienne, Clarence, Jon, Kellie, Karah, and the rest of the 47North team for your encouragement and continued diligence. And thanks again to Shasti O'Leary Soudant for her beautiful cover concept.

APPENDIX OF BORROWED WORKS IN THE PUBLIC DOMAIN

1. Old Scottish saying taken from *Scotland: Social and Domestic* by Charles Rogers (1869).
2. *Romeo and Juliet* by William Shakespeare.
3. "Dream-Land" by Edgar Allan Poe.

ABOUT THE AUTHOR

Photo © 2018 Bob Carmichael

Luanne G. Smith is the Amazon Charts and *Washington Post* bestselling author of *The Raven Spell*, *The Vine Witch*, *The Glamourist*, and *The Conjurer*. She lives in Colorado at the base of the beautiful Rocky Mountains, where she enjoys hiking, gardening, and a glass of wine at the end of the day. For more information, visit www.luannegsmith.com.